Heart OF THE Ocean

Heart OF THE Ocean

A NOVEL

HEATHER B. MOORE

OTHER WORKS BY HEATHER B. MOORE

A Timeless Romance Anthology Series

The Aliso Creek Novella Series:
Third Time's the Charm
The Daisy Chain
Lost, then Found
One Chance

The Newport Ladies Book Club series:
Athena
Ruby's Secret

PUBLISHED UNDER H.B. MOORE

Esther the Queen
Finding Sheba
Daughters of Jared

PRAISE FOR *Heart* OF THE *Ocean*

"*Multi-award winning author Heather B. Moore writes with a new voice in her paranormal historical romance, Heart of the Ocean. Meet her host of enthralling characters in a story set against the backdrop of Puritan New England, gossip driven New York society, and nineteenth century Europe. Experience a love that grows over time to rescue Eliza Robinson from mortal danger and ghostly terror.*"
—G. G. Vandagriff, Whitney Award Winning Author, The Last Waltz

"*A tortured spirit seeks restitution on the rocky cliffs of New England, but only Eliza Robinson hears her voice. Eliza must solve the crime that took the woman's life, before she loses her own, or her heart. Heather B. Moore brings readers a perfect blend of mystery and romance in this tale of ghostly spirits, unsolved murders, and unwanted proposals.*"
—Lu Ann Brobst Staheli, Best of State Educator & Author, A Note Worth Taking

"*Heart of the Ocean by Heather Moore is a story that will appeal to all readers, no matter what genre you like to read. It is a well-written historical romance, with a ghost story, heart pounding suspense, and very strong characters. I was immediately pulled into Heart of the Ocean from the first page with Heather's excellent way of storytelling.*"
—Mindy Holt, minreadsandreviews.blogspot.com

Thus sing I to cragg'd clifts and hils,
To sighing winds, to murmuring rills,
To wasteful woods, to empty groves,
Such things as my dear mind most loves.
—Dr. Henry More, 1614–1687

One

SEPTEMBER 1839

"*J*ump."

Eliza swung around, searching for the source of the voice—a woman's voice. Wind tugged at her wool coat, and streaks of rain pelted her face. Maybe it's the wind. Again. It was the same voice she heard on her walk out to the cliffs. But that's impossible. There's no one here. She turned to face the sea and realized she was only two steps from the edge of the cliff where the jagged rocks sloped into the surf dozens of feet below.

"Jump now."

Eliza backed away from the cliff's edge, heart pounding as she peered into the gray drizzle for any sign of the woman. I'm imagining it . . . or it's in my head. She shuddered and pulled the coat tighter around her body.

Shunning the treacherous drop-off a few steps away, Eliza closed her eyes against the incoming storm. Waves crashed below, sending vibrations through her body. The seagulls had long since abandoned their screeching cries and had found shelter among the jutted rocks. *Am I losing my mind?* With what she'd endured the past few months, it was entirely possible.

"Don't be afraid."

New cold shot through her at the sound of the woman's voice. Eliza opened her eyes and stared at the furious foam dashing against the dark rocks below.

"Who are you?" she yelled into the wind.

No response.

What's happening to me? "Now I'm talking to myself *and* hearing voices," she muttered. Feeling a sudden dizziness, she took several more steps away from the edge, as the ocean surged and spat out sea spray. The menacing clouds compressed into a deeper gloom, and the wind picked up its pace, as a force outside her seemed to urge her forward.

Aunt Maeve had said the New England coast was not for the faint-hearted, and Eliza understood why. Not only was September the most active month for hurricanes, but apparently the ghost stories she'd heard in town had just proven themselves credible. *Unless the voice is inside my head. Then I've truly lost my sanity.*

She turned from the cliff's edge and hurried to the lighthouse, clutching her coat and bending against the furious gale. Eliza had told her aunt she'd only wanted to see the incoming storm for a moment. But by the time she reached the crumbling lighthouse, she was panting, shivering, and thoroughly soaked.

"Come back," the voice said, slicing through Eliza. As she increased her pace and focused on the lighthouse door, she tried to block out everything else. *Just get there.*

The splintered door swung wide before Eliza reached it, and the wind slammed it against the wall. Aunt Maeve stood in the entryway at the base of the stairs, bundled up in a thick cloak and heavy boots, lantern in hand.

Her aunt was here, real and solid. Relief surged through Eliza. She wasn't in a horrible nightmare.

"'Bout time you came back." Maeve glared at her. "I thought you'd decided to take a swim." The woman's white-streaked auburn hair had come loose from its customary bun, wispy across her shoulders. It looked almost pretty.

Eliza knew better than to believe her aunt was cross. "I'm ready to go back to the house."

Maeve held the lantern high and narrowed her gaze, but through her stern Puritan demeanor, a twinkle showed in her eyes. "It's a good thing, too. I almost had to come for you myself. There aren't any men near enough to send on such an errand." She tilted her head, motioning for her niece to follow.

No men indeed. Precisely why Eliza wanted to come to this Puritan farm in the first place. She'd had enough of men, and their deceitful ways, to last her a lifetime. Maeve gripped Eliza's arm, bringing her thoughts back into focus. In the few seconds that Eliza had been inside the lighthouse, the wind had multiplied in strength. She clung to her aunt as they exited, and together they ran to the cottage, sodden skirts whipping their legs. The distance was not far, but with the wind slicing through their clothing, time seemed to slow, and it felt an eternity had passed by the time they reached the front door. Once inside, it took both of them to push it closed.

Maeve clasped her hands to her chest and fought for normal breath as she leaned against the wall. "On my life, it's going to be a big 'un. Leave your wet things here. We'll clean up later."

Eliza stripped off her coat then removed the wool scarf covering her head. Her hair was plastered against her cold face.

Maeve chuckled. "You look like a wet dog."

Eliza pulled her dark blonde hair free of her face, grateful to be inside the cottage—away from the cliff, away from the voice, and most importantly, away from the judgments of men.

"Aye, you're shivering as a dog would," Maeve began.

"And so are you," Eliza countered with a smile.

"I'll put the tea on." Maeve left the entryway and hurried to the kitchen.

Eliza moved into the hearth room, knelt before the fireplace, and threw a thin log onto the starving glow. She settled onto her heels, trembling from getting soaked, and from hearing that strange woman's voice. Her skin prickled as gooseflesh rose on her arms. *Was it my imagination? Or was there someone out there?*

Here, inside the humble, yet comfortable, cottage, it was hard to believe she'd heard a voice out on the cliffs that had commanded her to jump. *It must be my imagination.* That was it—the wind, the rain, the churning ocean—it had all combined to disorient her.

Eliza exhaled, feeling relieved as she looked around the room and let the familiar calm embrace her. Aunt Maeve's cottage was plain, a welcome change from Eliza's home in New York City. The whitewashed walls, a rocker, a pair of stout chairs positioned near the hearth, and a threadbare sofa against the wall made up the simple room.

Soon the warmth from the fire began to thaw her stiff fingers, and when they were nimble again, she combed them through her wet hair. A burst of wind blew down the chimney, making the fire waver. Eliza shuddered again, thinking about the woman's voice. *Jump . . . Don't be afraid.* What did it mean? Why did the voice want her to jump from the cliff?

Eliza leaned toward the fire, letting her hair fall over her face to dry in the heat. She'd been in Maybrook for nearly a month now. Everything about it was different than her high society life back in New York. No complaining mother, no docile father, no stab-you-in-the-back suitors. Even now, her stomach churned at the memory of her recent beau.

Mr. Thomas Bertram Beesley III. Even the name was repulsive. So proper; so arrogant. *Plump* was putting it nicely. *Kind* was overdoing it. And *filthy rich*, an understatement. He'd be mortified to see her in such modest surroundings now. Why couldn't the wealthy men also be handsome, humble, and totally and completely in love with her?

Eliza smoothed her hair back and pulled her knees up to her chest. She gazed at the flames, relishing the peace and absolute quiet save for the crackling fire.

Her aunt lived a humble life, though it hadn't always been that way. Maeve had once been a young debutante in New York, but she had fallen in love with a Puritan man and moved to Maybrook, where she had remained ever since. *What would it be like to throw all conventions in society's face? Live my own life, free from the shackles of high-brow culture?* Sparks shot out from the fire, close to Eliza's skirt, so she scooted back, shaking out the dancing sparks.

Maeve entered the room, two teacups in hand. "Here you are."

Eliza turned and accepted a steaming cup. "Thank you." Dry enough now to sit on the sofa, she sat as the wind howled its way around the house, sounding nothing like the voice on the cliff.

"There now, dear, you'll grow used to ol' Mr. Wind," Maeve soothed. She retrieved a bit of mending from the nearby basket and settled into the rocking chair. After threading a needle, she began to sew even stitches along the torn hem of an apron.

Eliza brought the teacup close to her lips and inhaled the sweet fragrance. She sipped the liquid, relishing the warmth moving down her throat. The wind suddenly increased its tempo, sending rapid bursts through the chimney and into the hearth. Eliza shivered and looked at her aunt. "When you're here alone, don't you feel afraid?"

Glancing up from her sewing, Maeve said, "When my husband was alive, I never gave the storms a second thought. After he was gone, I found I didn't mind the weather, even being alone. I believe this old house protects me."

Eliza gazed about the room—the glow of fire reached to the far corners, making the place look cozy. She understood how her aunt felt secure. But what about the voice on the cliff? Had her aunt experienced something of that sort?

"What did your mother say in her letter?" Maeve asked. She set down the apron and reached for her cup of tea.

"She'd like to come and visit." Looking again at her aunt, Eliza took in the woman's now carefully arranged hair and twice-mended pinafore.

"That would be nice," Maeve murmured, with a slight lift of her brow.

Eliza refrained from letting out an exasperated sigh. "I don't want her to come. I don't want to hear about the latest dance, or what everyone wore," she said. "It's hard enough to read her letters, but at least I can put them away and forget about the things that don't truly matter. Having her here— that would be . . . it would be unbearable!"

Maeve nodded before taking another sip. "I had the same feelings once. Felt I was drowning in an ocean of greed." She hesitated then leaned forward on the rocker. "When I met Edward, I saw my escape. It was probably an extreme choice to leave everything behind, but I loved him, and I've been happy here."

The nostalgia in her aunt's voice enveloped Eliza like a soft blanket, calming her spirit. "Maybrook is so unassuming," Eliza said. "As long as you're an upstanding citizen, no one cares which house in Paris made your dress, or how many people attend your coming-out party."

"You're guaranteed none of that here," Maeve said.

But there were other things here, things Eliza hadn't encountered in New York City—like a ghostly woman's voice. "Do you believe in ghosts?" she blurted, immediately regretting such a foolish question.

Maeve's forehead creased. "Have you been listening to the village stories?"

"No." Eliza wished she could take back her question. Her parents had specifically told her to ignore the superstitious tales among the Puritans. It was one of the agreements Eliza had made before coming.

"It's true that Maybrook is nothing like New York City." Maeve lowered her gaze. "But things around here are not always what they may seem."

"What do you mean?" A slow chill crawled up Eliza's neck. The same chill she'd felt at the edge of the cliff. She placed her tea cup and saucer on the floor beside her.

"As I said, in this house, I'm protected." Maeve lifted her gaze.

Eliza nodded and folded her arms. The room remained cold in spite of the fireplace.

"But what I'm about to say . . . your parents would have me hanged for."

Eliza inhaled. What could Maeve possibly tell her that would have her parents so upset? "I won't say anything."

"You are nineteen now, a grown woman, and it's time you knew about such things," Maeve said in a slow voice. "To answer your question, Eliza, yes, I do believe in ghosts." Her eyes seemed to glow as she took up the mending again. "The woman who lived in this house watches over me."

Flinching, Eliza clasped her hands together. "Oh . . . I . . ." Her aunt's response did not bode well, not after the voice, not after the order she'd heard on the cliff less than an hour ago. She wanted to tell her aunt what had happened, but no words would come.

A smile tugged the corners of Maeve's mouth. "You think I wouldn't believe in ghosts?" She gave a long, slow look toward Eliza, then continued, "Everyone dies and leaves their body. We just don't talk about what happens when a spirit refuses to leave our world."

"Have you . . . seen or heard the ghost?" Eliza practically whispered.

"I didn't say that." Maeve tied a knot in her stitching.

Her aunt hadn't actually seen or heard anything, so maybe it was Eliza's imagination too? Relaxing her tightly gripped hands, the blood returned to Eliza's fingers, creating a sharp needle-like pain. Just then, something banged on the window. Both Eliza and Maeve jumped.

"Only a falling branch." Maeve tied a second knot and snipped the end of the thread.

Questions whirled through Eliza's mind. Her aunt's words were far from comforting, and with such a wild storm outside, it took everything in her not to start at every sound. She retrieved her cup with trembling hands and took another sip of the tea, hoping the hot liquid would put some calm into her. Another piece of debris hit the window, and the cup shook in her hand.

"She was about your age, and her name was Helena Talbot," Maeve went on, oblivious to the tempest outside.

"Who?" *The ghost?* Eliza's mind added the second question. She wasn't sure if she wanted to hear this story on such an awful night. She couldn't very well excuse herself. And do what, stay awake in the dark? Listen to the frightful storm alone?

"His name was Jonathan Porter," Maeve continued. "Some say he was ten years her elder. I suppose he could have been even older than that, for all the places he'd seen."

A shrill whistle knifed its way through Eliza's chest as the wind vibrated the clapboard walls. She huddled against the sofa, wishing that the fire were brighter and the storm had already passed.

"It's been twenty years since Helena was lost. Some say she'll come back." A soft smile spread across Maeve's face.

"Others say they can hear her voice on nights like this." She paused as the wind screeched in confirmation. *The voice.* The one she'd heard on the cliffs. Eliza tried not to tremble.

"Scandal surrounded Helena, and Helena's mother never forgave her, never even visited her daughter's illegitimate baby," Maeve said. "It's said that ol' Mistress Talbot went mad from hearing her daughter's tortured spirit cry during the night."

Tortured spirit? "What happened?"

"Helena disappeared. Then her mother lost her mind. The townspeople said that Helena had thrown herself off the cliff, but a body was never found." Maeve smoothed the apron on her lap and began to rock slowly. "Ole Mistress Talbot used to comb the cliffs looking for her daughter. One night during a terrible storm she climbed upon a horse, driven to search for her daughter yet again, but she plunged off the cliff and fell to her own death. Mother and daughter were both gone in the same year."

Why had Mistress Talbot mounted a horse in such a storm? The woman had been mad indeed. Had she heard her daughter's voice at the edge of the cliff? Eliza could very well imagine the absolute terror of the mother. Eliza's eyes stung as she imagined the poor woman, lost, cold, wet, falling to her death.

"I suppose I'm getting ahead of myself. You see, after Jonathan Porter returned to England, Helena discovered she was with child." Maeve's voice brought Eliza back to the story. "Mr. Porter was a wealthy bachelor, and he should have married her properly. Weeks passed with no word from him, and eventually the minister and town authorities banned Helena and her growing belly from public sight."

"She was banned from *sight*?"

"Helena's shame was so great, she couldn't even accept visitors," Maeve said, her expression grave. She sipped at her tea, closing her eyes briefly. "The poor dear lived alone—couldn't face her own family or any of the townspeople for the disgrace of it."

A pang twisted inside Eliza. *Alone. Pregnant. Disgraced.* "Wasn't there anyone she could turn to?"

"Oh, some took pity and left baskets of food at her doorstep, but only on the darkest of nights." Maeve looked past Eliza as the candles in the room flickered. "The night of her son's birth, there was a violent storm—the townspeople had never experienced such a one. By morning, Helena's place was hardly recognizable, yet she'd delivered a healthy boy despite it all. She stayed away from town for the first year. Her mother never came to visit the baby."

What sort of mother refuses to see her own grandchild? Eliza wondered. The madness of Mistress Talbot must have been a mixture of grief and guilt.

"I still remember his dark locks and black eyes . . . He was only three years old when his mother disappeared." Maeve stared at the fire as if seeing it all in her mind. Her voice quavered, and after a deep breath she said, "Someone found the boy wandering the edge of the cliff all alone, looking for his mother. Many think his mother drowned."

Thinking of a little boy out in the dark all by himself, made Eliza feel ill. She twisted her hands, trying to comprehend the incredible tragedy—for Helena, for her mother, for her baby. "What happened to the boy?"

Maeve folded the apron she'd been mending. "Little Jon? Reared by the old spinster Ruth. The boy was a quiet lad. He moved to the big city some years back, and the town hasn't seen him since." She rose and busied herself with collecting the tea things. "I found Helena's journal in the lighthouse a few weeks ago. Strange that it would show up after all of these years. Maybe you can help me read it since my eyes aren't what they used to be."

"Can I see it now?" Eliza asked.

"Later. I left it in the lighthouse. It seemed disrespectful to move it. For all I know, I found it exactly where she put it."

Eliza wanted to know what was in the journal. The wind outside had mellowed, but it was still raining hard. Rising to help Maeve clean up, Eliza said, "Maybe her journal will tell us what really happened to her."

"Perhaps." Doubt crossed Maeve's face. "It may answer why her spirit can't rest, but I don't know if that's such a good thing."

"Why not?" Eliza felt a bit lightheaded.

Maeve hesitated. "Because, my dear, this is the house where Helena delivered her poor child and where she lived the three years until her disappearance. Was it an accident? I don't know. But I do know that her sorrow of raising a fatherless son must have been inconsolable, because each time a storm rolls in, people claim they can still hear her crying."

Two

After Maeve retired for the night, Eliza lay curled in her bed underneath a heavy goose-down cover. What had become of Helena Talbot? And why had her lover never returned? The voice Eliza had heard had to be Helena. Had the woman thrown herself off the cliff? And if so, was her spirit now obsessed to make another person to do the same? The thoughts rocked through her.

Eliza burrowed deeper into the covers, but warmth wouldn't come. She closed her eyes, desperate to take her mind off of the deep chill that Maeve's story had brought. What would her parents think about the sordid details of a despairing ghost? Eliza's parents had decided that if she spent a few months with her aunt, it would give the gossip columns a chance to cool over Eliza's rejection of the pompous Mr. Thomas Beesley. When he had made his intentions clear, and she turned down his marriage proposal, her family was spurned by the inner circles of New York society.

Eliza's face grew hot with familiar indignation. It hadn't happened all at once, but with subtle nuances here and there.

A dropped invitation, a neglected garden party. *It isn't fair.* Why should she have to marry a forty-plus-year old man, because he was her father's business partner and very wealthy? She cringed at his image in her mind. Thomas was shorter than Eliza by several inches, and his middle so large that she wondered how he laced his shoes in the morning. What appalled her most was his constantly running nose— and commentary to match.

When rumors circulated that Thomas was about to ask for her hand, Eliza had brushed them off. Her parents had always respected and spoke highly of the man, but they had never alluded to a possible union. To her dismay, a short time later at the company's annual charity picnic, he proposed on bended knee. Over the sound of exploding fireworks, he took her hand and asked, "Miss Eliza Robinson, will you bestow upon me the honor of becoming my wife?"

She had stared at him, wondering if she had heard right. Her mind spun as Thomas smiled with hope and waited patiently.

"I'm sorry," Eliza began, but quickly stopped when she saw his reddened complexion deepen to purple. She had made a fool of him. He left in a hurry, and by the next morning Eliza discovered that it was too late to make her apologies. Thomas had already confronted her father, who apologized profusely, then came straight up to lecture her. But Eliza refused to change her mind, and by evening, the gossip columns were in full swing, painting her as a heartless flirt.

At least, she thought as her eyes grew heavy, *Helena never had to worry about printed gossip columns in Maybrook.*

❦

The sound of shattering glass startled Eliza awake. Head pounding, she bolted out of bed and grabbed her robe. The

13

windows in her bedroom shook from the howling wind—ready to burst. Had her aunt broken something? Fallen? Eliza slipped on her shoes before hurrying out of her room.

"Aunt Maeve?" she called. She nearly stumbled as she descended the stairs in the dark. When she reached her aunt's room, she found the door locked. Eliza pounded on the wood. "Are you all right in there?" A burst of cold air hit her bare ankles as she shook the handle. "Aunt Maeve!"

The whining grew louder—or was it crying? Gooseflesh on her arms spread to her neck until the hair on her head prickled. Something was wrong. Her aunt couldn't be sleeping through all of this commotion.

Eliza frantically kicked at the heavy door, but there was no give. She dashed into the kitchen and scrambled in the dim light for anything to use to break the door handle. Finding a cast iron skillet, she hurried back to her aunt's room.

She froze. The door now stood ajar.

"Aunt Maeve?" she called again in a shaky voice. "Can you hear me? Are you all right?" As she stepped into the room, a cold wind cut through her muslin nightgown. Shards of glass lay haphazardly on the plank floor. Eliza's gaze moved to the broken panes of her aunt's bedroom window. And then Eliza looked toward the bed. Maeve lay motionless, her face turned away, hidden in the shadows.

Eliza gripped the skillet in one hand and walked to the bed. "Aunt Maeve?" There was no answer.

As she circled the bed, terror caught in Eliza's throat. Maeve's head was facing her, eyes closed. Eliza reached out and touched her aunt's hand. It felt like cold clay.

Eliza felt as if she'd been punched in the stomach. She backed away from her aunt, staring in horror at the still figure.

Aunt Maeve was dead.

She slowly backed out of the bedroom. As she passed through the doorway, she turned, her hands stretched out before her. She made her way down the hall until she reached the kitchen. Her foot caught on the rug, and she fell headlong into the sideboard.

She cried out. Her forehead burned with pain and her ankle throbbed. But she couldn't stop to examine or tend to her injuries—she had to find help. She took several breaths then pulled herself up by holding onto the sideboard.

Dizziness stunned her, and she sank to the ground, pain pulsing through her. She exhaled as tears burned her eyes. This wasn't the moment to give into the pain. *I have to get help.* Eliza crawled to the front door. She had to get to the barn and saddle the horse. When she reached the front door, she pulled herself up by the handle, and opened it. Debris swirled everywhere outside.

Rain drove nearly sideways in the fierce wind. Limping precariously on her injured foot, Eliza made her way through the yard. She was soaked in seconds and wished she'd put on her coat.

Her head pounded, and she realized that the sound she thought was in her head was really that of an approaching horse. She turned to face the horse as the animal grew closer, shielding her face from the driving rain to see.

The rider reined in his mount, stopping mere inches away from where Eliza stood. She stretched out her arms. "Help me," she gasped.

∽

Eliza awakened with a start. White curtains above her billowed in the soft breeze. *Where am I?* She rose to her elbows and groaned. Her head throbbed something fierce, and her mouth was parched. Sinking back into the pillow, she carefully touched her forehead, finding it covered with a bandage. The sleeve of her nightgown was different, and she realized she was wearing someone else's, faded but clean. What had happened to her own clothing? She turned her head and saw that she was in a small simple room. A rocking chair stood in the corner, with a patchwork quilt thrown over the back. Her gaze roamed to the opposite corner, where a lone basin sat atop a washstand.

The sound of lowered voices reached her ears. It was *his* voice—the man who had saved her last night. As Eliza strained to hear the words, the memory of the previous night returned.

She squeezed her eyes shut at the images—finding her aunt's body, falling against the sideboard, crawling through the house, facing the storm, a man riding into the yard on a horse. Despite the chaotic weather, the man's face was etched in her memory—dark eyes and black hair as wild as the storm's surf. Opening her eyes again, Eliza stared at the white curtains fluttering above her. Where was she? The voices from the other room had fallen quiet. A door shut.

"Don't leave," Eliza whispered. She wanted to find out who had helped her. Pulling herself out of bed, she stepped onto the wooden floor. She gasped in pain when her foot touched the ground, but she gritted her teeth and hobbled to the window. A horse came into view, and for a brief moment, Eliza saw the man's profile before he turned and galloped away from the house. It was him—the man who had found her.

"Up already, love?" came a voice from the doorway.

Startled, Eliza turned and looked at the wizened woman who had walked into the room. "Where am I?"

The woman's blue eyes peered through delicate folds of aging skin. "Thou are in my house."

"And who are you?"

"Ruth." The woman flashed a nearly toothless smile. "Thou hast had quite a night. Why don't thou climb back into bed, dear, and I'll bring thee a hot cup of tea."

Eliza obeyed and drew the covers around her. She would ask more questions of the Puritan woman when she returned. Tears burned as she thought about her aunt. What had happened to her? Was Maeve's body still in the cottage?

"Here thou are."

Eliza took the cup of tea gratefully.

"Jonny said he found thee outside Maeve's cottage."

Perhaps the woman didn't know that her aunt was dead. "Maeve is my aunt. Last night I found her . . ." She bit her lip. "I know about Maeve. Thou told us last night. And I knew Maeve had her niece, Eliza Robinson, staying with her." Ruth placed a gnarled hand over Eliza's arm. "I'm sorry we haven't met until now."

Eliza blinked back tears. She was sorry too, sorry for a lot of things.

"Don't worry, dear. Jonny went to fetch the constable," Ruth said. "Has Mistress Maeve been ill, dear?"

"No," she whispered, finding it difficult to speak. She took a sip of tea. The flavor was strong and burned her throat as she swallowed, making her eyes water more.

Ruth patted Eliza's shoulder and said, "It's my special medicinal tea. Thou wilt gain thy strength back quickly."

Eliza blew on the tea before taking another scorching sip.

"We'll have to make arrangements for thy aunt." Ruth's voice was kind. "Doest thou know what her last wishes were?"

"No," Eliza said, new tears forming. "I have no idea."

Ruth sighed. "She never did want to outlive her husband."

Eliza thought of her uncle, who had died a few years back. He was a quiet man with a warm and steady manner. Maeve and her husband had come to visit her family in New York once or twice, but their simple ways were out of place there. The Sunday activities were unbearable for them, and they had spent the day in the guest room, reading the Bible. Later, her father explained that laughing and speaking in a loud voice was prohibited on the Sabbath for Puritans, along with other worldly activities.

Ruth crossed the room and opened the window wider, letting in the morning breeze.

"Is Jonny your son?" Eliza asked.

Ruth turned, a flicker of sorrow in her eyes. "In a manner of speaking, yes. His mother died when he was young, and I took him into my care."

And then Eliza knew. Jonny was . . . "His mother was Helena Talbot?"

A shadow passed over Ruth's face. "Thou hast heard of her, I see. Aye, Helena was her name." She pursed her lips and fell silent. She seemed reluctant to say more.

Exhaustion pulled at Eliza; she closed her eyes. Ruth murmured something about sleeping, and Eliza was grateful to oblige, as she allowed herself to sink into nothingness.

Someone touched her shoulder, and Eliza startled awake.

An elderly woman stood over her. Eliza remembered it was Ruth and that she was in the woman's house because of the awfulness of the night before.

"The constable's arrived," Ruth said. "He'll want to ask thee a few questions."

Eliza smoothed her hair as Ruth left to answer the door. She sat up, adjusting the quilt about her. Her head throbbed, and her throat felt thick. A few moments later, Ruth led the constable into the bedroom. He bore a striking resemblance to Thomas, with a plenty wide girth. Eliza swallowed nervously.

"Good mornin' miss. Sorry t' hear about thy aunt."

The constable's dark eyes glinted in the morning light, and his mouth worked beneath his heavy mustache. It was his nose that reminded her most of her rejected beau—it twitched and sniffed persistently.

"About what time didst thou find her?" the constable continued, shuffling a step closer.

Eliza clasped her hands to steady their trembling. "I'm not certain. The sound of breaking glass woke me. It wasn't very late, but with the storm, we went to bed earlier than usual. Her door was stuck . . . and when it opened, I found her . . ."

The constable frowned. "Did thou hear any other sounds coming from her room?"

"Only the wind and . . ." She paused.

"And?" the constable prompted.

Eliza stared past him. "The wind sounded so strange. I thought I heard someone crying."

A sudden movement from Ruth caught Eliza's attention. Ruth's hands were gripped into a tight ball and her face had drained of color. "Crying?" she whispered.

The constable looked at Ruth, then back to Eliza, his thick eyebrows raised. "Most likely the *wind*, ma'am. Or perhaps the poor woman was crying right before her murder."

"*Murder?*" Eliza whispered.

His eyes hardened. "That's right, miss. Thy aunt was murdered. God rest her soul."

It took Eliza a moment to comprehend. "How?"

He looked from Ruth to Eliza as if unsure what exactly to say. In a quiet voice, he said, "Thou must tell me, Miss Robinson."

"How would I know?" Surely the constable didn't think that she . . .

His eyes bore into hers, and she shuddered involuntarily.

"You can't think that I . . ." She looked to Ruth for help.

Ruth folded her thin arms. She stared straight at the constable. "Now, sir. You can't believe this poor girl is a murderer."

He turned his gaze on her. "Maeve O'Brien's skull was crushed. I aim to find who did it to her, even if I have to imprison a few people to do it."

19

Eliza covered her mouth with her hand. Ruth rushed to her side and spoke quietly, as heaving sobs tore at Eliza's chest. "How could this happen?" Eliza cried out. Disbelief and anger and horror coursed through her. Hours before, Maeve had been telling her a ghost story, cozy in the hearth room, sewing on her lap.

Ruth sat on the bed and wrapped her arms around Eliza. "Hush, dear. The constable will find whoever did this."

"Thou are correct. I will find the culprit." He cleared his throat. "Thou wilt have to come with me, miss." He took a step forward. "Thou are under arrest for the murder of Maeve O'Brien."

Ruth rose from the bed. "Sir, is that really necessary?"

The constable said nothing, merely stared Eliza down.

Ruth reached out and patted Eliza's hand. "Go along now. Thou wilt be cleared soon." But her trembling voice betrayed worry.

In a daze, Eliza rose from her bed. *This can't be happening.* She stepped on the cold floor, and pain shot through her sore ankle.

"Wear these," Ruth said, handing over the shoes that Eliza had been wearing the night before. They looked like they'd been cleaned.

"This way," the constable said.

Eliza followed him, her mind numb as they left the house and walked to the waiting buckboard. Ruth followed and placed a cloak about Eliza's shoulders before she climbed in.

"Thou are making a mistake, sir," Ruth said. "The girl's harmless."

The constable turned and faced the woman. "Are thou willing to stake thine own reputation on it, woman?"

Eliza's heart sank as Ruth took a step back, shaking her head. Eliza hadn't really expected Ruth to risk anything for her, but the woman knew the town and the law better than Eliza did—where would she be without her?

"Jonny will tell thee—" Ruth began.

"Jon has to worry about his own neck right now," the constable interrupted. "Until I know why he was at the O'Brien house last night, he's a suspect as well."

Eliza stared at the constable. He'd arrested that man who'd helped her too? Panic shot through her. She couldn't go with the constable. Her parents knew nothing about this. She had to send a message to them. How could she face jail? She gripped the seat and made a move to stand, but the constable climbed in next to her and urged the horse into motion.

She fell back against the seat. It was too late.

Three

*E*liza stared through the dark iron bars. The cold cellar was damp, with water dripping from the ceiling in a rhythmic fashion. *This crude jail is no place for a woman,* she imagined her father saying. She pulled the cloak given to her by Ruth around her shoulders. Shivering, she thought of how last night she was snuggled in her warm bed; tonight she was surrounded by concrete walls.

A low curse from the next cell reached her ears. It had to be Jonny. When she arrived at the jail, she'd been led past his barred cell, feeling his eyes watching her. The constable already arrested Jonny before going to Ruth's place.

Eliza let out a breath, gathering her courage. "Are you all right?" she called.

Silence greeted her.

She tried again. Maybe he hadn't heard. "Are you ill?"

"I'm in jail," he said with a scoff. His deep voice seemed to fill the small space with an echo.

Eliza bit her lip. It was her fault he was here. "I'm sorry."

He spoke again. "Did you kill her?"

She drew a breath in sharply. "No." How could he accuse her? Because she lived with her aunt? How did he arrive so fast at the cottage—how had he known to come? Suspicion knotted inside her. "Why were you riding by the cottage in such a storm?"

There was a brief moment of silence, as if Jonny had realized what she was accusing him of. "I thought I could make it all the way to Ruth's in the storm, but it grew worse than I expected. I knew Mistress Maeve lived nearby, so I planned to take shelter in the barn until the worst passed."

She didn't know this man. Could she believe him?

"It's God's truth," he said.

Exhaling, Eliza realized she did believe him. She couldn't explain why, but she decided to trust her instincts.

"I'm sorry about what happened to your aunt. She was a good friend to Ruth over the years, although I didn't know her well." There was a shuffling sound from the other side of the wall, and then he spoke again. "As soon as my father's lawyers find out, the constable is going to be sorry."

This surprised Eliza. If Jonny was Helena's son, then . . . "Your father's alive?"

"I see you've heard the local gossip." Bitterness was evident in his voice.

"Only from my aunt—" She cut herself off.

A door banged in the distance, and soon a man appeared with a trencher of gruel. He slipped the wooden dish through the bars and set it on the floor in Eliza's cell. "Thank you," she said. The man grunted and shuffled to Jonny's cell. There was no spoon with the gruel, so she had to sip the nourishment.

Night came and along with it, inky blackness. Eliza huddled on the moldy cot and hugged her arms against her body. Her heart seemed to beat in tandem with each passing second. The occasional sound of a door banging reached her. Otherwise the jail was silent as a grave, and she heard no sound from Jonny.

She had almost forgotten the companion adjacent to her when he spoke.

"I'm Jon Porter, by the way," he said in the quiet stillness. "We haven't been properly introduced."

Eliza swallowed. "I'm Eliza Robinson, niece to Maeve. My parents sent me here for a while to . . . help my aunt."

He said nothing for a moment, then, "My father recently died. I never met him. He sent money to pay for my education, but there was never a personal letter or an invitation to meet him. You can pass that onto the townspeople."

A rebuttal caught in Eliza's throat. She didn't know what to say. Seconds turned into minutes, and presently she smelled the sweet, robust scent of cigar smoke. She knew it would be futile to try to explain things to him. He must hate her, and it was her fault.

Quiet tears slipped onto her cheeks. Soon her body trembled. How long would she have to remain in this dreadful place? It wasn't until dawn began to invade the cell that Eliza at last fell into an uneasy slumber.

⌀

"Wake up, girl."

Eliza opened her eyes. As the cloudiness of sleep disappeared, she recognized the figure standing over her.

The constable studied her with ill-concealed contempt. "Thou are free to go."

"How—"

"The evidence against thee isn't strong enough yet. Therefore I must let thee go, but thou wilt have to stay in town until the charges can be formally cleared." The constable turned and left, leaving the barred door wide open.

Eliza listened to his footsteps echo down the corridor. She licked her cracked lips. Glancing around the damp cell for the last time, she rose from the cot and adjusted the cloak about her shoulders. She ran her fingers through her tangled hair as she walked out of the cell, still limping. The corridor was quiet as she passed by Jon's cell, which now stood empty. When she reached the stairwell, she paused, sensing someone behind her. She turned to see a rat scurry past.

She walked up the stairs, her legs stiff and cold from the night in the cell. A jail guard waited for her at the top and motioned for her to follow him outside. Heavy clouds discolored the sky, looking pregnant with rain, although not a drop fell now. She followed the guard around the building and stepped through another doorway into a narrow room with a bench and two desks. A grizzled man was seated at one of the desks.

The guard said nothing, and Eliza stood in front of the desk for a moment, waiting until the man looked up. Finally, he noticed the visitors and peered at her through his spectacles. "Thou must be the young lady who was released."

"Yes, have they found my aunt's murderer?" Eliza clenched her hands in front of her.

The man shook his head. "The constable is still investigating."

Eliza blew out a breath, disappointment filling her.

"After you sign this release, thou are free to go," the man said, pushing a piece of parchment toward her. "When Mr. Porter was released, he petitioned for thy freedom as well."

"*He* freed me? But how?"

"Why, turns out he's a lawyer." The man grunted. "And he told the constable, 'You can't keep that girl without evidence.' Thou had best be going, miss, before the constable finds another excuse to keep thee 'ere. Mr. Porter left for the city and won't be available to help again."

Relieved she was free, yet disappointed she couldn't thank Mr. Porter properly, Eliza bent and signed her name on the parchment. "Thank you."

The old man nodded, then said in a gruff voice, "May God keep thee."

The guard stepped aside as she passed through the doorway. The last few hours seemed like a dream. Had she really spent the night in a jail cell? She clasped the rough woolen cloak about her and started toward the road that led to Maeve's. She dreaded going back to the place where her aunt had died.

Yet she had no choice but to return. The main road passed right through the commons, and as luck would have it, today was market day. People stared at her as she hurried by. At least the adults averted their eyes, but the children watched her with open, curiosity. Untidiness was a disgrace to the Puritans, and she must be a sight to behold, in addition to the fact that she'd exited the jail. She wished she could disappear inside her cloak.

Skirting around the market stalls, Eliza thought she heard someone call her name. But when she turned, no one was looking at her. At least it wasn't the voice of the woman from the cliff. That voice had been silent since the night before.

Eliza watched two plump boys battling with sticks next to their father's bread cart, making her realize how hungry she was. She wouldn't be able to eat for a while, since the walk back to her aunt's was nearly an hour. Wishing she had paid more attention to her aunt's acquaintances, she approached the cart. Perhaps the man would give her some food on credit.

She dodged a rather large puddle to reach it. "Good day, sir. I don't have money today, but I'll repay you tomorrow if you could be so kind to give me a bit of bread."

The merchant's eyes appraised what was sure to be a dirty face and a stained nightdress beneath her borrowed cloak. Not to mention uncovered hair. Finally he nodded. "I cannot turn away a beggar."

She wanted to tell him she wasn't a beggar, but instead she kept silent, deciding it was best not to argue with the man.

Making grand gestures, he eyed his neatly arranged loaves and scratched his head. Then he elaborately chose a loaf that looked a bit over-baked and handed it to Eliza, wrapped in a cloth.

She took the bread and thanked the merchant. This wasn't a time to be choosey.

"Good morrow, Eliza," a voice spoke behind her.

She turned and saw Nathaniel Prann, a young, blond man whom she'd met during Sabbath services on her first visit to the Meeting House.

He looked her up and down, as if he couldn't believe her appearance. "Art thou well?"

The merchant squinted at them with curiosity. "Thou knowest this girl?"

"Of course. She's Maeve O'Brien's niece."

"Ah. I didn't recognize thee," the merchant said. "I am sorry to hear about thy aunt."

"Thank you," Eliza said, feeling completely mortified that Nathaniel was seeing her in this state.

"What happened to thy aunt?" Nathaniel asked, his usually merry blue eyes somber.

The words stuck in Eliza's throat. The merchant was only too eager to supply the information that Maeve had died. Nathaniel turned his concerned gaze back to Eliza.

"I didn't know." He led her away from the peering merchant. "What can I do? Doest thou need a place to stay?"

Hot tears filled her eyes. "I haven't been back to the house since . . . I spent the night in jail." She nearly choked on the last sentence.

Nathaniel's eyes widened. "Thou must come to our place. Mother will help thee clean up. I'm on my way home now. I came into town to pick up the post."

Eliza was too exhausted to turn down such a kind offer. She followed Nathaniel to his horse, sure that all eyes of the market were watching. Nathaniel Prann was the eldest of a large family. He had been friendly right away, but she knew she could never become like him. A Puritan.

Nathaniel helped her onto the horse, then took the reins in hand and guided the horse down the road. "My house is up the coast from thy aunt's. We don't get the post delivered yet—too out of the way, I suppose."

He chatted most of the way back to his place, but Eliza wasn't listening. Her mind churned with thoughts of her aunt's death and the night in a cell, with Jonathan Porter on the other side of the wall. He'd saved her twice. It seemed that beneath his aloofness was a caring man.

"—it would be a fine place to live," Nathaniel was saying.

Nodding absently, Eliza murmured, "Mm-hmm."

He pulled the horse to a stop and stared up at her. "Thou thinkest so too?" The grin on his face was broad.

Eliza reddened when she realized the trap she had stepped into. What had she agreed with? She knew that look, had seen it in opportunist's eyes—yet Nathaniel was not much more than a boy.

Nathaniel continued, his voice a happy lilt. "I'm nearly twenty-one, not so much older than thou are. Perhaps . . . perhaps thou wouldst consider allowing me to court thee?"

Eliza opened then closed her mouth. Speechless.

Nathaniel chuckled. "I have shocked thee. I apologize." His eyes were trained on her, though with a boldness much older than his age. His hand grasped hers. "Perhaps a kiss would make my intent more clear."

Before she could protest, Nathaniel lifted her hand and kissed it.

Trying to hide her shock, she said, "Are you sure that's not a sin, Mr. Prann?"

He laughed. "'Tis not, I assure thee."

Eliza smiled at his laughter. He was misguided in his quick attachment to her, but that was sure to fade as quickly as it had bloomed. After all, she wasn't even Puritan. Surely there was some law about marrying outside the faith, and she wasn't willing to convert like her aunt had.

Nathaniel tugged at the horse's reins. Eliza's smile faded when she realized she couldn't share this amusing experience with her aunt. A lump tightened in her throat. Who could have harmed her aunt, and why? She was glad Nathaniel was looking straight ahead and didn't notice the quiet tears slipping from her eyes. As they neared the Prann homestead, the sun broke through the clouds and a gentle breeze lapped at the hem of Eliza's nightdress.

"Here we are," Nathaniel said, obvious pride in his voice.

Before them stood a plain two-story clapboard house with a porch that wrapped around the entire front, substantial by Puritan standards. Eliza hadn't been this far up the coast before. When she'd taken the horse out, her aunt had cautioned her to stay near. Nathaniel extended his hand and helped Eliza to the ground. "What doest thou think?" he asked, his gaze eager.

Eliza hesitated. "Why, it's so large, I thought—"

"My parents have eight children, so the size of our house is quite prudent."

"I didn't mean . . ."

He winked. "Of course I'll build my bride her own house."

"Nathaniel, I don't think you should—"

"There thou are," a merry voice called from the side of the house. A stout woman appeared, carrying a basket of sun-dried laundry. She wore a blue scarf tied about her head, although pale strands of hair had fallen out, framing her round face.

Nathaniel went to greet his mother while Eliza lagged behind. But Mistress Prann would not tolerate timid behavior. After hugging her son, she wrapped Eliza into her ample arms and squeezed. Now Eliza knew where Nathaniel had inherited his friendliness. "I've heard about thy aunt and the trip to jail. How ghastly. Thou must have had such a dreadful night. Come inside, and we'll give thee a proper bath."

Eliza drew away from the woman. "It can wait until later. I don't want to be any trouble."

"Nonsense, child. The water only takes a moment to heat." She turned to her son. "Nathaniel, find Rachel and tell her to bring a change of clothes to the kitchen."

Eliza followed Mistress Prann into the warm room, where a metal tub sat in the corner, next to a parted curtain. Mistress Prann moved the butter churn away from the tub then dragged it forward and poured water into it from two buckets stationed in the corner. She added a kettle full of steamy water. Then she refilled the kettle and waited for the water to heat. When several inches of water covered the bottom of the tub, Mistress Prann instructed Eliza to undress.

Eliza pulled the curtain closed and removed her soiled nightgown.

"Give me thy clothes to clean," Mistress Prann said.

Eliza handed the garment through the opening, then gingerly stepped into the fast-cooling water. She sat down and ladled water over her skin.

"There's lye soap behind thee on a shelf, and some hair cleanser in a jar."

Locating the soap, Eliza began to scrub furiously. She poured a dollop of hair cleanser into her palm, smelling the scent of roses. It felt good to get clean. She did not even mind the draft that seeped through the curtain, causing gooseflesh to rise. The bath couldn't warm her entirely from her night in a damp cell.

"Here thou are." Mistress Prann handed a large square of cloth through the curtain.

"Thank you." Eliza took the coarse fabric, stepped out of the tub, and rubbed herself dry.

"Thou must spend the night here," Mistress Prann's voice came through the curtain. "I can't bear the thought of thee sleeping in an empty house, especially after . . ."

Eliza pulled on the petticoat that had been handed to her then dressed in a lightweight cotton dress. It was obvious the Prann family didn't have warmer clothes to spare and had to bring out their summer wear to accommodate Eliza. "I'd appreciate the place to sleep." She wasn't ready to return to Aunt Maeve's home yet. Tomorrow, with the storm clouds gone, she would make the journey.

She stepped out from behind the curtain, pulling her damp hair into a bun. The Pranns' kitchen was cramped, filled with a rough-cut square table, surrounded by four solid benches. The oven protruded from the bricked hearth, blackened by years of greasy smoke.

"Girls," Mistress Prann called to her daughters. "Eliza is dressed. Come prepare the meal."

Three girls bustled into the room, all Nathaniel's younger sisters. One carried a baby, whom the girl strapped promptly to the highchair. The young child started to wail until a wooden rattle was fetched.

Over the banging of the rattle, the eldest sister, Rachel, called out instructions. One sister descended through a trap door in the floor. She brought up a section of beef, then on her second trip she carried a basket full of sweet potatoes, parsnips, and carrots.

"It'll be stew tonight, dear." Mistress Prann looked over at Eliza.

"How can I help?" she asked.

"Thou must rest. Sit at the bench and entertain little Prudence, who'll be glad for the attention."

Eliza settled next to the baby. She was greeted by a toothless grin and loud babbling.

Mistress Prann set a noggin of cider in front of Eliza. She smiled gratefully and took a sip. The Puritans in this small town were experts in making cider, and the Pranns' was as good as her aunt's.

Eliza watched Rachel swing the iron kettle on its pothook, then lift the heavy lid and stir the contents. Not long after, the wafting aroma reached Eliza, making her realize how hungry she was. She'd only eaten jail gruel and a bit of bread over a day's time. Before that was the tea at Ruth's house.

Rachel set out clean napkins on the table next to the porringers, which had been scrubbed and readied for the stew. She cast a sympathetic smile at Eliza.

A commotion sounded at the door; the men were home from the fields. The deep voice of Master Prann filtered into the kitchen from the hall, speaking to his sons. "If you've pulled the last of the onions, then tomorrow we'll start on the corn."

"Dinner's almost ready," Mistress Prann said and ushered the boys into the room.

At the sight of Eliza, Master Prann raised his eyebrows. He was similar in appearance to Nathaniel, tall, broad, white-blond hair, and Eliza felt as if she were looking at the future Nathaniel.

"Thou rememberest Eliza Robinson, Maeve O'Brien's niece," Mistress Prann said. "She needs shelter and food tonight."

"Thou are welcome to stay here, Miss Robinson."

Eliza nodded politely, then caught Nathaniel's eye. He'd come in right behind his father. His blue gaze soaked her in. She hid a sigh, knowing she'd have to deflate his hopes sooner rather than later.

Following the prayer, Rachel and Mistress Prann served the food. Eliza was surprised at how quietly the family ate; there was little conversation as they passed the platters of food around and helped themselves. Even Nathaniel, who had been talkative every time they were together, remained solemn. Dinners in New York were always lively, often accompanied by music, and conversation was animated with the latest gossip. When the last porringer had been emptied, the girls rose to clear the table. As Eliza stood to join them, Mistress Prann motioned for her to remain seated.

Eliza obliged and settled next to the contented baby.

"Nathaniel will read tonight," Master Prann said to no one in particular.

Nathaniel's face reddened at his father's suggestion, and Eliza wondered why. Surely he had read for his family many times before. Seats were taken again, and the smaller children hushed. The older girls pulled out samplers to stitch. Eliza caught Nathaniel's eye as he opened the large Bible in front of him and removed the marker. She offered an encouraging smile, but he broke the gaze and lowered his eyes.

"Psalm 46. God is our refuge and strength, a very present help in trouble . . ."

Nathaniel read deliberately, enunciating each word. Master Prann closed his eyes and nodded in rhythm to the phrases. Mistress Prann and the two oldest girls bent over their embroidery, making even stitches in the dimming light. Eliza tried to focus on the holy words, but each verse sounded the same as the last.

Her mind wandered. Soon she wondered what Nathaniel would be like if he'd been born in New York. He'd no doubt be an apprentice of some sort, and not under his parents' eye, ever watchful for sin. Would he be the same man if he were able to express himself freely and have the opportunities afforded other American men?

After the evening prayer, Rachel told Eliza, "Thou mayest sleep in my room."

"Thank you," she said, and followed Rachel up the narrow staircase into the girls' bedroom. Eliza put on her nightgown, which Mistress Prann had cleaned and repaired. Climbing into bed, Eliza moved close to the wall and kept her body straight, so as not to disturb Rachel. It was ages before she fell into a troubled slumber.

Four

onathan Porter stepped off the hissing train in New York City. Breathing a sigh of relief to be on familiar ground again, he walked briskly to the busy road and hailed a carriage to take him home. After settling into the bumpy ride, he thought about the previous night he'd spent in jail. It was a miracle he'd escaped Massachusetts without further interrogation. If it hadn't been for his father's death two months ago in England, he would have never returned to the Puritan town. Though it was nice to see Ruth, the only mother he'd ever known, he had returned only for one thing—his official birth record. He needed it to claim his inheritance from his father since he had other children, and Jon's half-sister would inherit if Jon couldn't produce proof of his parentage.

But Ruth didn't have the document, so he had risked bad weather to locate the magistrate. When the magistrate then denied having the document in the courthouse or the Meeting House, there was only one place left to look—the home his mother had last lived in, now Maeve O'Brien's place. Perhaps the record was stored in the attic of the old house. But the storm had raged, and when he dared set out, he doubted if he'd make it in one piece to the O'Brien cottage.

When he finally came into view of the cottage, he saw the distraught figure of a woman emerge from the front door. That's where everything had all gone wrong. *Of all the damned nights. She looked like a drowned waif and was obviously limping.* He couldn't just pass her by. And now he couldn't very well go back to search through a crime scene. He'd be delayed again.

The carriage lurched over a pothole, and Jon realized they were near his neighborhood. He tapped the driver in front of him. "Turn here." The driver obliged and maneuvered onto a narrow street lined by two-story homes that were dated but elegant.

"Number twelve, on the right," Jon instructed. The carriage pulled to a stop, and he alighted. After unloading his single piece of baggage, he paid the driver.

The front door opened as he started up the stairs.

"Oh, Mr. Porter, what a welcome surprise." It was Sarah, the parlor maid. "You've arrived a day early."

Jon tipped his hat. "Are there any messages for me?"

"The letters are on the hall table, sir." Sarah bobbed her head then made herself scarce.

Jon had the hallway to himself. On top of the letters was a familiar envelope. The pale pink seemed to wink at him. Jon smiled, knowing the letter was from Apryl, his fiancée.

Walking into the library, Jon thumbed through the other envelopes—nothing but business. He settled into the over-sized leather chair, imported from England, and brought the pink letter to his nose. The faint scent of roses still remained. He opened the envelope and read the looped writing.

Dearest Jonathan,

I know you're still away, but I'm anxiously awaiting your return. This Friday night my parents are hosting a dinner. It would be wonderful if you returned in time to attend.

Yours truly,
Apryl

Jon was tempted to pay her a surprise visit then thought better of it. She hated anything unexpected. He remembered the day he had surprised her as she was walking in the park, only to discover that she was embarrassed about being seen wearing a hat from the week before. So he penned a reply, which he sent Richards, the butler, to deliver. Attending an extravagant dinner was what he needed to take his mind off the woman who had landed him in jail.

He next turned his attention to the drawer of the heavy oak desk and removed his father's will. Scanning the familiar words, he thought about how different things would have been if only his father had married his mother. He would have been brought up in a wealthy home. He would have attended the best private schools in England. And his mother would still be alive.

Jon leaned back in his chair, thinking about the mother he could barely remember. Were the rumors true? That she drove herself mad with grief and took her own life? Had she truly drowned on that stormy night? The fierce storm of the other night in Maybrook had him realizing how easy it would have been for anyone to become disoriented.

Ruth's quiet words played in his mind. "Thy mother was unconventional for a Puritan. Oh, she went to Meeting and always obeyed the Sabbath. But some said she had a strong will—too strong. She learned to swim, and often in the early evening, she swam to the Old Rock. Of course, she never dared do so with anyone around. I'm set in my ways and believe in the good Bible, but I never believed that only witches could float in water. Not everyone believed that though, and she would have fallen under suspicion if anyone had seen her."

Whoever decided that only witches could float?

Ruth had continued her story about how his mother had gone out for a swim on the night of the impending storm.

Now, sitting in his leather chair, Jon furrowed his brow. That was the part of the story he didn't understand. How could his mother not see billowing clouds gather, hear the wind pick up speed, or feel the swift raindrops? And if she did know the storm was coming, why did she still go swimming?

Ruth had told him that his mother was lonely and often stared out to sea for hours at a time with a journal in her lap. "Your mother was unusually smart for a woman—could read and write with the best." But Ruth said that when she cleaned out his mother's house, she didn't find any books, journals or letters. "No matter," Ruth had said. "All the furniture was burned, and the house purged of sin."

Purged of sin. As if his mother was evil.

Jon closed his eyes against the flickering candles. The town he grew up in was another world, a place he was glad to be rid of. If only he hadn't stumbled into the mess at poor Maeve O'Brien's house and found that girl staggering through the mud.

And if he hadn't then been thrown into jail!

Otherwise, he might have searched the attic of his mother's old house and found his birth record—something he believed still existed.

⟨✕⟩

At six o'clock sharp on Friday evening, Jon rang Apryl's bell. The door was opened by a straight-faced butler, whom Jon followed into the immense hall, where he shrugged off his overcoat. Mr. and Mrs. Maughan stood at the base of the stairs.

"Jon, how good of you to come," Mrs. Maughan purred, leaning her long face forward for a kiss. She wore her signature red tonight, setting off her gypsy-coloring, a low-cut bodice displaying her curves. She was a woman who had no problem competing with her daughter. And Apryl didn't seem to mind one bit.

Jon kissed the hostess's cheek, his gaze straying to the drawing room.

Mr. Maughan chuckled in his booming voice. "Apryl eagerly awaits you."

Jon shook his future father-in-law's hand. "I'll go to her, then."

Entering the drawing room, Jon was met with a dizzying array of finery, from the formal English furniture and the imported Italian tapestries, to the Persian rugs. But nothing could compare to the elaborate creature who greeted him.

Apryl, a younger version of her curvy mother, rose. Her apple cheeks flushed, and her deep green eyes lit with pleasure. The tight-fitting bodice only accentuated her spilling bosom, supported by indigo brocade. The ribbons adorning her velvet sleeves fluttered as she crossed the room. "You've come, my love."

Jon took her jeweled hand and winked. Kissing the weighted fingers, he cocked his head to one side. "Miss me?"

Laughing, Apryl tilted her Grecian hairdo, her coiled black ringlets swaying. "Of course." She led him to the center of the room, where other guests were visiting.

"May I introduce Mr. Thomas Beesley, and his kind sister, Jessa."

Jon bowed. "It's an honor to meet you both." Beesley was familiar, but Jon couldn't place the name. The large man appeared to be about forty, and the fact that he was accompanied by his rather plain sister revealed that he was perhaps unmarried.

When dinner was served at half past six, Jon was seated with Thomas Beesley to his right and Apryl to his left. Amid the animated conversation, Jon couldn't help but notice intermittent sniffing coming from Mr. Beesley. Jon was about to offer his handkerchief when he noticed Thomas already clutched one in his meaty fingers.

"Are you fighting a cold?" Jon asked his neighbor.

"Ah yes," Thomas answered, producing a prominent sniff. "It's the confounded city air. I often retreat to my place in the country to find relief."

Perhaps the man was single and wealthy. "And is there a Mrs. Beesley who shares in the same relief?"

The conversation around the table faded into awkward silence. Apryl placed a hand on Jon's arm.

"I gather you've been away on business," Thomas said in a distressed tone.

The tension was palpable. What had Jon said? Apparently it was the wrong thing, yet, how was he supposed to know the history of a man he'd never met? He'd been at Yale for the past few years and hadn't been involved in society.

"I was nearly engaged once," Thomas said.

Knowing murmurs of sympathy echoed around the table, and a few whispers were quickly suppressed by Apryl's glare.

Jon brought his hand up to his collar automatically, trying to loosen a tightness that had suddenly formed. "I-I'm sorry, I didn't mean—"

"It's all over with now. I'm on to better things, right?" Thomas leaned forward over his girth and looked at Apryl.

Jon was surprised to notice a blush creep up his fiancée's neck. He looked back to Thomas, but the man had turned to his sister. The conversation resumed around the table, more hushed now.

"We'd be so pleased if you could join us," Apryl said.

Jon looked at her. What had she been talking about?

"What's the matter, love?" she asked, patting his hand. "Too much wine?"

"No, I . . ."

"Then what do you think?" Apryl pressed.

He adjusted his collar again. "About what?"

She covered her mouth and stifled a giggle, then nudged him. "Spending next weekend at the Beesleys' country home?"

His face warmed. "Of course. I'd love to."

Apryl beamed, and Jon smiled back. She really was quite beautiful, and he was once again grateful she'd bestowed her favor on him.

Thomas clapped Jon on the shoulder. "It's all settled, then. We'll have a grand time in the fresh air. Be sure to bring your riding habits."

"I haven't ridden since I was a girl," Apryl said.

"Then I'll be your personal escort," Thomas offered.

She leaned forward to meet Thomas's eye and laughed. "I guess I have some shopping to do."

Thomas's appreciative gaze dipped to Apryl's bosom.

Jon's hands clenched into fists. He was about to say something, but the servants appeared to clear the dinner plates. Jon scooted his chair forward to block Thomas's direct line of vision toward Apryl. Jon didn't entirely care for Mr. Thomas Beesley.

Five

liza ran into the dark room and saw the window open, wind gusting through it in sharp bursts. Pulling the window shut, she turned to see her aunt. Moonlight cast dancing shapes upon the bed. "Aunt Maeve, are you all right?" She stepped closer to the side where her aunt lay. "What happened?" Reaching over, she touched her aunt's motionless shoulder. Just then, a shadow fell across the bed, causing Eliza to turn and stare at the dark form standing behind her. She tried to scream, but a heavy hand clamped down on her mouth.

Eliza sat up in bed, perspiration soaking her hairline. She clutched the quilt to her chin, shivering. The room was still dark, and the faint sound of breathing came from Rachel. *It was only a dream.* Eliza tried to calm herself.

But doubt crept over her. What if Jonathan Porter had come to seek revenge? What if he'd been making his escape when he heard Eliza calling for Maeve? He had definitely seemed bitter about the way his mother was treated and about how the town continued to gossip about the circumstances surrounding his birth.

"Canst thou sleep?" A quiet voice spoke behind her.

"No . . . I had a bad dream."

Rachel was quiet for a moment. "About thy aunt?"

Eliza nodded.

"I'm very sorry."

Tears dropped from Eliza's eyes, making round wet circles on the quilt in her lap. "I need to send a telegram to my parents. They'll undoubtedly come to fetch me." She felt a warm hand on her shoulder, offering comfort. Rachel had risen to sit next to her.

"Doest thou want me to come with thee to gather thy things tomorrow?"

Eliza felt overwhelmed at the kindness from her new friend. "That would be nice."

"We'll bring your things here. Thou cannot stay in that empty house, not after what happened. Thou must stay with us until thy family arrives."

"Thank you," Eliza whispered. It was another hour before she fell into a fitful sleep, trying to keep the nightmares from returning.

When Eliza finally aroused from her troubled sleep soon after dawn, the house below was in full motion. She changed into the dress Rachel had lent her the day before. Smoothing the dark brown cotton fabric over her narrow hips, she noticed a row of starched bonnets hanging on the wall. She walked over to them and fingered the ties on one, remembering her aunt. Maeve had let Eliza wear a straw hat on weekdays, but on the Sabbath insisted she wear a Puritan bonnet to Meeting, out of respect for the townspeople.

Descending the stairs, Eliza was surprised to see Nathaniel at the table, cracking walnuts.

Mistress Prann greeted her cheerfully. "Good morning, dear. Nathaniel stayed home from the fields so he could take thee back to thy aunt's house and gather thy belongings."

43

"Thank you," Eliza said.

"Rachel said she would like to help too," Mistress Prann continued. "She will be in shortly with the eggs."

The day was overcast, as if it couldn't let go of the storm, fitting with Eliza's somber mood. As they rode in the Pranns' buckboard, she couldn't help but wonder what the house would be like with her aunt gone. Rachel and Nathaniel kept up a light chatter, and Eliza joined in only when necessary to be polite. For the most part, she was content to watch the changing landscape as they traveled the narrow road. The brilliant-colored leaves seemed to whisper to her from their branches.

"*Turn back.*"

It was the voice again. Eliza looked behind her. Rachel and Nathaniel were quiet. Had they heard it too? Eliza's breath stuttered—she didn't dare ask them. Wouldn't they say something if they'd heard it? She hadn't heard the voice since leaving her aunt's, but now it was back. What did it mean? Tears stung her eyes, and she rapidly blinked them back.

As they approached the clapboard cottage, the events of the last few days seemed dream-like. She expected to see Aunt Maeve's bustling form fill the doorway upon the sound of the approaching wagon. But no one came out to greet them, and when Nathaniel reined the horse to a stop, they sat in silence for a moment until Nathaniel jumped from the buckboard and helped the girls to the ground.

Eliza looked at the mud beneath her. It hadn't dried completely from the storm, and its twisted rivulets mirrored the feeling in her stomach. Nathaniel hovered near her, as if he wasn't sure whether to follow.

"You should check on the horse," she said.

Nathaniel nodded, seemingly relieved to be given direction, and he headed toward the barn.

Eliza stepped carefully around the more sodden parts of the ground and headed for the house, with Rachel close behind. As she reached the front door, Eliza realized that the last time she'd entered this door, she was running to get out of the storm, with Maeve right beside her.

"Do you want me to go in first?" Rachel asked.

Eliza shook her head then turned the doorknob and pushed the heavy door. The first thing she noticed was a set of muddy footprints on the oak-planked floor. They were large—the size of a man's boots. Eliza hesitated, staring at the footprints. Could they be the murderer's?

Rachel spoke behind her. "They probably belong to the constable."

Relieved at the thought, Eliza nodded in agreement and looked at the sideboard cabinet that stood its ground, silently taunting her to trip against it again. She scanned the room, her pulse a nervous flutter. Nothing had been moved. The hearth was dark and still, the water in the iron kettle quiet, and the air stale.

Everything reminded her of Aunt Maeve—the quilt thrown over the rocking chair, the forgotten ball of yarn and needles, the painting of a lighthouse, and the stack of brittle firewood. But the house felt empty—empty of her aunt's spirit, the woman who had once loved and laughed within its walls.

Eliza continued into the kitchen and stopped, staring at the disarray, caused either by herself on the night of the storm or the constable searching for evidence. The table had been moved, cupboards left open, with pots strewn about. She took a deep breath, turned and walked to her aunt's bedroom door. Images of that night surfaced. Taking a deep breath, she decided she wasn't ready to enter Maeve's room and ascended the stairs to her own bedroom instead. She removed the traveling trunk from under the bed and loaded her belongings. The room seemed to grieve for Maeve; even the patchwork quilt on the bed, made by her aunt, seemed sorrowful. Eliza lifted the quilt and tucked it into her trunk.

"Can I help?" Rachel asked from the doorway.

Eliza wiped a stray tear.

"I'll carry it out," Rachel said. "Take the time thou needest."

Listening to Rachel's retreating footsteps, Eliza sank onto the bed. She tried to memorize every detail of the room, knowing this might be the last time she'd see it. It was furnished with only a dresser, washbasin and bed. The curtains covering the narrow window were of plain, homespun fabric. She rose and opened them, letting the sunlight warm the room.

Finally she descended the stairs and paused, glancing again at her aunt's bedroom door—it seemed to beckon to her. Eliza resisted, not able to bear seeing the room where her aunt had taken her last breath.

The sound of an approaching wagon came from outside, and Eliza hurried to the porch. The constable had arrived and sat perched on top of his black horse, a disapproving look on his face. He blew his nose haughtily into a handkerchief, which made his bulging paunch vibrate.

"Thou shouldn't be here," he said. "This house is still under investigation."

Eliza opened her mouth to answer, but Nathaniel came out of the barn and said, "We've come to gather Miss Robinson's things."

The constable looked at the three people before him, and then his gaze focused on Eliza. "Thou should have notified me before coming. Best be on thy way."His eyes narrowed for a moment, and his mouth formed a thin line. "Tuesday after the funeral, thy aunt's will is to be read, and thy presence is expected. It will be in the Meeting House."

"Thank you, sir," Eliza said, though she didn't feel entirely grateful. Under the constable's gaze, she climbed onto the Pranns' buckboard, settling next to Rachel. She clasped her hands together to conceal their trembling.

Nathaniel set the horse into motion and turned the buckboard around. Eliza stared straight ahead as they passed the narrow-eyed constable. She felt his gaze on her back, and although it made her cheeks burn to be stared at, she held her head high.

"Too bad the previous constable died," Nathaniel said. "Master Perry was an agreeable man."

Rachel squeezed Eliza's hand. "Master Perry was gentle-mannered and would have never treated thee so harshly."

Eliza's shoulders sagged as she remembered something. "I must post a telegram to my father. Could we pass through town?"

"I thought thou mightest desire to do something like that," Rachel said. "I brought an extra bonnet just in case."

Nathaniel chuckled. "My sister thinks of everything."

Eliza smiled. The gloom the constable had brought with him had dissipated. She donned the bonnet. Once they reached Main Street, Nathaniel pulled the buckboard to a stop in front of the post office. Eliza descended, followed by Rachel, and together they entered the oblong room. A dour-faced clerk looked up as they walked in. He looked like he was straight out of the 1600s, wearing a heavy English wool jacket, a leather hat, with an over-starched white collar.

"Good day," he said in a voice worn with years.

"My friend would like to send a telegram," Rachel said.

The postmaster's eyes widened. "An unusual request for such a young lady. Perhaps thou hast better ask thy father to come in."

"The telegram is to her father, who lives in New York City. He must be notified of his sister's recent death," Rachel said.

Eliza was more than grateful that Rachel had taken the lead in this strange conversation.

"Ah. Thou are Maeve O'Brien's niece? I was sorry t' hear the news."

47

"Thank you," Eliza said.

The postmaster left the counter and returned a moment later with a card to fill out.

Eliza accepted the dip pen and ink well and began writing the brief message. Both the postmaster and Rachel read each word as she wrote. Eliza tried not to let their prying eyes bother her. When finished, she handed over the money, and the postmaster double-checked the message.

When they left, Eliza asked, "Is that man always so nosey?"

"Yes," Rachel said with a laugh. "But he's sending the message, so he would be reading it anyway."

It seemed nothing was private in this town. By the time they arrived at the Prann homestead, Eliza felt restless. She knew she should offer to help with the chores, but she wanted to be alone. Mistress Prann noticed her troubled face and offered consolation.

"I'd like to take a walk, if that's all right," Eliza said.

Mistress Prann nodded. "Doest thou want Rachel to walk with thee?"

"No, thank you. I need some time alone." She thanked her hostess again and stepped into the front yard. One of the younger boys was chasing a chicken. When he saw her, he waved merrily. Eliza smiled and waved back.

The afternoon shadows stretched across the rutted road. For a moment she thought about borrowing a horse but then thought better of it. The Pranns didn't ride horses for pleasure. Without planning her destination, she headed east toward the shoreline. She reached the jagged cliffs and realized she was only about a mile from her aunt's lighthouse. Had it only been two days ago that she had stood on this same rocky shore, facing the incoming storm?

Eliza shuddered. The changing sky above her brought new clouds, swallowing up the shadows cast by the sun. Gone were the brilliant golds, reds, and yellows of the tree-rich landscape. In their place stood muted browns and grays.

The wind began to stir the wispy grass beneath her, and the long, green fingers whipped her ankles. It was time to head back. The tip of her ears had grown cold, and her feet ached. Maybe tomorrow she would take one last look at the old lighthouse. She was about to turn away from the incoming tide when she heard a whisper in her ear.

Don't leave me.

Eliza spun and looked behind her. It was the same voice—the one she'd heard on the night Maeve was murdered. Now, as then, no one was in sight.

Six

The dance was underway in the Maughans' newly remodeled ballroom. Jon took the first number with Apryl, but he paid careful attention to Thomas Beesley, who danced quite close to them with another partner. Apryl chatted about the shops she would have to visit to obtain a proper riding habit, and Jon was only required to nod from time to time.

More than once, he caught Thomas gazing at Apryl. When the first dance ended, Jon asked Thomas's sister, Jessa, to dance. She remained quiet as they danced and nodded at Jon's occasional comment. Thomas ensnared Apryl and waltzed her around the dance floor. Surprisingly, Beesley was light on his feet despite his bulk. Laughter floated from their direction. Jon frowned, looking at Jessa.

"How long has your family known the Maughans?" he asked.

Jessa looked up at him. "My brother has mentioned them once or twice, but this is the first time we've been invited for dinner."

What intentions did Thomas have about Apryl to make him pay such particular attention to her? She was not a wealthy heiress. Her family came from new money procured in the financial markets. Any future son-in-law would well know the risk of such a volatile industry.

Because of his own recent inheritance, Jon would be far wealthier than Mr. and Mrs. Maughan. It would be only a matter of time before his future father-in-law would pose the indelicate question of what his estate in England was worth. Of course, as the fiancé to Mr. Maughan's daughter, Jon expected the questions. After all, New York society marriages were often based on assets, not love.

Jon didn't expect to be in love with his wife, but he did expect mutual affection and respect with his future wife. Most of the women he had been introduced to were too self-centered for his taste. That's why, when he met Apryl, he was pleasantly surprised. The size of her figure told him she didn't care for the conventions of the corset fashion, though her clothing was designed after the latest Parisian styles. And her animated eyes and vivacious conversation kept him entertained. She would make a lively wife. More than ever, Jon wanted to produce an heir for his imminent fortune.

"Have you been engaged long?" Jessa asked, interrupting his thoughts, her pale brown eyes studying him.

Jon answered, "A month. We met only a short time ago through a mutual friend. Apryl is hard to ignore."

The corners of Jessa's mouth twitched. It was the most animated Jon had seen her all night. "That she is."

Mr. and Mrs. Maughan retired after an hour, letting the younger guests continue to enjoy themselves. It was after midnight when Jon left the house, amid enthusiastic farewells from the guests.

Apryl followed him out to the carriage and kissed his cheek. "You'll call tomorrow?"

"Of course," Jon said, tipping his hat. "Unless you would rather see Mr. Beesley."

Apryl lowered her gaze. "Oh, don't tease me about him. I thought he was rather too forward tonight."

Jon snorted. "You didn't seem to mind." When he saw Apryl's irritated expression, he softened his comment by saying, "You were the belle of the evening and naturally the center of attention."

"You're not angry?" Apryl's gaze was hopeful.

He took her hands then kissed each one. "How could I be angry with a cherub such as you?"

Apryl laughed. She pressed against him and gave him a rather illicit kiss on the mouth.

Jon's resentment toward Beesley faded. Jon might not be in love with his fiancée, but he could still enjoy her. He was tempted to stay a bit longer to explore the depth of her kisses, but his carriage driver was all eyes, and there were still guests in the house. He drew away from her. "Tomorrow, then."

Apryl smiled up at him. Jon climbed into the waiting carriage and lifted his hand in a wave. As the driver pulled away from the walk, Jon saw Thomas exit the house and step behind Apryl, placing his hands over her eyes in some sort of game.

⁓

The following afternoon, a formal invitation to the Beesley country estate arrived by post. Jon opened the card in the hall. As he read the details, he knew he would have to attend, if only to thwart Thomas's advances toward his fiancée. A note from Apryl was in the stack of correspondence.

Dearest Jon,

I assume you've received the Beesley invitation by now. Would you like to travel with my parents

and me in our carriage? We leave Friday at 3:00
p.m. Don't forget your riding habit.
All my love,
Apryl

Jon folded the scented note. There was no mention of meeting before then, although she had asked him to call on her today. Seeing her flirt with Beesley the night before created a sour pit in his stomach; he decided not to make the call. Maybe it would be good for Apryl to wonder and worry about him. He'd wait until tomorrow to reply. Meanwhile he wrote a hasty note to the Beesleys, accepting the invitation to their country home.

The next letter in the mail stack troubled him. It was from his deceased father's lawyer, informing him that the original production of his birth record was required by law to claim his father's estate in England. Damnation. It was as he thought, and the reason he'd traveled to Maybrook in the first place. The last thing he wanted to do was return to Maybrook and face the volatile constable again. Maybe there was a loophole that a solicitor well-versed in estate and property law could uncover.

Donning his hat, Jon selected a polished mahogany cane. The afternoon was still warm as dusk descended. He began the stroll to the solicitor's building. When Jon arrived at the office front, he noticed the sign hanging over the entrance: *Doughty, Franklin, and Harmon, Solicitors at Law*—very formal and impressive. He hoped their services would be equally so.

A man with well-oiled hair greeted him at the front entrance. "Do you have an appointment, sir?"

Jon sized up the fellow and determined that he looked too shabby, what with his soiled silk cravat and threadbare jacket, to be one of the lawyers. "I have but a small matter to discuss with . . ." He thought of the first name on the marquis. "Mr. Doughty."

The man nodded. "Who may I say is calling?"

"Jonathan Porter."

The man spun on his heels and ascended the narrow staircase to the left of his desk. Moments later he returned and motioned for Jon to follow. He was led into a dim office, where books were stacked everywhere. The two bookcases were stuffed as well. A balding man looked up as Jon entered. The man's gray-blue eyes surveyed him over spectacles.

Jon offered his hand. "Jonathan Porter, sir."

The man waved his hand away. "Christian Doughty. Please be seated and state your business."

Jon scanned the cramped space for a place to sit.

"Set the books onto the floor and excuse the clutter," Doughty said. "Mr. Franklin's office is being renovated. I'm housing his books until the work is completed."

After creating a space, Jon took a seat. "I was hoping you could help me reconcile my father's estate. He passed away recently, and I am the sole heir."

Mr. Doughty nodded gravely. "My condolences on your father's passing. Being the sole heir will make settling the estate simple."

"My father's estate is in England, and I was born in Massachusetts."

"No problem."

Jon continued. "England requires a birth record, which I don't have."

"Was it lost or destroyed?"

"I don't know." Jon shrugged. "My mother died when I was young, and my father never met me. You see, he was supposed to come back for us in Massachusetts, but he never did. I was raised by a neighbor."

"Did you check the church records?"

"Nothing is recorded there. My mother was an outcast in the town. She and my father weren't married . . . She was from a staunch Puritan family that—" He broke off.

Mr. Doughty was silent for a moment. "Puritans won't bite, son. My grandfather was a Puritan. Even if your birth was swept under the carpet, there should be at least a private record at the Meeting House, if not a public one."

Jon's eyes narrowed. "Because of other circumstances, I'd rather not return to the town to pursue the matter. Is there another way?"

"What do you do for a living, Mr. Porter?"

"Litigation."

"Ah, an-up-and coming profession. Had any luck?"

Jon relaxed a bit and smiled. "Actually, with my training, I was able to get myself out of jail."

Mr. Doughty raised his eyebrows. "Interesting!"

"I traveled to Massachusetts last week and went to my mother's former home to search the place. Unfortunately I walked into a murder scene and was thrown into jail with another suspect. The next morning I freed myself and haven't looked back."

Mr. Doughty smiled. "Those are words you may have to swallow. Despite your wish not to do so, you'll have to return to find recorded evidence of your parentage."

Jon leaned forward and clasped his hands together. "There must be another way. Look at all these books." He waved his hand.

The solicitor chuckled. "What are you afraid of, getting thrown in jail again? Won't happen. Unless . . . you *did* have something to do with that murder."

"Of course not." Jon leaned back.

"Then there's nothing to fear," Mr. Doughty said in a mellow voice. "If you want your father's money, you'll return to Massachusetts."

Jon blew out a breath. "Isn't there another choice?"

"Not unless you want to travel around your birth town and ask acquaintances to sign affidavits, testifying to your parentage."

Jon hesitated. Ruth was the only one who'd probably be willing to sign something like that. And her friend, Maeve, who was no longer alive. "If I hire you to represent me, will you accompany me to Maybrook?"

Mr. Doughty gave a curt nod. "I can leave Tuesday."

On Monday morning, Jon scrawled a brief note to Apryl and a second to Thomas Beesley, declining the invitation to Beesley's estate, citing important business that couldn't wait. By afternoon, he'd cleared his appointment book. Once he collected the inheritance, he could live a gentleman's life and pursue politics if he chose. Maybe he would refer his current clients to Mr. Doughty.

His father, Jonathan Sr., had paid for his college education at Yale. Yet the older Jon became, the more tortured he felt knowing that his father had been alive and well, but refused to meet his own son. What had his father been afraid of? Was the idea of facing his past really so awful?

Upon graduation, Jon had purchased a steamship ticket to England, determined to meet his father and discover why he'd abandoned his mother. But the day before departure, Jon had received notice of his father's death.

The door to his past had been cruelly slammed shut. Then an envelope arrived with a copy of his father's will, and Jon learned he would be financially independent. That was when he decided to propose to Apryl.

A knock sounded at the library door around 3:00 that afternoon. "Mr. Porter?" Richards said. "Miss Maughan is here to see you."

"Send her in, please."

Apryl entered with a flurry of rustling yellow silk. Ringlets protruded beneath the delicate straw hat she wore, tilted jauntily on her head. Jon crossed the room and kissed her cheek.

"You've come alone?" he asked.

"My maid is in the carriage, but I don't want her to overhear," she said, her eyes watering.

"What's wrong?"

She glanced at the floor then met his gaze. "Can't your business wait a week?"

Jon tried to conceal a smile. "Is that what you're upset about?"

A stray tear fell onto Apryl's flushed cheek. Surely she couldn't be this upset over his business trip. "You look tired." Jon took her arm and guided her to a chair next to the window. "Would you like a drink?"

Apryl bit her lip. "No. I can't stay long. My parents are going to a violin performance, and I must accompany them." She folded her arms. "It won't be any fun in the country without you."

Jon tried to suppress a smile. Apryl could be absolutely childlike sometimes. "I seriously doubt that. Thomas seems to be the most accommodating host."

Apryl grabbed Jon's hand. "Please, Jon, you must come with us."

He looked at her in surprise. She had never acted so distressed before. "Has Thomas done something to make you reluctant to visit him?"

Apryl lowered her eyes, her face flushing. "No."

So there was something between them—some sort of attraction, it seemed. But Jon didn't want to drag it out of her. "Then what is it?"

She gave him a coy look. "I'll just miss you, I guess."

Perhaps that was all it was. That could be a good sign.

Suddenly, she reached for him and pulled his head down to hers, kissing him on the mouth. Jon returned her kiss, but did so with a bit of reluctance. If he kissed her as fervently as she was kissing him, they would certainly cross the line of propriety, one that he dared not cross. Scandals abounded in New York City, and Jon had had his share of that in Maybrook. He would never want her to face any sort of speculation, not knowing what his mother had gone through. No matter how Apryl tempted him, or how her curves pressed against him, he must keep a level head.

He drew away from Apryl's ardor and placed his hands on her shoulders, keeping his distance. "I won't be gone that long, my dear."

"Oh, Jon," she said, her mouth trembling. "I want to know how much you truly care about me."

Instinct made Jon want to laugh—she was like a toddler. He refrained from teasing her, saying, "Of course I truly care for you. How can you think otherwise?" He gently lifted her hand that sported her engagement ring. "Are you not my fiancée?"

"Of course." She blinked rapidly. "I have been silly."

Jon squeezed her hands. "I am doing this for us. My inheritance depends upon this business trip, and I can't put it off any longer." He lowered his voice. "It will do you good to be in the country. You look quite pale today. Go enjoy yourself. I'll be back before you know it."

Her face brightened. "I guess it won't be so bad. Although his sister, Jessa, seems a little boorish."

Jon chuckled. "You, my dear Apryl, can make any situation lively."

She raised a hand to his cheek and stroked it. Moments later she was out the door.

When she was gone, Jon let his smile fade and began to pace the room. He had never seen this side to her before— unsure, pleading, throwing herself at him. He was the one who should have been insecure about their separation. Maybe he should cancel the trip to Massachusetts. But once he had his inheritance secured, not even Thomas Beesley could measure up.

Seven

The following morning, Jon met Mr. Christian Doughty at the train station. Amidst the noise of fond farewells of other passengers and train signals, they entered the passenger section and found an empty compartment.

"Did you bring a copy of the will?" Mr. Doughty asked as soon as they were settled.

"Yes." Jon reached into his traveling bag and pulled out the document.

As the train rolled into motion, the compartment door flew open. A tall man in a brown tweed entered. "Sorry for the interruption. Is this seat taken?"

Mr. Doughty shook his head. Jon placed the will back into his bag and watched in amusement as the stranger removed his overcoat and hat, methodically folding the coat before placing it in the rack overhead. The man sat next to him and stretched out his legs. Jon noticed the dull polish on the man's expensive shoes. He was probably well-to-do, but didn't invest much time in the upkeep of his appearance.

Across the aisle, Mr. Doughty was scrutinizing their new guest too. "Business in Plymouth, Mr.—?"

"Philip Robinson," the man said, leaning across the aisle and extending his hand. "I'm traveling to my sister's funeral."

Mr. Doughty expressed his condolences, and Jon murmured in agreement.

But Mr. Robinson was eager to expound. "Sent my daughter there for a couple of months to stay with my sister, Maeve. A few nights ago, my sister died." He paused and rubbed his face. "Murdered."

"How dreadful," Jon said. This must be Maeve O'Brien's brother. Thinking about the poor woman reminded him of Eliza. He'd barely caught a glimpse of her as he transported her to Ruth's house that night, and from there, Ruth had taken over. Eliza Robinson had seemed to be quite young, and thin, and extremely distressed. And this man was her father.

"I don't know any details," Mr. Robinson said, as if he needed to talk to someone about his situation. "Received the telegram yesterday and decided to catch the first train out."

Mr. Doughty stared at the man. "We wish you all the best in finding the person responsible."

"Thank you. It's quite baffling. A quiet town and all."

Jon stared out the window at the passing scenery, growing more and more uncomfortable. He had to know for sure if this man was who he thought he was. "What town did your sister live in?"

Mr. Robinson cleared his throat. "Maybrook. It's probably not even on a map. It's a secluded Puritan settlement that managed to survive all these years. My sister fell in love with a Puritan and decided to convert." He shook his head. "Imagine that. My parents would have turned in their graves . . ."

Mr. Robinson was Eliza's father, without a doubt.

"We're traveling to the same town," Mr. Doughty said.

Jon groaned inwardly and cast Doughty a warning glance. *Please don't tell Mr. Robinson our names.*

Interest brightened Mr. Robinson's face. "Do you have family there?"

"My client and I," Doughty said, tilting his head in Jon's direction, "are on a business trip."

"May I ask what line of work you are in, sir?"

"Christian Doughty, estate lawyer, and my client . . ." He paused.

"I'm in litigation," Jon said, trying to decide what exactly he wanted this man to know.

"Litigation? Interesting," Mr. Robinson said.

Jon desperately wanted to change the direction of the conversation. "And what is your profession, sir?"

"I'm a furniture dealer." At the surprised expressions, he laughed. "Heard of Robinson-Beesley & Trade Co.?"

Mr. Doughty rubbed his chin. "I think my wife ordered a bedroom set from your company several years ago."

"Could very well be."

As the two men talked, Jon stared out the window, thinking about this man, who was Eliza's father. He seemed to be a reasonable sort. Too bad he'd gotten caught up with Thomas Beesley. Soon the conversation took another turn.

"I hope my daughter has come to her senses since living in Maybrook," Mr. Robinson said. "Eliza is quite heady for a young lady and doesn't appreciate the opportunities she's been given."

Jon listened to every word, his pulse quickening at the mention of Eliza. It was entirely possible he'd see her again now, especially after meeting her father. The town was just too small.

"It was quite an honor when my partner, Mr. Beesley, asked for my daughter's hand in marriage. To tell you the truth, I was flattered, and my wife was excited to see our daughter settled with a secure future."

"I can imagine," Mr. Doughty murmured.

"I had no idea that Eliza would be fool enough to turn the man down."

Jon bit his lip, wondering if he could keep himself from laughing. He knew very well why Mr. Robinson's daughter would turn away a man like Thomas Beesley. Even with his brief encounter with Eliza, Jon could tell the delicate young woman was no match for Thomas. How old was she anyway? Seventeen?

Why was he thinking about her so much? With Mr. Robinson also in Maybrook, Jon might run into Eliza as well. What would her reaction be to seeing him again? She probably despised him—he hadn't been able to keep her out of jail and had spent a dismal night being abrupt with her. She wouldn't want to see him and be reminded of his rudeness.

One thing was certain: Apryl would find this story amusing.

After helping Mistress Prann with morning chores, Eliza set out across the fields on horseback. Mistress Prann had been worried about the swirling clouds overhead and told her to take the chestnut mare. Eliza was more than happy to be riding again and even more important, it allowed her to go to the coast. She hoped to find Helena's journal in the lighthouse.

Maeve's funeral was being planned by the town, and Eliza's father was on his way, which meant she'd be returning home to New York soon. Today might be the last chance she had to find out more about the ghost, as long as she could find the journal. The voice hadn't spoken to her since her last visit to her aunt's place. It seemed the woman only spoke in the area of the lighthouse or Maeve's home. If what Maeve had believed was true—that Helena Talbot's spirit had never left—then the voice belonged to her.

Eliza heard the ocean surf before it came into view. She rode the mare right up to the cliffs, and at the noise below, it became jittery. Eliza urged the mare south, toward the lighthouse. When she neared it, she stopped near a lone tree and tied the horse to the trunk.

The lighthouse towered above her. It had seen better days, but the size and construction were still awe inspiring. Eliza ran her hand along the side of the rough, chipped wall—the coats of whitewash had long since been faded by the weather. Grasping the rusted latch, she was surprised to find that it wouldn't budge. The door was locked. She circled the building, looking for another entrance. Then she stopped in front of the door again and frowned. Had her aunt locked it the night of the storm?

Eliza remembered only the mad dash toward the house. Aunt Maeve couldn't have taken time to lock the door. Eliza fingered the giant keyhole—there was no lock mechanism inside.

The door had to be stuck. Eliza pushed hard then used her shoulder against it. Finally it flew open. A couple of roosting doves fluttered at the movement and flew past her.

Stepping inside, Eliza realized she'd never really inspected the old structure. A thick layer of dust seemed to cover the walls, but when she moved closer, she realized it was mold. In the middle of the floor, a winding staircase rose to the landing above, as if reaching to the heavens. One by one, she ascended the steps, passing narrow windows on the way. At the top, she was surprised to find how cozy the loft was. A hay-stuffed chair stood in the middle of the circular room, and a stack of books sat on the floor.

Eliza picked up a leather volume and traced the title— Frankenstein, by Mary Shelley. Interesting. Not something her aunt would probably choose to read. The buzzing of a lazy fly caught her attention, probably the last one of the year. She leafed through the remaining books, but none were journals. Checking beneath the chair, she found only dust and a lone cobweb. Eliza felt along the crevices of the wall, but nothing was loose, and the floorboards underneath her feet seemed solid enough.

The door to the lighthouse banged. Eliza froze—was it the wind? Then she heard footsteps on the stairs below.

Eliza turned with a start. Someone had entered the lighthouse. She walked to the head of the steps, heart hammering, trying to decide what to do. Please don't be the constable. Then she realized that she had as much right to be here as anyone. After all, the lighthouse used to be run by her uncle.

She stepped into the stairwell and called, "Who's there?"

No one answered, but she heard the footsteps continue up the staircase. She moved behind the chair, waiting to see who came into view, her breath coming fast.

A shock of rust-red hair appeared first, then a young man's ruddy face covered in pockmarks. Eliza found herself staring at the most brilliant blue eyes she'd ever seen.

"What're 'ee doing 'ere?" The man spoke with a thick and garbled tongue.

Perhaps he was older than she was, or younger by a year or two; it was difficult to tell.

"I'm visiting. Who are you?"

He took a step forward. "I'm the lighthouse keeper. I never see'd thee before."

A dank stench coming from the man reached Eliza. She tried not to breathe in too deeply. "I'm Maeve O'Brien's niece. My uncle used to own this lighthouse."

He shifted his stance awkwardly. "I liked ole Mr. O'Brien, tho' his wife was too nosey."

Eliza hid a smile. "I didn't know there was a lighthouse keeper. I've never seen you here before either."

"Don't need to come much since they closed it. But I reckon I should keep an eye on the place, all the same," he said.

Something about his movements weren't quite right. He licked his lips a couple of times, and his arms hung heavily at his sides. "What's your name?" she asked.

His eyes narrowed. "Thou asks a lot of questions."

"You know my name."

He studied her for a moment then replied, "Gus. My dad was the lighthouse keeper, and his dad before 'im. We're all Gus." He grinned, revealing gapped teeth. His gaze seemed to swallow her, and he inched closer.

Eliza felt an urgent need to get out of the building. "Are these your books, Gus?"

He nodded. "I read 'em over and over."

"Perhaps I could bring you more books sometime."

Gus's eyes lit up. "Sure."

"But I'd better hurry home now." She took a step forward and was relieved when he stepped aside and let her pass.

She escaped down the stairs without trying to make her hurry obvious, but Gus followed her.

Reaching the bottom, she pushed open the door and stepped out in time to run into someone standing outside the entrance. Arms encircled her, steadying her feet.

"Sorry," Eliza sputtered, fervently hoping the person holding her wasn't Gus Senior.

"What's the hurry?" came a deep voice.

Eliza looked up at the man. She knew those dark eyes. *Jonathan Porter.* She tried to hide her surprise. "What are *you* doing here?"

Gus barreled out the door, panting. "Why didst thou go so fast?"

She turned. "I'm expected back home soon. I can bring by a book another day and leave it here for you."

Gus's face broke into a wide grin, and then he looked at Jon. "Hallo, sir."

"Keeping the lighthouse in good condition?"

Gus's chest puffed out. "That I am, sir."

Eliza watched the interchange with surprise. Jon seemed almost . . . friendly. Not the imposing, irritable man she'd known so far. She took a quick glance in his direction. She hadn't realized how tall he was—he practically towered over her.

Jon asked Gus about his family, whom he proudly offered up information about.

"Thanks for watching out for Ruth," Jon said.

Gus grinned. "She gave me sweets."

"That's because you helped her out so much."

Gus nodded vigorously. When he left a few moments later, Eliza felt strangely relieved.

Except now, Jon's full attention was on her. "Enjoying your freedom?" His dark eyes seemed to penetrate into her.

Was he teasing? Upset? The eyes that Eliza could have sworn were black were actually a dark brown. "I thought you'd left Maybrook."

"I did," he said in a stiff tone. "But now I'm back."

There was his aloof manner. She folded her arms, tired of being made to feel guilty when she was around him. After all, her aunt had been killed, and everything else that followed was minor in importance. "Even though you have a foul temper, and can't seem to manage a civil word to a lady, thank you for helping me out the night of the storm."

Jon's mouth lifted at the corners. Was he laughing at her? Heat spread through her neck at the insult.

"What do you mean *I* have a foul temper?" he said, looking down at her. "Can you blame me? I went to *jail* because I helped you."

"I—I know. But I apologized earlier." Eliza's face reddened as he continued to stare at her. What was going through his mind? Did she have to apologize every time she saw him? "Thank you for getting them to release me."

Jon stared at her until she had to look away.

"Is there something you wanted to say?" she asked.

He blinked as if he were coming out of some sort of trance. "I thought you were much younger." He looked away.

What did her age have to do with anything? She wondered about this man who seemed to be two different people. "Tell me about Gus," she said. "I've lived here a month and never met him before now."

Jon's gaze moved back to hers, but was less intense than before. "Gus is harmless. He's not quite all there in the head, as they say."

"I see," she said.

Jon turned toward the ocean and scanned the horizon. "Looks like another storm is coming in."

Eliza studied his profile. Jon could be considered by some a handsome man, but his manner was too curt for her. That alone made him quite unappealing. She closed her eyes, wondering why she was studying him at all.

When she opened her eyes, she realized Jon was right. Dark clouds were racing across the sky, right toward them. The storm had returned.

Eight

*J*on's gaze slid to Eliza as she stared out across the ocean. Her brow was furrowed and her pale green eyes troubled. He found himself comparing Eliza to Apryl, who had dark green eyes. Eliza's were like a watercolor painting, as if different colors had been blended together. It appeared as if she'd attempted a simple bun in her hair, but now it had come loose, and tendrils of gold-brown hair hung down her back, reaching nearly to her waist.

Seeing her coming out of the lighthouse had stunned him—first that he recognized her immediately, and second, that she wasn't a girl of sixteen or seventeen. She was a woman of at least nineteen, perhaps twenty. And in a few moments, she'd established that she wasn't a wilting flower and wasn't about to mince words.

"Any more news on your aunt's accident?" he asked.

She looked at him then. "You mean her murder?" Instead of tearing-up, her gaze was like steel. "The constable hasn't shared anything with me, but in a town this size, I would have likely heard of any new developments anyway."

Again, Jon thought of her spending that horrible night in the dank cell. At the time, he'd been quite furious, but now, seeing her putting on a brave face, he felt awful about his actions, and that his actions could have resulted in her being put in jail in the first place.

"My father is on his way," she said. "For the funeral."

"I met him on the train."

Interest lit her eyes. "You did?"

"We shared the same compartment on the way here. When he introduced himself, I discovered the connection." He tried to contain his smile at her change in countenance. "I wondered why you didn't speak like a Puritan when I first found you— much less act like one."

A slight smile crossed her face, but she turned away quickly.

Jon couldn't help but smile as well. She looked quite beautiful when she smiled—but why was he even noticing?

"You thought I was Puritan?" Eliza laughed and looked over at him.

His breathing faltered, and he took a step back. This woman was . . . he didn't know what she was, but he suddenly felt unsure about everything he'd ever said to her. "I assumed . . . being in Maybrook and all . . ."

Her face tilted as she studied him, like he'd said something she finally found interesting. "I'm not sure if I should take that as a compliment."

Jon exhaled. "It's not, really—a mistaken assumption."

Her gaze held his for a moment, and he couldn't think of a single thing to say.

Finally, she broke the silence. "I suppose I should head into town and find my father. He's probably looking for me now."

"Yes," he said, but neither of them moved. He decided to be direct. "I came back to look for a record of my birth."

He hesitated. "Do you think I could search your aunt's house for any papers that my mother might have left behind?"

Eliza bit her lip. "I don't think there's anything to find in the house, but my aunt did mention a journal by . . . Helena Talbot."

"My mother." He placed a hand on her arm before he realized what he was doing. "Where is it?"

Eliza pulled away from him, alarm in her eyes.

"Sorry," Jon said. "You don't know what finding my mother's journal would mean to me." He took a breath. "I don't know what to believe about her death. Ruth told me one thing; the villagers say something else."

He found himself waiting for her response. Had she already read the words of his dead mother? Had he divulged too much?

"My aunt said she found the journal in the lighthouse," Eliza said. "Maeve left it there, and that's why I came today, but I couldn't find it. I'm sorry that I can't tell you more."

Jon took a step closer. "Where have you searched?"

"Only the upstairs room."

His mother's journal was somewhere in the lighthouse! His mind churned with possibilities. It might have the answers he was looking for—the location of his birth record, and what really happened to her. He couldn't waste another moment; he turned and walked to the lighthouse door.

"Wait!" Eliza called after him.

He paused in his step. "Will you help me search, then?" He hoped his voice didn't sound too desperate.

Someone interrupted before she could answer, calling out, "Eliza!"

Jon turned toward the direction of the voice. A young man was riding toward them, and by the looks of him, he had to be a Prann boy.

"I've been searching for you," he called to Eliza. "A storm's coming in."

The rider looked over at Jon, and their gazes met for a brief instant. The curiosity was plain in the Prann boy's expression.

"I was about to return," Eliza answered, walking to where the boy had pulled his horse to a stop.

The boy climbed off of it and held out his hand toward Eliza. She took it and said, "What is it, Nathaniel?"

Jon didn't like the familiarity he showed toward Eliza. Nathaniel Prann, it seemed.

"Your father's in town," Nathaniel said.

Eliza nodded and released his hand. "Yes, I know."

"You know?" Nathaniel looked puzzled and cast another glance in Jon's direction.

Eliza shrugged. "I sent him a telegram, didn't I? I assumed he might arrive today, as the funeral is tomorrow morning."

So she wasn't going to mention his encounter with her father, Jon thought. He exhaled and turned away. It also appeared that Eliza was otherwise occupied and wouldn't be helping him today after all.

He stepped into the lighthouse and waited for his eyes to adjust to the dimness. In the few moments since Nathaniel's arrival, the sky had grown even darker.

Jon climbed the stairs, his footsteps slow and heavy. The voices outside faded until he could no longer hear them, although that didn't stop him from remembering Eliza's upturned face and Nathaniel's obvious interest and concern for her. A rock formed in his stomach. From the loft in the lighthouse, he was drawn to the window.

Eliza had mounted the horse she'd brought and was riding away, followed by Nathaniel in pursuit.

You fool, Jon chided himself. Foolish because of the way he had let her make him feel. And foolish because he was very securely engaged.

The day of Aunt Maeve's funeral dawned misty and gray. By the time the incoming storm hit land the night before, it had dissipated into a harmless drizzle. Eliza was still glad Nathaniel had come to fetch her before she spent more time with Jonathan Porter. The man was confusing— one moment he was harsh and angry, the next, he was kind to that strange man. Then Jon was practically pleading with her to help him find his mother's journal. And why had he been moody again around Nathaniel?

"Are you ready, Eliza?" Mistress Prann's voice came through the door to the room Eliza shared with Rachel.

"Another moment, then I'll be out." Eliza pulled on the bonnet Rachel had lent her. It matched her most conservative dress of dark gray she'd brought to Maybrook.

Her thoughts turned back to Jon—she'd been touched by the acute sorrow in his eyes. She'd known when she saw them that he did have a heart, and he did care, at least about his mother. How would it be to have lost your mother at such a young age and not have any answers about the circumstances?

Eliza left Rachel's room, making sure it was tidy behind her. Her father waited on the porch. When she stepped out, she grasped his hand and gave him a kiss. She'd been quite nervous to see him when he first arrived—after all, it was her actions that led to the trouble with his business. She hadn't even dared to ask him about Thomas, and her father hadn't said a word either. Perhaps the situation would wait until after the funeral.

"You look almost Puritan," her father said.

"Mother would not be too pleased."

Her father smiled. "No, she would not."

It was good to see him smile at a time like this. Her father didn't seem to care too much for the fashions of the day; he was more interested in turning out fine furniture.

"Nathaniel is bringing around the buckboard now," her father said.

She heard it before she saw it. Even Nathaniel looked properly somber. They rode in silence to town, and when they arrived at the Meeting House, the place was nearly full.

Eliza linked arms with her father, and they walked inside the building together, taking their places near the front. Her wood casket was at the front of the room, closed.

The place didn't feel much like a church. The benches were made of rough oak boards, and the clapboard walls rattled as the wind persisted outside. Eliza noticed the Tithingman's discipline rod propped in the corner. Attached to one end was a squirrel's tail—a light brushing of the squirrel's tail was meant to rouse a sleeping woman during services, whereas a rap from the rod was meant to rouse a dozing man.

Eliza had dutifully attended Sabbath meetings with her aunt. It was strange to be here not for services, but for her aunt's funeral. Behind her, the boys sat separately from the rest of the congregation, like they did on Sabbath. The Tithingman's rod hung from a peg on the side of the room. At least the Tithingman wasn't strolling the aisles and looking for anyone not paying attention.

Eliza remembered asking Aunt Maeve about the patrolling Watchman. She told her that he walked the streets on Sundays, making sure no one broke the Sabbath by laughing or worse.

The Puritans attended their services all day, with a short break to eat, when everyone gathered in the Sabbath house for a meal of cod and pottage. The sermons were heavy and solemn; the room felt as solemn now. Eliza was used to the fact that even young children respected the importance of sitting quietly.

When everyone was settled, the Reverend stood and read the eulogy. Eliza was surprised by its short length. It seemed that Aunt Maeve had lived a very simple life. The audience murmured, "Amen," and then everyone rose.

Eliza and her father followed the pall bearers to the cemetery behind the Meeting House, where an iron fence surrounded the modest grave markers. Many were wooden, while some were made of stone. She slowed as she passed a grave dated from the 1620s, marked by a grisly death head.

Her father noticed it too. "Thank heaven they've done away with that tradition."

Eliza nodded, eyeing another grave marked by a winged skull. When they reached the corner of the cemetery where her uncle was buried, she began to relax. This was the newer section. Here, the grave markers seemed more ethereal, with winged cherubs, urns and willows.

As the coffin was lowered into the ground, the Reverend spoke a few simple words. "Here rests the body of Maeve O'Brien, wife of Edward O'Brien. May God have mercy on her soul."

❦

"Good evening, ladies and gentlemen," the magistrate said in his gravelly voice, standing at the pulpit. "Thanks to all for attending this meeting in such short order. We'll commence immediately to read the last will and testament of the recently deceased Mistress Maeve O'Brien. God rest her soul."

Eliza glanced about the Meeting House, surprised to see how many townspeople had remained after the funeral and were now sitting behind them. The Pranns had stayed, but that had been expected. She clutched her father's hand, and he squeezed hers in return. She was relieved to be out of the cemetery and back in the Meeting House, but wasn't the reading of a will only family business?

Eliza focused on the robed men before her, wearing their white wigs and lace cravats—as if they were living in the eighteenth century. Tomorrow she would accompany her father to the constable's office and make sure all of the charges against her had been cleared. Then perhaps this business would be done.

Oh, Maeve, I miss you so.

The magistrate cleared his throat and read. "'I, Mistress Maeve O'Brien, daughter of Philip and Rebecca Robinson, do hereby bequeath all my earthly possessions and property to my niece, Elizabeth May Robinson.'"

Eliza gasped. Aunt Maeve had left the house and property to her. It was supposed to have gone to her father. She covered her mouth with her hand then stole a glance at her father, expecting his face to be red in anger or disbelief. But he was smiling. Smiling! He reached over and patted her hand.

Oh, did she have questions for him.

After the reading, Eliza and her father rose, as they'd been instructed beforehand. They walked before the judge and signed their names on the witness forms. Eliza's signature was shaky, just like her hand that held the pen. The magistrate handed another document to Eliza.

"This is the deed to the O'Brien estate. You will sign your name here." He pointed to the bottom, below some beautiful calligraphy.

Eliza took a steady breath and put the pen to the paper, then signed her name. She was now a woman of property.

Her father rested a hand on her shoulder and said in a quiet voice, "Congratulations. Maeve left her property in the best hands possible."

Eliza looked up at her father, a dozen questions on her mind. But here wasn't the place to ask them, especially with the stern-faced magistrate listening in.

She thanked the magistrate, who barely gave her a nod, then turned to face the people. Many stepped forward and congratulated her, but most wore looks of disapproval. She was an outsider, that was for certain, and not one of them.

When they were nearly alone in the Meeting House, Eliza said to her father, "It should have gone to you."

His smile was genuine. "Nonsense, I am established in life and have a successful business. But you're young and have a whole future ahead of you. Maeve knew what she was doing."

"Father—" Eliza began.

Two men strode into the Meeting House. Eliza looked over to see Jonathan Porter and another man. Her father crossed the room easily and warmly greeted both gentlemen while Eliza followed behind.

Jon was still here? He seemed to fill the room with his presence, and Eliza forced herself to look away from him. Had he found his mother's journal in the lighthouse? She felt his gaze on her—and imagined his brown eyes turned black.

"This is my daughter, Eliza," her father was saying to the men, "whom I told you about on the train. Eliza, this is Mr. Doughty and Mr. Porter."

Mr. Doughty smiled and extended his hand. Eliza turned toward him and shook it.

"I've had the opportunity to meet your daughter already, sir," Jon said.

Eliza met his gaze for an instant. Something passed between them—like familiarity—something Eliza couldn't quite explain.

Her father glanced at her, then back to Jon. "Well, then, all for the better. You must join us for supper at the dining hall."

Mr. Doughty accepted at once. "Of course."

Jon's gaze went to Eliza. "Perhaps another time. We have business to attend to."

"It won't take long," Mr. Doughty said, smiling. "We'll meet you at the dining hall shortly."

Something in Jon's eyes flickered; was he annoyed with his friend's acceptance of the invitation?

"Very well then." Her father shook their hands again. "We have much to discuss tonight. My daughter has become a land owner."

Eliza lowered her eyes, avoiding the questioning look from Jon. Her cheeks burned at her father's openness. But he was always open, honest, and sometimes that was a detriment. As she left the Meeting House with her father, she felt Jon's gaze on her back.

Half an hour later, Eliza and her father were seated around a well-worn table, opposite to Jon and Mr. Doughty. The dining hall was one of the modern additions to the town. A pleasant-faced woman approached them with four mugs of ale. "Here thou are," she said, sloshing the overfilled mugs on the table.

Eliza listened absently as the men talked, uninterested in the subject of politics, until it turned personal.

"Eliza has inherited my sister's estate," her father said.

Doughty's eyes went to her. "And will you take up residence there, Miss Robinson?"

"Oh no," Eliza said. "I have no plans to live in Maybrook. I don't think I could convince my parents to change locations to live with me."

Doughty chuckled. "I suspect not."

"So you will sell it then?" Jon said.

Eliza looked at Jon with surprise. He seemed genuinely interested. "Eventually. I'd like to stay here for a few more weeks." She glanced at her father.

Her father nodded. "Yes, there are matters at home that are a bit delicate for Eliza right now."

She was thankful that neither of the men pressed for more information.

"How did you meet my daughter, Mr. Porter?" her father asked.

Eliza froze. How would he answer?

"Maybe your daughter should tell you the story," Jon said.

She looked away from his intense gaze. It was strange to be sitting across from him, having this conversation around her father, as if everything was completely normal. But in truth, she'd just become a land owner. She was sitting across from a man she never thought she'd see again, and she was aware of every movement he made and ever look he gave her.

"He was visiting Maybrook too," she said, knowing that wasn't the whole truth. Thankfully Jon didn't add anything more.

Her father nodded. "We have important business to settle tomorrow morning with the town constable."

"Oh?" Mr. Doughty asked.

"When my sister died, the authorities put my daughter into jail. Imagine that. Poor Eliza." He patted her hand. "A lawyer was able to have her released. If I could thank him . . ."

Eliza's gaze met Jon's across the table. He was waiting for her to make the first move, she realized. "You can thank him now, Father. It was Mr. Porter who argued my case."

Her father looked at them in surprise. "You mean . . . but, how?"

Knowing that the whole story would come out sooner or later, Eliza took a deep breath. "On the night that Aunt Maeve was killed, I was desperate for help. I hurried out of the house to saddle the horse, and there was Mr. Porter." She kept her eyes on the table, not wanting to see Jon's reaction.

"What were you doing there?" her father said to Jon.

"Actually, I was planning a visit to Maeve. I was seeking documents that might have been left by my mother, who used to live in that house." Jon looked from her father to Eliza. "I was born there, and my mother died when I was very young. Upon the recent passing of my father, I was instructed to obtain a birth record." He lowered his voice. "When I saw Eliza staggering in the storm, I knew something was wrong. Before she fainted, she told me her aunt had died."

The memory of her fear and desperation that night resurfaced. "Jon helped me to a safe house and warm bed."

Her father put a hand on her shoulder. "What an awful night! I'm grateful Mr. Porter was there to help."

"I awoke in a neighbor's house," Eliza said, looking up into Jon's eyes. She well remembered his anger once they were in jail together. But here, now, his face was gentle, his eyes kind. "The next thing I knew, I was being arrested for the murder of my dear aunt."

Jon gave a slight nod then summarized how they both ended up in jail. Their eyes met again.

"When I was released," Eliza said, "I discovered that Mr. Porter was the gentleman who came to my aid—a second time." As she spoke, she realized Jon had come to her aid a third time, at the lighthouse that afternoon.

"I'll toast to that," her father said, raising his mug. "Since Mr. Porter already has experience defending my daughter, would you gentlemen be willing to accompany us to the constable's office in the morning? I need to make sure the charges against Eliza are cleared and that the investigation into my sister's death is moving forward."

"Certainly," Mr. Doughty said. "We'd love to help."

Jon's eyes found Eliza's before he said, "Of course."

Nine

'm going straight to hell. At least I would be if I were Puritan. Jon stared at the spreading light on the ceiling above him. He lay in bed with his hands crossed behind his head, welcoming the chill of the morning. He'd barely slept, and what little sleep he did get was consumed by thoughts of Eliza Robinson.

She'd decided to invade his dreams, no . . . haunt them. The soulful expression in her eyes when they'd talked about the night of her aunt's death seemed to burrow into his soul. He wanted to protect her, and wished he could have protected her more.

Like a brother protects a sister. He shook his head at the notion. She was nothing like a sister, and she was completely different than Apryl. Eliza was like an innocent spring day compared to Apryl's full summer flirtatious ways.

It didn't help that last night, Eliza had looked at him like he was some kind of hero. *She's damned alluring, that's what she is.* And she didn't even know it. Jon let out a breath of frustration. It wouldn't do him any good to keep thinking about her. After he returned to New York, he'd never see her again. He'd be busy focusing on his future and planning his wedding with Apryl.

As it well should be.

Cracks of light spread across his quilt; dawn was here. This day he must find his birth record. He needed to concentrate on that, and only that. Then he could clear his mind for his future as a wealthy man and husband.

After Eliza left the lighthouse the previous afternoon, he'd discovered a stair with an unusual angle. It looked like someone had recently tried to repair the step. As he'd fiddled with the wooden plank, it came loose in his hands. Beneath the step was a hidden box. His heart had hammered as he removed it, feeling almost as if his mother were watching him, whispering encouragement.

But the box had been empty.

Jon sensed that the contents had been recently taken. Perhaps Eliza had taken his mother's journal and hadn't told him about it—was she capable of that? Was her innocence a ruse? Had Gus taken the journal? Jon was determined to find out before the afternoon train. He didn't want to stay in Maybrook one more night.

Squeezing his eyes shut, he tried to concentrate on his fiancée, her laughing face and smiling eyes. He thought of how she'd pressed against him, demanding that he kiss her, to which he had happily obliged. Then the deep green eyes paled, and the dark hair lightened. What would it be like to kiss Eliza? Did her innocence extend to men and kissing? Had she allowed Thomas Beesley to touch her?

Jon opened his eyes in exasperation. His thoughts were out of control. Why couldn't he get Eliza off his mind? The answer was to return to New York as soon as possible. He would never do what his father did to his mother—abandon her and break his promises. No matter how distracted his thoughts were about Eliza, he'd stay engaged to Apryl.

"Are you awake, Jon?" Mr. Doughty called through the door, lightly knocking.

"I'll be ready in a minute." He'd told Mr. Doughty that he wanted to get going at first light. He climbed out of the covers and drew on his trousers. His shirt hanging over the back of a chair still looked presentable. Peering into the scratched mirror over the basin, he realized he needed a shave. It would have to wait until he returned to New York. Every moment counted now. As he dressed, he caught himself humming as he thought of Eliza. He immediately scolded himself.

At the breakfast table, Jon listened with half an ear to Mr. Doughty. "We'll have to search your mother's home today. The constable might have to come with us if it's still closed for the investigation. If we can't find anything, we'll round up some townspeople who lived here at the time of your birth and get them to sign an affidavit as witnesses."

Jon nodded, his thoughts moving again to Eliza. When Mr. Doughty finished his breakfast, Jon pushed away his untouched plate and rose.

The short walk to the jail house brought back the memories of the night he'd spent there with Eliza. He could have certainly been kinder to her, more comforting. He doubted she'd ever spent a night in such dismal conditions. At the front of the building, Mr. Robinson and Eliza stood waiting. Jon's pulse involuntarily quickened, and he silently cursed his reaction at seeing her.

In the morning light, he was struck with how vulnerable Eliza appeared, how her pale skin contrasted with the rich gold-brown of her hair, and how there was a bit of a flush on her cheeks when their gazes met.

He cursed himself again. He had to stop thinking about her—he should be more concerned about how Apryl was doing. But shadows played under Eliza's eyes, making him wonder if perhaps she'd slept as poorly as he.

"Good morning," Mr. Robinson said.

Mr. Doughty shook his hand, and they talked as they entered the constable's office together.

Jon lagged behind so he could speak to Eliza. "I found a box hidden under the lighthouse stairs."

Her eyes flew to his face. "The journal?"

"It wasn't there. You didn't take it?"

"No."

But it was too late to discuss the matter further. They'd reached the doorway where the constable greeted everyone.

Instead of a grim face, Jon was surprised to see the constable smile at his guests. "Welcome. I have some good news. We've found thy sister's murderer."

Jon almost felt Eliza's shock reverberate through him as she grasped her father's arm.

"Aye," the constable continued. "We received a telegram early this morning in regards to a transient arrested for a similar case in the state of Connecticut. He all but confessed to the murder of Maeve O'Brien."

"He's in custody, then?" Mr. Robinson asked.

The constable nodded. "He'll be tried in Connecticut, and, depending on the sentence he receives, he may receive two death sentences. But he'll probably not need to be hanged twice."

Everyone in the room chuckled, except for Jon. It was too easy, too neat. "How can we find out what the sentence will be?"

"You can read the papers or telegram the Connecticut office," the constable said. "I'm grateful that it's over."

Jon wanted to question the constable further. Could the case be closed so easily? Was the man not to be convicted in Maybrook also? But everyone around him looked pleased, Eliza included.

"Well," Mr. Doughty said amid the congratulations, "I guess that clears Eliza and Jon as suspects."

Mr. Robinson laughed, and even the constable chuckled with relief.

"With that good news, we have another item of business," Mr. Doughty said. "Could you give us a few names of the townspeople who lived here twenty-four years ago?"

"Why?" the constable asked.

"My client, Jonathan Porter," he said gesturing in Jon's direction, "needs proof of his birth in this town."

The constable surveyed Jon. "What were thy parents' names?"

Jon wanted to laugh. Everyone knew everyone in Maybrook. Surely the constable remembered him as well, but instead of arguing, he obliged. "Jonathan Porter and Helena Talbot."

The constable's eyebrows arched. "Helena Talbot was thy mother?" he said in a wary voice.

"Did you know her?" Jon asked.

The constable's answer came rather quickly. "I heard about her tragic ending. It was quite odd. Some said she could swim, so why she drowned is beyond understanding."

Jon stiffened. He hated this town. Hated the gossip. Hated that this man was speculating about his mother's death. He didn't even notice that Eliza had come to stand beside him until her hand brushed his. He definitely noticed that.

The constable continued, his tone sympathetic now. "Aye, I could come up with some names. But it does seem strange. That is, if she didn't drown, why a young mother would leave her only child."

Rage pulsed through Jon. It was everything he could do not to knock the man to the ground. The silence in the room was tangible. Jon clenched his hands at his side. Eliza moved closer and touched his arm.

"Jon," Eliza whispered. "Come outside with me."

Her voice and touch seemed to pour some sanity back into him. He became aware of everyone in the room staring at him.

Eliza turned to her father and Mr. Doughty. "Please bring the names with you."

Jon let her guide him out the door, where they stopped on the side of the jail house beneath a group of maple trees. Eliza kept her hand tucked beneath his arm. Jon focused on his breathing, each moment getting easier. Eliza must think him a silly fool.

"I certainly don't blame you if you despise everything in Maybrook," she said quietly.

Jon looked down at her, into those watercolor eyes, his trance broken. "I don't hate everything in Maybrook."

The sides of her mouth lifted. "That's good to hear. Ruth seems like a good woman."

"Ruth is," Jon said, his breath calming, his body warming at Eliza's nearness. "And the ocean is quite beautiful."

A smile escaped Eliza's mouth. "Very true—in calm and in storm."

Jon couldn't take his eyes from her. Her hair was pulled back into a twist, but a strand had come loose, falling against her cheek. Before he could consider what he was doing, he tucked it behind her ear. "And I discovered another good thing in Maybrook . . . only recently."

Her face flushed, and Jon decided it was one of the most charming things he'd ever seen.

"Jon . . ." Her breath seemed to shorten, but she didn't say anything more, and let his name hang in the air between them. Yet she didn't move away from him, and he found he liked having her at his side, her hand tucked in his arm. It felt comfortable, natural.

"Maybrook seems to be a nice sanctuary for you though," he said. "I heard about why you left New York."

Her face paled. "I hate the gossip columns."

"It wasn't the gossip columns, Eliza," he said. "I'm only telling you this because I think you should know. I met Thomas Beesley at a dinner the other night. He told me about it himself, and when I met your father on the train, I put it together."

"Thomas is still talking about me?" Her eyes flickered away. "Why does the man persist? He's already made things difficult for my father."

Jon felt something inside his heart stir. Again he wanted to protect Eliza, and the more he learned about Beesley, the more he didn't like the man. "I don't blame you for turning him down."

Her eyes lifted to meet his, gratitude reflected in her expression. "Really?"

He nodded, unsure if he should say more. They fell into a silence for a moment. Finally, he said, "I don't have the answers about my mother, and neither does the town. The constable was right—how could a mother abandon her baby?" He studied Eliza, lost in her closeness. He felt like he could talk to her with frankness, ask her anything. "Would *you* abandon one you love, Eliza?"

She blinked and looked away. Were those tears in her eyes?

"Jon, you can't think of your mother like that. Whatever happened, I know she loved you and didn't want to leave you." Her eyes were back on his, and for a moment, he believed her.

But how could Eliza know?

Voices belonging to Mr. Robinson and Mr. Doughty reached them. "We've plenty of names to go on," Mr. Doughty said confidently when he spotted the couple.

"Very well," Jon said. Eliza released his arm and folded her hands together. He noticed the distance immediately, like a warm blanket being drawn away on a cold morning. He regretted that their privacy was over. "Let's go."

"It's been nice to see you folks again," Mr. Doughty said. "We're grateful things are resolved with your sister, Mr. Robinson. Perhaps we'll cross paths again in New York."

"We would like that," Mr. Robinson said, shaking Mr. Doughty's hand.

Jon felt Eliza's gaze on him, but when he looked over, she was walking toward her father and Doughty. "Thank you, Mr. Doughty, it's been a pleasure," she said.

After Eliza and her father left, Jon stared after them.

"What a nice family," Mr. Doughty said. "Too bad they've had to endure such a tragedy."

"Yes," Jon said. Why had he let himself become so wrapped up in her? It wasn't like he was living in Maybrook, and she was the best thing it had to offer. He lived in New York City, and there were many women, not to mention his lovely fiancée. Maybe it was because she was so different than the socialites he knew.

The constable appeared in the entryway. "Ready, gentlemen?"

"The constable will let us into Maeve's home and help us search for documents, and if none are to be found, we'll seek out the townspeople," Mr. Doughty explained.

Jon followed them to the constable's buckboard. He didn't want to be in the constable's presence, but there was no help for it. The sooner it was over, the better. He hoped that Maeve had forgotten that she'd brought the journal to her home, and then he'd be able to find it. After that, he'd leave Maybrook and never return.

The ride to Maeve O'Brien's house was short but bumpy. The recent storms had left gouging ruts in the country road. Jon caught himself watching Mr. Doughty, who seemed unperturbed by the turn of events and was conversing easily with the constable.

Am I the only one who is worried that Maeve O'Brien's murderer was found so easily? Jon shook his head. The solution to her untimely death was too simple.

Arriving at the deserted cottage, the three men climbed off the buckboard. The constable unlocked the door and entered, but Jon hung back for a moment, letting Doughty enter first. Jon couldn't remember any details of this particular childhood home. He had left it when he was three and moved into Ruth's home.

He walked inside to see the disarray of the kitchen. He thought of Eliza here, of the night that she'd come stumbling out of the cottage, injured and frightened. It all seemed dreamlike in the harsh light of day.

"We'll start at the top, in the attic," the constable said. He and Mr. Doughty disappeared up the stairs.

Jon walked about the rooms on the main floor. He picked his way through the kitchen, pulling drawers and opening cupboards. Then he stopped in the sitting room with its blackened hearth. A fire would make this room cozy, but now it was silent and cold.

He ran his fingers along the hearth, feeling for any loose bricks that might conceal a hiding place. The oak planks on the floor were solid and well-worn. Nothing on the wall looked out of the ordinary. He felt along the crevices of the sofa and discovered a forgotten handkerchief. Elegant embroidered letters had been stitched in the corner, "E. M. R." It had to be Eliza's. Without a second thought, he tucked the handkerchief into his coat pocket.

Leaving the sitting room, Jon paused before the open door of the bedroom. This must have been Maeve's room. He walked into the quiet sanctum, stepping noiselessly on the rug. Trinkets sat upon a small desk in the corner. The bedding had been stripped from the mattress tick. A quilt was folded neatly on a chair in the corner. It was a patchwork, with intricate hand-stitches securing the fabric swatches together. It reminded him of something he'd see in Ruth's house. A board covered part of the only window—glass shards still lay on the floor where they had fallen.

"It's not too late."

Jon spun around and stared at the doorway—but no one was there. Had the noise been merely the wind coming through the broken window? But there was no breeze.

A draft brushed near his ankles; he must have left the front door open.

"Mr. Doughty?" he called out. "Constable?"

They didn't answer, so they must still be in the attic. He was more tired than he thought. He walked out of the bedroom and heard the constable and Mr. Doughty descending the stairs.

"Any luck?" the constable asked when they came into view.

"Nothing yet," Jon replied, noticing that the front door was shut tight. "And you?"

"Nothing."

"Mind if I check up there myself?" Jon asked.

"Go ahead," the constable said. "We'll have a look around down here."

Jon climbed the narrow staircase and paused before the bedroom door on the second landing. This must be where Eliza had slept. He opened the door and was surprised by how large it was. The room was bright and cheerful, although all personal effects had been removed. Only a bed, a sturdy dresser and a washbasin on a stand remained.

Crossing to the window, he looked out the mottled pane of glass at the lighthouse in the distance. Should he tell the constable about discovering the empty box? The missing journal?

His thoughts were interrupted when the constable called out to him, "We're going to the barn."

"All right," Jon called back, then knelt and tested the floorboards, checking to see if any of them were loose. He lifted the mattress from the bed and patted it down. Nothing felt unusual. Checking behind the dresser, he still found nothing. By the time he left the cottage, Doughty and the constable were coming out the barn.

They stood in a circle for a couple of moments, talking. "We'll have to go with our backup plan," Doughty said. "And hope it's enough to satisfy a British solicitor."

Jon nodded. "It will have to be." Claiming his inheritance was the next step in his plan to marry and enter into politics.

Ten

"hank you so much for everything," Eliza said, standing in the Prann kitchen.

Mistress Prann brushed off her flour-spotted hands and pulled Eliza in for a tight hug. "Must thou leave so soon?"

"I've encroached on your hospitality long enough," Eliza said. "I'm staying at my aunt's place until my mother arrives."

"But dear, wilt thou be safe alone?"

Eliza's stomach fluttered, but she ignored it. "They've caught the criminal. He's never coming here again."

"If thou needest anything, we are here for thee," Mistress Prann said.

"I'll be all right," Eliza said. "As soon as my father returns to New York, he'll send my mother back on the next train. She wants to look over the furniture to decide whether any of it will be of use in New York. But I'm afraid she'll be disappointed, as Aunt Maeve lived quite simply."

"I know, dear. Thy aunt was unpretentious. She'll always be missed." A frown creased Mistress Prann's forehead. "I worry for thee."

"Don't worry," Eliza said and smiled. One more embrace followed, and Eliza stepped into the sunshine. The day promised to be a new beginning. She was now a young woman of independent means and would be setting foot on her own property.

Nathaniel helped Eliza into the front seat of the buckboard, then climbed up and sat next to her. Traveling through the early-morning countryside glistening with an early frost, Eliza breathed in the cool air. The beauty of the autumn leaves and deep blue sky, combined with the invigorating air, made her feel more alive than she had in a long time.

Nathaniel was unusually quiet on the way to Maeve's house. Eliza stole a glance at him and saw his eyes narrow as he stared straight ahead.

"Is something wrong?" Eliza asked.

At first Nathaniel didn't seem to hear her, but then he slowed the buckboard until it came to a stop.

She fiddled with a button on her skirt. Why was he acting so strange?

"Eliza," Nathaniel said, his voice hesitant. He released the reins and turned. Then he took her hands in his and held them tight.

She had put off speaking to him, and now she realized she'd waited too long. His hands were hot and sweaty, and beads of perspiration dampened his forehead.

"Don't say it," she said. "Let's leave things as they are."

"I can't wait another day, Eliza. From the time I first saw you, I felt something inside. I love thee. And I want to marry thee."

Marry? Hearing the word sent a dagger through her. This had gone much farther than she'd thought. He looked so trusting, and she didn't want to hurt him.

"I—I have no intentions of marrying anyone soon, Nathaniel. You're young and have much to look forward to." *And I don't love you, and you're Puritan, and . . .*

Nathaniel's cheeks flushed. "My father has promised me a parcel of land, and with thy aunt's house, we'd have a place to live in the beginning. I'll build thee a new house, and we'll farm the land. Thou can be happy here—I know it. My parents married a year younger than our age, and I wouldn't make thee go to Meeting, unless thou wanted to . . ."

Eliza stared hopelessly at him, tears brimming. He viewed life so simply, and now she had to break his heart.

"Surely there was a girl you had your eye on before I came," she said, hoping to make the moment cheerful—how things had always been between them. "I'm more than satisfied being friends with you for many years to come."

"Friends? Do you mean friends who marry?"

"No," she said, her throat tight. "I don't want to marry, you or anyone. Not now."

He stared at her as if he couldn't quite believe her.

She pulled her hands away from his grasp. "Please, take me to my aunt's." She looked straight ahead, avoiding Nathaniel's soulful eyes.

He scooted right next to her and pulled her into his arms. She felt his lips on her neck as he kissed her.

Was kissing before marriage even allowed among the Puritans? "Nathaniel, you're—"

But then his mouth was on hers, his kisses soft and clumsy at first, then hardening into deliberate urgency.

It was not horrible, but she knew she couldn't allow him to kiss her. "Stop," she said, pushing him away.

Nathaniel fell back, his face red. "Forgive me," he whispered.

"No, forgive me, for letting you think I'd welcome a marriage proposal." His face went ashen, and Eliza felt like she might be sick with guilt. How could she have led Nathaniel to believe she'd want to marry him? Was there something wrong with how she communicated with men? First Thomas, now Nathaniel. She climbed down from the buckboard and went to the back to retrieve her traveling case.

"Please don't, Eliza," came his voice, clear and strong again. "I'll take thee to thy house, and I swear I'll not touch thee again."

She hesitated. If Nathaniel was anything, he was honest. Knowing it would be quite impossible to drag her belongings the remaining distance, she secured the case onto the buckboard again and climbed into the rear seat, relieved at Nathaniel's promise.

He didn't turn to look at her. Instead he urged the horse into a trot, and before long, Aunt Maeve's house came into view.

After Nathaniel pulled the horse to a stop, Eliza climbed down to fetch her traveling case. In an instant, he was by her side and lifted it down. When his arm brushed hers, a faint smile crossed his lips.

"I'm sorry," he murmured. He followed her into the house and set the case down, waiting for further instructions.

"Thank you," Eliza said, dismissing him with a half-hearted smile. But he didn't make a move to leave.

Instead, Nathaniel gazed at her, confidence in his eyes. She glanced away, not sure what to say.

"I'll wait for thee, Eliza, as long as it takes."

She opened her mouth to protest, but he turned and walked outside. She heard him whistling as he climbed into the buckboard and snapped the reins. *Don't wait for me, Nathaniel Prann. I'll be gone before you know it.*

Sinking onto the sofa, she couldn't picture herself living out her days in this complacent Puritan town. Then she began to laugh. Maybe she should accept his proposal and insist he move, to New York City. His innocent eyes would be assailed by all the evil-doers. He'd turn and run at the first sight of a misdeed.

She sighed, not knowing what to think of Nathaniel. After all, he had just kissed her—passionately. Maybe she didn't know him as well as she thought.

∽

Eliza spent the afternoon cleaning the cottage. A layer of dust had settled over the floors and furniture. Her mother would be arriving in a couple of days, and there was a lot of work to be done before she arrived. When the place was presentable, Eliza ventured into the garden. Aunt Maeve had kept an immense herb collection, growing lavender, comfrey, and rosemary. Eliza gathered a variety of the stubby plants and took them into the kitchen, and hung them upside down to dry.

In the late afternoon, Eliza heard the sound of an axe splitting wood. She left the kitchen and walked around the house towards the sound. A man with a shirt tied about his waist stood in front of the shed, chopping wood. Eliza found herself staring at the man's back and its mass of heavy scarring, as if he had been whipped multiple times. The color of his rust-red hair told her who it was.

He turned. "Good day, miss."

"Hello, Gus."

He started to split the wood again, raising the axe over his head then brought it down with an earsplitting thud.

Before the next chop, Eliza asked, "What are you doing?"

He paused and relaxed his grip on the axe. "Chopping Mistress O'Brien's wood."

"Remind me what she pays you."

"Eggs. Sometimes she gives me a whole basketful."

Eliza watched him chop for another moment. Did he not know that Maeve had died? He acted like Maeve had recently asked him to chop the wood. He really was a strange man.

95

Eliza would have to see about some eggs. She walked into the barn to check on the chickens. They perched in the coop, their feathers fluttering with each cluck. A sack of feed had been opened, and its contents were spilled onto the dirt. At least they hadn't gone hungry.

She reached under one hen that protested loudly and collected its egg from the nest, then moved onto the next hen. When Eliza had filled a basket, she left the barn and went to hand them over to Gus. But he was no longer at the chopping block. He was stationed by the well, drinking water in large gulps from a ladle.

Placing the basket of eggs on the edge of the well, Eliza said, "Thank you."

Gus wiped his mouth with the back of his hand. "Thank 'ee, Miss. But where's Maeve?"

Eliza took a breath. "She . . . died last week."

Gus's eyes widened. "She died? But 'ow?"

"She was . . . killed. But they've found the one who did it."

Gus's eyes watered, and tears rolled down his cheeks. He brushed away the tears and looked past Eliza. "I have to go." He scrubbed at his face, took the basket of eggs, and walked away. She watched him go, baffled that he hadn't known about Maeve's death, and feeling bad about being the one to tell him.

Eleven

*J*on cursed again as the ink smudged the paper. The train ride didn't make writing easy. He poised his dip pen over the half-filled page and scanned the first paragraph:

> *Miss Robinson,*
> *I was pleased to find you safe and sound upon my return trip to Maybrook. I appreciate the aid you gave me after the constable's unfeeling words. But as I said, not everything in Maybrook is painful to me.*

He scratched the words out, then wadded up the paper, and started fresh on a new paper.

> *Miss Robinson,*
> *I was pleased to find you safe and sound upon my return trip to Maybrook. I hope you are recovering from the past week. Mr. Doughty mentioned that as a lawyer, he'd be happy to help*

you with any matters regarding your new inheritance.

There. That was a better start. Formal, yet concerned. Not too personal.

If you happen to find my mother's journal, could you please write to me at the address below? I will come personally to Maybrook to fetch it.

He signed the letter and added his address, then sealed it into an envelope. He'd post it as soon as he reached New York. The signed affidavits were in Mr. Doughty's carrying case; they'd been able to get four signatures from Maybrook townspeople who remembered his mother's pregnancy and Jon's birth. At least that business was over, and he could move forward in claiming his inheritance.

Jon wouldn't have to return to Maybrook ever again . . . unless he received a letter from Eliza about the journal. That would be the only reason he'd return. He leaned into his seat, glancing at Mr. Doughty, who dozed across the aisle. There was no Henry Robinson sharing their compartment this time. But Mr. Doughty had procured the Robinsons' New York address, which would come in handy if Jon had to follow up on the journal after Eliza returned to New York.

He closed his eyes, hoping to get some rest. The nights in Maybrook had proved difficult to sleep through, but that should be remedied with the absence of Eliza. He didn't have to worry about running into her. He allowed himself to admit that he was drawn to her—quite unexpected, but he decided it was due to the unusual circumstances in which they'd met and her connection to his mother's house.

He'd also been drawn to her innocent beauty, but what man wouldn't be? It was only a natural appreciation, nothing more than that. Jon had no intention of changing any of his marital plans. He'd committed himself to Apryl, and she was his future.

He dozed, the image of Eliza on his mind, making his sleep quite restless. What seemed like only moments later, the train came to a halt, and Jon awoke with a jolt.

"We're here," Doughty said.

Jon gathered his things, and the two men stepped off the train together and shook hands.

"I'll send the witness documents right away," Doughty said. "And I hope to hear back within a month."

Jon blinked, still trying to clear the fog of the nap from his mind. "I look forward to it." As he moved into the milling crowd, he felt lighthearted. Things were beginning to fall into place. He would soon claim his inheritance, and, with Eliza on his side, he hoped to solve the puzzle of his mother's death. But that was as far as his acquaintance with her would go. He was looking forward to seeing Apryl again, and getting Eliza off of his mind. Jon hailed a carriage to take him straight to Apryl's. He wanted to tell her the news.

When he arrived at the Maughans, he climbed the steps and rang the bell. But Apryl wasn't home. According to the housemaid, the family was gone and wouldn't return for two days; they were still enjoying the country life at the Beesley estate. Jon left feeling confused. Had she not been anxious about staying at the Beesleys without him—so why had she prolonged her visit? She must be enjoying Jessa's company more than she'd expected. By the time he reached home, Jon had decided to repack his bags and take up Thomas's invitation after all.

Time to get to know the man who Eliza turned down.

Just as the sun was sinking below the horizon, Jon arrived at the long driveway leading to the Beesley estate. The house was a stately two-story, surrounded by sprawling lawns and gardens. The carriage pulled around the circular driveway, and Jon alighted with his overnight bag and stood before the house, ablaze with lights and music flowing from the open doorway.

A butler must have heard the carriage and now waited as Jon ascended the front staircase. He removed his overcoat and hat, placing them on the outstretched arms of the butler. "I'm Mr. Jonathan Porter."

The butler bowed and said, "I was told you might arrive. Mr. Beesley is in the garden, but you're welcome to wait for him inside."

So they were expecting him? Certainly that was evidence of Apryl's optimism. Jon stepped into the grand hallway and looked at the chandelier lit with hundreds of candles, blazing their welcome. To his right, the music poured from the drawing room, but no one was dancing. In fact, except for the musicians, the room was vacant.

He walked back to the butler. "I'll find them in the garden, I suppose."

The butler dipped his head. "It's this way, sir."

Jon found the garden path easily enough, which was lit with oriental lanterns. The heavy scent of blooming roses assailed him as he walked, reminding him of Apryl.

He came to a clearing, expecting it to be filled with several guests, including Apryl and her parents. But on the bench on the far side, only Apryl and Thomas sat together.

Their shoulders were touching, and their hands intertwined. Jon's throat tightened. The bench was rather small, but they appeared as intimate confidantes. It might be nothing, but the longer he stood there unobserved, the more he doubted his own thoughts.

Apryl saw him first. Her mouth fell open, and she rose, practically stumbling over her white gown of lace and ribbons. "Jon!" Her face paled two shades. Behind her, Thomas rose and clumsily straightened the velvet vest over his generously cut shirt.

Jon walked forward, pretending that everything was normal. He even shook Beesley's hand, which he found to be quite damp. The man was perspiring—had he been all along? Or just now at the sighting of Jon?

"Welcome, welcome," Thomas said, removing a handkerchief from his breast pocket and wiping his nose.

Jon could have broken that nose.

Apryl smiled and gave Jon a kiss on his cheek. "You've returned early. I'm so delighted you decided to join us. I was hoping you'd come."

Even though Jon felt like decking Thomas, he smiled at the two. "I didn't expect Apryl to still be here, but when I learned of her extended stay, I decided to join the fun."

"W—well, of course," Thomas stuttered then cleared his throat. "Perhaps I'd better see if your parents have made themselves comfortable in the library." He hesitated as he met Jon's gaze. "And when you're ready, I'll have the butler, Mr. West, show you your room."

Jon offered a mock bow and watched Thomas waddle down the garden path. Jon turned and looked at Apryl, whose face had grown quite flushed. Holding out his arm, he asked, "Care for a stroll?"

"Let me fetch my wrap," she said, turning back to the bench.

No "love" or "dear." It made him sick to think of what was so obviously transpiring between his fiancée and Thomas.

Jon guided Apryl along the trails of the garden in the gathering shadows. When he couldn't stand the suspense any longer, he stopped and faced her. "Do you want to break our engagement so you can court your bloated host?"

Apryl's eyes widened, filling with tears. "Of course not, Jon. I—I wouldn't dream—"

"I saw the two of you together, pressed together like fish in a tin—"

"It was nothing. He's easy to talk to, and he's fun to be around, but he's not like you. You're . . ." Her voice broke.

"What am I, Apryl? Easy to talk to? Fun to be around? I thought we had an understanding, a commitment." Frustration boiled inside of him. "I don't want a wife who will always be looking for the next entertaining party, or the next man who romances her—who's *not* her husband."

Tears trickled down her cheeks. But even in the rising moonlight, her eyes blazed, her cheeks aflame.

"Why can't you tell me, Jon?" she asked, her voice trembling.

His eyes hardened. "Tell you what?"

"That you love me. Why won't you say it?"

Because I don't know if I do. Jon gaped then watched her face dissolve into sobs. How had this suddenly become his fault? "Did I not ask you to marry me? Have I not shown you every courtesy? Just because I'm not a dandy, or some tripe that composes poems."

"Don't be ridiculous. Thomas doesn't compose poems. But he doesn't hold back his affections, either."

Jon stared at her, his face heating up. "Are you saying you've kissed him? Have you been intimate with him?"

She gasped and turned from him, her shoulders shaking.

Jon needed a man to punch. Had Eliza and Thomas . . .? He couldn't let himself think about that. The thought of them together was mortifying. He had no desire to comfort her, to tell her the words she wanted to hear.

"So you'll not tell me you love me." Her voice trembled. "Your silence is my answer."

"You won't answer me about Thomas, yet you make proclamations about my intentions and my feelings?"

"Jon," Apryl said, her voice pleading. "Tell me if you love me."

He opened his mouth to say it, but something stuck in his throat. He'd never said those words to someone else. What did they mean anyway? He swallowed at the dryness in his throat, but try as he might, he couldn't bring himself to say what she wanted to hear. "Isn't my anger at seeing you with that beast of a man enough?"

Apryl wiped furiously at new tears coming down her cheeks. "Jonathan Porter, you're the most infuriating man I've ever known." She turned and fled along the path.

Call her back. Tell her you love her, that you want to marry her and that you forgive her. But his words froze as he watched her disappear into the trees.

When Jon entered the Beesley home, the musicians had stopped playing. He found Mr. and Mrs. Maughan in the library, who greeted him pleasantly. He was surprised to see Apryl sitting near the fire, leafing through the pages of a book. She watched him as he came into the room. He'd have thought she would have run to Thomas. Jon waited for her eyes to offer welcome, but she lowered her gaze and ignored him.

Mr. Maughan asked, "How was your trip to Massachusetts?"

"I didn't find what I needed, so I'm working on another solution." Jon thought he saw Apryl raise her head.

Mrs. Maughan nodded. "I've heard the coast there is lovely this time of year."

"Yes." Although the loveliness that he had experienced had nothing to do with the landscape.

"Why don't you read us something, Apryl?" Mrs. Maughan asked, breaking into Jon's thoughts.

Apryl looked down at the book she was holding, turned a few pages, and began to read aloud. Jon relaxed in the wing-backed chair and lit one of Thomas's imported cigars, listening to his fiancée's melodic voice reading Bryant's "Green River."

When breezes are soft and skies are fair,
I steal an hour from study and care,
And hie me away to the woodland scene,
Where wanders the stream with waters of green;

Jon closed his eyes, picturing Maybrook. In his mind he was walking through the woodlands bordering the fields near Ruth's house. Then he saw Eliza. She stood near the edge of the trees, waiting for him. As he approached, she walked towards him, smiling.

And gaze upon thee in silent dream,
For in thy lonely and lovely stream,
An image of that calm life appears,
That won my heart in my greener years.

The poem ended, and Jon opened his eyes, surprised to see Apryl looking at him expectantly. He exhaled a cloud of smoke. "Very nice."

A slight smile crossed her lips. It appeared peace had been made, which was just as well for him.

❦

The following morning, Thomas appeared at the breakfast table, dressed in a riding habit. The tight jodhpurs and narrow riding boots only accentuated the man's poor figure in the worst possible manner. Jon nearly choked on a bite of cold ham. He wondered how Apryl could even pretend to be entertained by him—let alone kiss him, if that's all that had happened.

Thomas tossed a newspaper onto the table. "It's finally happened. My foolish partner has broken the last straw with his increasingly poor reputation. His daughter landed herself in jail earlier this week."

The Robinsons. Before Jon could read the article, Mr. Maughan snatched the newspaper and scanned the front page.

"No, it didn't make front page news," Thomas said in a snide tone, "but there it is on page two, all right, by the gossip section. See for yourself."

Mr. Maughan turned the page and began to read. "'Mr. Henry Robinson, well-known furniture dealer and connoisseur, has again disgraced himself in high society. It appears that his daughter, Eliza Robinson, has become independently situated, but only on the occasion of her aunt's murder.'"

Apryl let out a small gasp and looked over at Thomas. "You did well to distance yourself from the family."

Thomas's smile was triumphant. Jon set his mouth in a firm line, ordering himself to stay silent.

Mr. Maughan read on. "'While Eliza Robinson enjoys her new property, her poor aunt is barely cold in the grave. Perhaps she was an accomplice in her aunt's unfortunate death, and therefore did not need anyone's hand in marriage to secure a fortune.'"

"Serves the girl right," Mrs. Maughan blurted out.

"Oh my goodness, Thomas," Apryl crooned. "You poor man. Do you think they're referring to you?"

Jon's stomach felt as heavy as lead.

Thomas's eyes gleamed as he loaded his plate with sausage, toast and marmalade. "Wouldn't it be something if she went to trial for murder?" A low chuckle rumbled from somewhere deep inside him.

Apryl leaned forward, her eyes intent on Thomas as he took the seat across from her. "She must have coveted her aunt's property all along, and was only waiting for the perfect opportunity get rid of the woman." Her face flushed as Thomas smiled at her.

"I believe so," he said in a conspiratorial voice, his eyes not shying away from Apryl's bold gaze. "I will have to terminate my partnership with Mr. Robinson, of course."

"Most definitely." Apryl nodded. "Please read the rest, Father."

Mr. Maughan cleared his throat. "'Mr. Robinson could not be reached for comment, but sources close to him say that he's grieving over his daughter's involvement, and that Mrs. Robinson has left home, with no word of her return or her whereabouts.'"

"I never did like her mother," Mrs. Maughan interjected, rosy circles forming on her cheeks. "Too snooty for me."

"Do you know the family, then?" Jon asked, genuinely curious as to how the Robinsons were connected to the Maughans.

"Not well, but I've seen Mrs. Robinson at social functions," Mrs. Maughan said.

Amid the speculating, Jon pulled the paper in his direction, his anger rising. It was all slander and gossip. Who could be idiot enough to believe any of it? Unfortunately he was in a room full of people who were doing just that.

"She didn't kill her aunt," he said sharply above the conversation. The talking stopped, and everyone looked at him. "Eliza didn't kill Maeve O'Brien."

"Who in damnation is Maeve O'Brien?" Thomas asked.

"Henry Robinson's sister. Maeve Robinson married a Puritan man named Edward O'Brien and settled with him in Massachusetts."

Apryl was staring at Jon now, twisting her napkin. "And how might you know this, Jon?"

He hesitated, but he suddenly didn't care about protecting his past anymore. All he wanted to do was see Thomas Beesley eat his words. "Because I grew up in Maybrook. Maeve O'Brien was my neighbor, and I know Eliza."

Twelve

*W*ith two hours of daylight left, Eliza decided to take a walk to the lighthouse. She scanned the area for any signs of Gus, but seeing none, she continued on her way. When she reached the lighthouse, she pushed open the door and called out, "Anyone there? Gus?"

She glanced behind her, but saw only trees swaying gently in the breeze. Entering the lighthouse, she watched the flecks of dust float in the air, illuminated by the sunlight filtering in through the narrow window behind her.

She examined the steps to find the one Jon had said was loose. Nails were missing on the third step. She lifted up the board.

Beneath was the same wooden box Jon had told her about. She lifted it out of the step, finding it weighted. According to Jon, it had been empty. With her anticipation mounting, she opened the lid. Inside sat a worn, leather-bound book. She carefully opened the cover and read *Helena Talbot, January 1815.*

Jon had said the journal was missing. How did it get back in the box? She replaced the now-empty box into the step, then left the lighthouse, clutching the journal to her chest. She ran the entire way back to the cottage in the growing dusk.

Eliza locked the front door of the cottage behind her and hurried into the kitchen. She lit two tapered candles with a trembling hand, deciding that supper would have to wait. She reverently placed the volume on the table, hoping she'd made the right choice by bringing it home. Turning to the first page, she stared at the long arched handwriting.

She skimmed the first few pages, where Helena had written about ordinary things—doing chores, sewing samplers, attending Meeting. Then Eliza stopped on the page dated January 8. It was the first mention of something different happening in her life.

January 8, 1815. A stranger came into town last week— he's a traveling salesman for the ship industry. He recruits sailors who travel the world, and he's been to the West Indies and to Australia, even China. The stories he shares are amazing and almost unbelievable. Father offered him a room at our house, and I can hear them talking long into the night about the many adventures he's had. I'm not allowed to sit with them after supper, because Mother doesn't want me to hear anything heathen. His name is Jonathan Porter. Doesn't that sound nice?

Nice, indeed. Little did Helena know that this was the man who'd abandon her. No wonder the Talbots had kept close watch on their daughter. A shiver traveled along Eliza's back, making her wonder if she should be reading Helena's words. But the journal was in front of her . . . waiting to be read. She turned the page. The next entry was written more than a month later.

February 15, 1815. Mother is an absolute tyrant. I've been doing my chores, attending Meeting, and keeping the

Sabbath perfectly holy, so there should be no room to complain—although Mother always finds something to criticize. Jonathan is still staying at our house, though he is not around very often—until today. He came home early from someplace and stood in the doorway, staring at me. Finally I asked if he needed anything. I know Mother would have never left to visit the widow Goodwife Harttle if she'd known Jonathan would be returning so early in the day.

I offered to fix him a meal, but he shook his head and continued to watch me work. Finally he went upstairs. I could hear him pace the floor like a caged animal. Then he came back down and asked if I would take a walk with him. You can imagine my surprise. A tall, handsome man wanting me for company—and he even knowing that I am only seventeen.

What he said to me I dare not write, but I discovered that Jonathan Porter does not see me as a child. Rather, he said that I'm a "beautiful woman." Those words are now etched in my memory.

It was all so sweet, but Eliza knew the bitter was about to come. Imagine being so proper, or so Puritan, that Helena couldn't even write out a conversation.

March 1, 1815. Perhaps I should burn this journal. But for now, I'll pour out my heart upon these pages. I have become used to Jonathan's kisses. Aye, he has kissed me. I suppose I feel bold in saying so. I have to write it down, or it won't seem real. I cannot stop thinking about him, nor stop my cheeks from flaming when I am in his presence. The private kisses are not enough for him, or for me. I yearn for his touch every hour I am not with him, and that is most of the day. When I hear his footstep upon the threshold, I have to refrain from flinging myself into his embrace. I love him. When we are secretly together, I chide him for looking at me the way he does in my father's presence. I'm surprised my parents haven't noticed—for I am truly a woman now that I've had a man's love. Jonathan says he will marry me after his job is completed. My parents will not want me to marry a non-Puritan, even one so important as Jonathan Porter.

The candles flickered rapidly. Eliza looked up and stared at the dancing flames, realizing that a window must be open in the house somewhere. She reluctantly left the table and went to the hearth room, but everything was shut tight. Walking upstairs, she scanned the rooms, finding all of the windows closed.

There was one last place to check for a draft—Maeve's room. Eliza went down the stairs to the main floor and stopped in front of the door. The door was shut, and there was no draft coming from beneath. She took a deep breath and opened the door. Sure enough, the broken window had been replaced, and the room looked neat and tidy, as if waiting for its occupant to come home. She shivered involuntarily. Then, as she shut the bedroom door, she thought she heard a voice.

"Thank you."

Eliza spun on her heels, her breath halting. The voice was back. *No,* she decided. *It's not a voice; it's the blasted wind.* The way it wove around the house made it sound like a voice. Except that there was no wind outside. Perhaps the sound was a lonely rat scurrying above, searching for a morsel.

Her mother would arrive tomorrow, and Eliza found herself looking forward to it. Being alone in the cottage was making her nervous. Feeling chilly, she went to light the fire, which proved a dubious task with trembling hands. When she had the fire roaring, Eliza brought the journal into the hearth room and pulled the rocking chair close to the fire.

March 23, 1815. Jonathan's contract is fulfilled, and he leaves in two days. He is secretly trying to steal more time to spend with me, and he's promised to return as soon as he can to fetch me. Then we'll leave this dull place for England. His father owns a big estate and will welcome his son's new fiancée. But my monthly time is delayed. Constance Kinder told me it is how one knows one is with child. Your monthlies stop. I feel ill just thinking about it. Every hour I pray to God that my sin with Jonathan will not be discovered. I am filled with anguish knowing I don't deserve God's benevolence now. If I am with child, my sins will be a permanent stain. I wish I knew for certain. Then I would tell Jonathan, and maybe he would take me with him now. But what if I am not with child, and he becomes angry at my deceit?

March 30, 1815. Jonathan is gone. I've been trying not to weep openly because Mother would guess what is wrong. I didn't tell Jonathan that my monthly was late, because I kept hoping it would start. But it hasn't, and I am so confused. Should I have told him? Am I with child? My breasts feel tender to the touch, and I can smell the cows a mile away. Am I becoming ill because of my sin? Will God ever forgive me?

Eliza stood and placed another log on the fire. She wiped a stray tear off her cheek. How would it be to feel so alone in the world that you couldn't tell anyone you were having a baby? She curled up on the sofa, pulling an afghan over her.

April 2, 1815. I write this inside my jail cell. Mother discovered my condition. After seeing me vomit day after day without a fever or chill, she guessed. On the fourth day of being sick, I was trying to pull some weeds in the garden, but doubled over and vomited in a bucket. Mother stood behind me, silently watching. Then she grabbed my hair and yanked my head back, her gaze boring into me. She called me filthy vermin. And for once, I agreed.

I tried to explain, but she wouldn't listen. Her voice sounded harsher than I'd ever heard her. She said I am

*carrying a devil child and that I am being punished by God for
my sins.*

*I sobbed and said that Jonathan would return and marry
me. She trembled and forbade me to speak his name again.
Then she called me a whore.*

*I reached out to her and clung to her skirts. But she shook
me off and spat in my face, forbidding me to enter the house.
She left me there, in the yard, lying upon the cold ground,
a sobbing mess. Even when my hysterics passed, I was too faint
to arise and clean myself.*

*When Father arrived home, he came immediately to my
side. Surprisingly, in his own way, he was compassionate and
sorrowful. He apologized for letting the devil himself reside
within our walls.*

*He directed me to clean myself and climb into the
buckboard. I will be staying in jail until the day of my trial
before the magistrate.*

Eliza shuddered at the image of going to jail and
standing trial because you became pregnant out of wedlock.
Too bad Helena couldn't have been secreted away to a
distant relative's . . . As I have done, but for different reasons.
Eliza looked at the dying flames and closed her eyes against
the image of Helena being treated like an animal by her own
family. She pictured Jonathan Porter, Sr. and the beautiful
and innocent Helena. Did she become desperate enough to
take her own life?

What would Jon think when he read this? Clutching the
journal to her chest, Eliza soon fell asleep on the sofa as the
crackling flames faded to glowing embers.

⌒✓⌒

Eliza stretched her cramped legs on the sofa. The
journal had fallen on her lap, and the fire had long since
died. Rubbing her sore neck, she sat up. The late-morning
sun seemed to wink merrily at her through the window. It
was strange to be in Maeve's house alone—to be anywhere

alone. Stretching, she rose and walked into the kitchen, remembering that she'd had no supper the night before.

She found an apple and bit into it as she looked around the room. The place looked presentable enough for her mother's arrival, but she knew it wouldn't be what her sophisticated mother expected. Mrs. Robinson would soon find out that having an independently wealthy daughter looked much better on paper. With an amused eye, Eliza scanned the kitchen. Perhaps her mother would like the drying herbs that hung so neatly in a row . . . or maybe she would take a fancy to the hens in the barn . . . or perhaps she would want the scarred kitchen table, with years of memories etched on the surface . . . Puddles of candle wax were hardened on the table. Eliza would have to scrape those off.

Laughing to herself, Eliza looked at the kitchen door and was surprised to see an envelope on the floor. The post must have come early this morning. She stooped to pick up the expensive-looking paper and examined it—from New York. She tore the envelope open and scanned to the bottom of the letter. Jonathan Porter? Her heart gave a jump before she realized it was from Jon, the son of Jonathan Porter and Helena.

She skimmed the letter then sat at the table and slowly read through it again, wherein he asked her to continue searching for his mother's journal.

I have it now, Jon. And I'll send it to New York. When she picked up her mother today from the train station, she would post a return letter to Jon. Eliza found some paper and a pen, and after rereading Jon's letter, she began her reply. It was easier to write to him than to talk to him. Without his dark eyes and moody expression studying her, she felt able to freely express herself.

> *Dear Mr. Porter,*
> *Thank you for your recent letter of concern. I'm*
> *curious to know when it was you discovered the box*

empty, as it was only yesterday that I happened to find your mother's journal, dates starting in 1815, in a box underneath the same bottom stair. My mother is coming to Maybrook for a visit, and she'll be returning to New York in another week or so. I will send the journal back with her.

    Regards,

    Eliza Robinson

    P.S. I hope you don't mind that I've taken the liberty to read a few pages.

Eliza bit her lip then rewrote the letter, this time leaving out the postscript.

⟨✐⟩

In the early afternoon, Eliza opened the barn doors and hitched up Maeve's horse to the wagon, something her mother would likely detest riding in. In fact her mother would be surprised she even knew how to prepare the wagon and horse—thankfully Maeve had taught her that. But Eliza had no other choice but to fetch her mother in the wagon. On the way into town, she stopped at Ruth's cottage. As expected, she was home, kneeling in her garden, furiously tugging at weeds.

"They'll die soon, won't they?" Eliza asked.

Ruth turned and squinted against the glare of the sun. "Well, on my soul, if it isn't Maeve's niece . . ."

"Eliza," she filled in for her.

"Yes, a beautiful name. Thou hast recovered from thy ordeal, I see. Jonny told me about what happened, and I've been praying for thee ever since."

"Thank you."

Ruth continued, "He seemed quite interested in thee and asked me several questions. I'm afraid I couldn't answer him."

"What kind of questions?" she asked, then wished she hadn't.

But Ruth didn't seem to mind. "About how long thou hast lived here, and whether you were of the faith, and . . . oh, I forget now."

"It's all right," Eliza assured her, reddening at the thought of Jon asking about her. "I've come to inquire about a young man named Gus, whom I've seen around lately."

Ruth brushed the dirt from her hands and stood. "What about Gus?"

"He was chopping wood at Maeve's house and seemed to think she was still alive."

Ruth's warm brown eyes studied Eliza. "Don't pay attention to that. He's not all there, one might say. Gus is a hard worker, though he could never do anything more than manual labor. Lives by himself now, poor soul. His father passed away a couple of years ago."

"Where does he live?"

Ruth hesitated. "Close to the cliffs in a little cottage not too far from the lighthouse. In fact, if there weren't so many trees surrounding his place, thou could see it from here."

Eliza looked in the direction of Ruth's gaze.

Ruth spoke rapidly. "Poor boy, he was born breech, so it's no surprise that he never had much intelligence. But he's a good lad, and he stays out of trouble, he does. His father and . . . his father always saw to that."

Eliza had only been at the station a few minutes when her mother's train arrived. A few people exited, and soon Mrs. Robinson came into view. Her fashionable sapphire chiffon and low-cut bodice was completely out of place in Maybrook. Thankfully, she wore a lace cravat, covering her bosom. Her dark blonde hair was done up in a chignon, topped by a pert hat. Behind her, the porter carried two bulging bags. Eliza crossed to her mother and kissed her cheek. It seemed ages since they had last been together.

"You're looking well, Mother."

Mrs. Robinson frowned. "I can't say as much for you, Eliza. What happened to your good dresses?"

Eliza glanced at her faded blue dress, which she used to wear for traveling—it had become her mainstay as of late. It was clean, and the collar starched in proper Puritan style, but the fabric lacked the luster it once had. "There's not much sense wearing my finery among the chickens on the farm. Maybrook is different from New York."

Her mother lifted her chin and glanced at their surroundings. "You don't need to tell me that, dear. It's quite evident already. Where's the carriage?"

Eliza led the way to the crude wagon and instructed the porter to load the bags.

Her mother stood rooted to the ground, her eyes wide. "You can't mean for me to ride in this."

Eliza hid a smile. "As I said, Mother, this isn't New York."

Mrs. Robinson let out an exasperated sigh, hiked up her chiffon skirts, and climbed into the wagon. "I hope my dress doesn't snag," she mumbled. "And my hair will look a fright without a proper carriage roof. How far is the estate?"

Her mother would find out soon enough that Maeve's "estate" wasn't what she was expecting. On the ride to Aunt Maeve's house, Eliza told her mother about the people with whom she'd become acquainted with. "Ruth Temple is our closest neighbor. You'll find her very hospitable, and you'll probably meet the Pranns, whom I stayed with for a few days. Harvest Goddard runs the only dress shop in town, although I'm afraid you'll find it somewhat lacking."

"What strange names," her mother said.

Eliza laughed, tightening her hands on the reins. "It's a Puritan town, remember? Multiply Aunt Maeve by a hundred, and you have the population of Maybrook."

Mrs. Robinson flicked at an unseen piece of lint from her skirt. "The society papers have stirred themselves up again over you."

"What are they saying now?"

"Oh, that you're an heiress, and you were thrown into jail as a suspect in your aunt's death."

Unbelievable. "They've twisted the truth, I imagine."

"They have." Mrs. Robinson pursed her lips. "And like your last scandal, this one will no doubt affect your father's clientele. Some of our oldest friends have dropped us from their invitation lists."

Anger bubbled inside Eliza, not because of the gossip journalists who managed to get their malicious words printed, but at her mother, who refused to defend her own daughter. Even when Thomas had proposed, her mother had seemed to take his side. Why did Thomas Beesley have to propose to her in the first place? It had set in motion a chain of unsavory events. And why was her night in jail being talked about? It wasn't anyone's business.

Her mother continued her self-indulgent talk. "I hear Thomas is doing well. Your father says he's working on a contract to implement mass production."

Her father had been set against mass production for as long as she could remember. "What does Father think?" Eliza slowed the horse a bit as they rounded a bend.

"Oh, you know him. He's old-fashioned, but I think he'll come around. The ladies at the club say it's the next step in industry, and anyone who wants to compete will have to start mass-producing ready-made furniture."

Her mother made it sound like there was no other choice. Eliza thought about how Jon had said that Thomas was still spreading the story of his rejection. "Has Thomas forgiven me?"

"What a question, dear. Thomas was deeply hurt. I

don't see him getting over the humiliation, especially working with your father on a regular basis."

If only the gossip columns would stay out of it, maybe Thomas would be more inclined to drop it as well. Maeve's house came into view. "There it is," Eliza said, glancing at her mother to gauge her reaction.

Mrs. Robinson noticeably flinched. "It doesn't look like much."

Eliza smiled. "I know, but I love it."

When they climbed from the wagon, Eliza unloaded her mother's baggage.

"Isn't there anyone to do that?" Mrs. Robinson asked, looking around.

"Just me." Eliza hefted the bags one at a time up the stairs and set them on the porch. "Come inside and have a look around, and then I'll make us some tea."

Mrs. Robinson's face brightened a little. She traipsed up the stairs and followed Eliza inside.

"What do you think?" Eliza asked.

Her mother looked around, walking slowly from the kitchen to the hearth room. "I, uh, it's very humble," she finally managed.

"They were Puritans, remember?"

"Of course," Mrs. Robinson said. "It's rather quaint, like a country home should be. I can't imagine how Maeve lived here all those years."

Eliza shrugged, expecting her mother's reaction. "The simple life made her happy. I think she was the most cheerful person I've ever known."

Mrs. Robinson scoffed. "Perhaps she didn't know any better."

Eliza saw no solution except an argument, so she ignored the comment. After all, there was no changing her mother's viewpoint. "Why don't you sit on the sofa? I'll stoke the fire and make some fresh tea."

"Thank you, that would be lovely," her mother said with a sigh.

Thirteen

$\mathcal{J}$on settled into the carriage seat, Apryl beside him. Mr. and Mrs. Maughan were seated in their own carriage, traveling a short distance behind, as they left the Beesley estate. Adjusting the fur covering over her knees, Jon hoped the courtesy would deflect the onslaught that was sure to come.

Apryl had barely spoken to him after learning that the small town he told her he'd grown up in was in fact, Maybrook, and that he was acquainted with Eliza Robinson. Not to mention that he had in fact, rescued her, twice. Two bright spots stood out on Apryl's cheeks as she stared forward in the chilled air.

"I think we wore out our welcome at the Beesleys," Jon said, in an attempt to make peace. The carriage jolted forward, and they were on their way back into the city.

She blinked and slid her gaze to his. He'd never seen her gaze quite so . . . icy.

"You've not been forthcoming, Jonathan," she said.

Ah. She is speaking. At last.

"The events didn't seem remarkable at the time," he said. "I did tell you about Maybrook, just not in connection with Thomas's ex-fiancée."

"And you don't see any reason for my concern?" Her voice was quiet, but strong. "What am I to think? You told everyone that you rescued the Robinson woman on the very night of her aunt's murder . . . and you had to get her out of jail as well." Apryl pulled the rug up higher and folded her arms.

"Am I being scrutinized because for once, I seemed to know more about the gossip than anyone else in the room?"

She turned her head and looked at him full on, and that's when Jon realized she was jealous. His heart thumped—although he wasn't sure if it was because he realized that Apryl might care enough about him to be jealous of another female acquaintance, or whether thinking so much about Eliza had brought on the rush.

"I'll concede that is quite a feat," Apryl agreed. Her lips quivered. "Tell me what she looks like."

"Whatever for?" It was true, then. Apryl was jealous. He exhaled. What he said next could determine Apryl's mood.

"Unless you want to keep that private as well." Her pouty tone was back.

"No . . . of course not . . ." Jon gazed out the window at the passing countryside. The first cold of autumn had arrived, and he found the chilly air invigorating. "The first time I saw the famous Miss Robinson, she looked like a wet rat."

Apryl gasped then giggled. "No!"

At last. His icy fiancée was thawing. "It was during a horrific storm, and I had meant to leave the next day, so I braved the weather and rode to Maeve O'Brien's doorstep. There Miss Robinson was, staggering in the mud, drenched to the bone."

Apryl scoffed. "And the handsome hero rescued the damsel in distress."

"If you want to put it that way, I suppose. But it was the wrong damsel." He met her gaze—her eyes had warmed. He wrapped his hand over hers. She didn't pull away. "Eliza is nothing like the lovely Apryl."

A smile touched her lips. "Is she at least fair?" Apryl asked.

"I suppose some men might think so. But I wasn't interested in making such an assessment. I felt sorry for the poor girl, that's all."

Apryl's smile turned triumphant. "Certainly not a predicament I'd wish on anyone."

"Of course not," Jon said. "She was hysterical and asked for help, telling me her aunt was dead. Naturally, I had to help her, so I loaded her on the horse and took her to Ruth's house."

"The woman who raised you?" Apryl interjected.

"Yes." Jon remembered how fragile and young Eliza had seemed at the time. He'd thought her merely a girl. He'd thought her hair dark at first, but when it dried, he realized it was the color between the early morning sun—

A nudge from Apryl brought him to full awareness.

"Ruth knew what to do and instructed me to help get her warm and dry." He stopped, his throat suddenly raw.

"Pray tell me how you accomplished that, sir Jon?"

Jon's collar felt itchy and the carriage stuffy. He could very well imagine Eliza's eyes on his—scared and desperate. He'd felt helpless at the time, wishing he could soothe the girl's fear. "I wrapped her in a blanket. She was delirious and kept saying that her aunt was dead." He shifted position, trying to dispel the heat spreading upward from his neck.

"Then you got her out of jail. What a gentlemen," Apryl said. "If nothing else, Jon, you're always a gentleman." She leaned her head on his shoulder.

Jon exhaled. Crisis averted. It seemed he was forgiven now.

Apryl's head remained on his shoulder, and the carriage soon lulled her to sleep.

My thoughts aren't always gentleman-like. Jon continued to stare out the window, remembering the morning after he had found Eliza. With Ruth dozing by the fire, he'd peered into the room where Eliza slept. As vividly as if it were yesterday, he could still picture her pale, delicate face, with dark eyelashes resting peacefully against her cheeks in slumber, framed in a halo of gentle waves of dark gold.

An hour later, with Apryl and her baggage unloaded from the carriage and settled into her house, Jon went home. When he reached his place and walked through his front door, he glanced at the pile of letters on the hall bench and decided they would have to wait—he was famished. But as he passed the bench, something caught his eye. Turning, he picked up the top envelope and scanned the handwriting. It was definitely feminine, but unfamiliar.

"Sarah?" he called.

A moment later, his maid appeared. "Yes, sir?"

"Bring me some hot soup in the library, please."

Sarah nodded and scurried away.

Jon walked into the library, tossed his coat over the chair, and sank onto it to read. He scanned to the signature—it was from Eliza. Her mother would be joining her in Maybrook. He wondered when Eliza might come back to New York. Had she read the journal? It was strange to think that he might meet her in New York—Eliza and Maybrook seemed to be an entirely different world.

A short time later, Sarah entered the room with a tray of steaming soup and a small loaf of bread. Underneath her arm she carried the evening paper. "It just arrived," she said.

Jon thanked her and dipped his spoon into the soup. The hot, spicy liquid felt wonderful as it warmed his throat. He scanned the front page and, seeing nothing new, he turned to the next. A heading caught his eye.

Connecticut Transient Sentenced to Death

He continued to read. *One such Byron Hatham, accused of a series of murders in the Massachusetts and Connecticut regions, has been brought to justice. Mr. Hatham's rampage began a little over a month back, with his final villainous act ten days ago upon the murder of Mr. Donald Barton, in Hartford, Connecticut.*

Jon reread the dates again and compared them to the timing of Maeve's death. He stilled. The dates weren't consistent. The transient blamed for Maeve O'Brien's death, couldn't have been in Maybrook the night of her murder. He was in Hartford killing the unlucky Donald Barton.

Damn it to hell. Jon stood and paced the room, running his fingers through his hair. That could only mean one thing—the killer was still in Maybrook, and Eliza was in danger.

In the light of the sinking sun, Jon sank into his chair until dusk had deepened into night, debating what to do. Was he overly worried? And why was he so concerned about something that had nothing to do with him? Finally, he made up his mind. He would send a telegram to the constable of Maybrook and write a letter to Eliza. And then he could put the matter out of his hands.

⌒⁄⌒

The following morning, Jon set out to see Mr. Doughty, thinking that the man might be interested in his discovery. The day was cold and blustery, with promise of rain to come, so he ordered Richard to bring the carriage around. He snatched the morning paper from the front hall table and scanned the pages for a follow-up story. There was none.

He arrived at the law offices. Mr. Doughty greeted him warmly, and led him into his cramped office. "Sorry again about the clutter. Renovations are taking longer than planned."

Jon stepped over a pile of books. "I've brought something for you to see," he said, handing over the newspaper clipping.

Mr. Doughty read the article. "So they've found the murderer guilty. That's good news, right?"

"Look at the date and location of the Barton murder," Jon said. "That was the same night Henry Robinson's sister was killed in Massachusetts."

"Ah, I see what you're getting at. This man, Byron Hatham, couldn't have been in two places at once," Mr. Doughty said.

"Exactly." John moved some books from a chair and sat down. "I sent a telegram to the constable. But there has to be something more we can do."

Mr. Doughty arched a brow. "We?"

"What if the murderer knew Maeve personally, and Mr. Robinson's daughter is the next victim?"

"I thought the family was back in New York. I happened to run into Mr. Robinson this morning," Mr. Doughty said.

Jon let the news sink in. "I received a letter from Eliza in yesterday's post, sent from Maybrook, and she said her mother is coming to stay with her."

Mr. Doughty leaned back in his chair. "You're being extremely gallant, Mr. Porter. I'm sure the constable will take care of it." He paused and steepled his fingers. "Forgive me for getting personal, but aren't you engaged, Mr. Porter?"

"Yes. Why—" He felt his face grow hot. What was Mr. Doughty implying? "My concern is only natural and stems from having met the family."

Mr. Doughty nodded his head in agreement, but didn't look convinced. "Of course. I'm sure the constable will reopen the investigation and see to the safety of his citizens." He peered at Jon closely. "Or perhaps we should pay another visit to Maybrook and warn Miss Robinson in person." Jon tugged at his collar. "Perhaps a telegram is enough after all. Thank you for the advice." He took the newspaper article back from Mr. Doughty and rose to leave.

Moments later, Jon stepped out in to the driving rain and made a dash for his carriage. Richards pulled forward as soon as the door was shut. Now sodden, Jon leaned back in his seat and exhaled. How could Mr. Doughty make the assumption that he was interested in Eliza as more than an ordinary acquaintance?

Terms with Apryl were back on track, and there was no reason for him to jeopardize that, especially after he'd remonstrated Apryl for being friendly with Thomas. He must let his mind be free of the Robinson girl, forget he ever met her. She would be protected by the constable in Maybrook. He would soon recover his mother's journal. Then he would never see or hear of her again.

He reached into his waistcoat pocket and drew out his handkerchief. After wiping his forehead, he discovered that it was the cloth that carried Eliza's initials. He folded it carefully and placed it in his pocket, reminding himself to remove it at home.

As he rode, the wind whipped about the carriage, which reminded him of the night he met Eliza.

"Enough," he told himself, pressing his fingers against his temples. Maybe he should accept a few clients to take his mind off things until his father's estate was ready to be settled.

Upon his arrival, Sarah met him at the door. "Mr. Thomas Beesley is waiting for you in the library. I hope you don't mind, sir," she said with a curtsy. "You said you wouldn't be gone more than an hour, and Mr. Beesley said he didn't mind waiting."

Jon tried to hide his annoyance. "Did he state his business?"

"No, sir," Sarah said, her eyes going to the floor.

"No matter. Thank you for making him comfortable." Jon left the maid standing in the hallway and entered the library. Thomas sat in a chair, leafing through a book. When he saw Jon, he rose, his massive form making the room seem insignificant.

"An unexpected pleasure," Jon said, staying decidedly calm.

"Your maid is gracious," Thomas said through his full lips.

Jon sat in a chair opposite. "Thank you. Please have a seat."

Thomas followed suit, his eyes gleaming. "You must be wondering why I'm here."

Jon watched the man's bulk settle into his chair. *I hope the legs hold.* "I suppose your country vacation is over, and it's time to get back to business?"

"Something like that." Thomas folded his hands over his girth. "I'm looking for a lawyer to represent my case against Mr. Henry Robinson. As you seem to know the family's quirks, I thought you'd be the perfect candidate. That is, if you feel you're up to it."

Jon rubbed the back of his neck. Becoming further involved with the Robinson family wasn't inviting, especially if it meant representing Thomas against Eliza's father. "I'm newly out of law school, Mr. Beesley, and I haven't yet established my practice."

"So I've heard." Thomas nodded. "Tell me, Mr. Porter, what are your future plans?"

"Once my financial situation is secure, I'll marry Apryl, of course. I've thought about doing something in government..."

"How very noble of you—a public servant. I hear the pay is pittance, but the benefits are immense." Thomas pulled out a massive handkerchief from his waistcoat pocket and blew his nose.

Jon flinched and waited for the noise to subside. "I'm not worried about money."

Thomas took one last swipe at his reddened nose and replaced the crumpled handkerchief. "You must be very rich, then, Mr. Porter, to be able to work for free and support a wife accustomed to a lavish lifestyle."

Jon gripped the edge of his chair, aching to punch the man. "Apryl will be well-taken care of, as will our children. I'm sorry I won't be able to represent you in this matter."

Glancing about the room, Thomas said, "You know where to reach me, Mr. Porter, if you decide to change your mind. I'm sure we can agree on a price we'll both be happy with." He rose awkwardly and lumbered across the floor. "Good evening, sir. I'll see myself out."

The door shut behind him, and Jon stared at it for some time. He'd just been grossly insulted.

Fourteen

*E*liza spent the day showing her mother the sights of Maybrook. It was a strange time. Eliza was still young, yet her station had risen, but the cutting remarks from her mother said she was somehow jealous of Eliza. How could her mother envy a run-down cottage, crumbling lighthouse, and fallow farmland? But her father had told her that the property was valuable, especially to non-Puritans who were encroaching on every side of Maybrook, buying up land where they could.

On the third morning, Eliza and her mother sat at the kitchen table with a list between them of all the items in Maeve's house and their approximate value.

A light scoff came from her mother. "There's nothing of real worth, except for the land. Your father said it might be best to sell that right away."

"Wouldn't he rather wait until the scandal has died down?" Eliza tried to keep the edge out of her voice.

Her mother looked up sharply. "We want to do what's best for you. This town is becoming smaller and less desirable. You'll only get decent money out of it from an investor."

"I don't think Maeve would have wanted it sold off that way," Eliza said.

"Then sell it to some foolish Puritan who values the secluded farm life." She said with a wave of her hand. "How about the Prann family? You seem to be on friendly terms with them."

Eliza was sure that Nathaniel would be more than delighted to take over the property, if a bride were to be thrown into the bargain. But she doubted he could afford to buy it.

The sound of an approaching wagon caused both women to rise and look out the window.

"Speak of the devil, Mother. It's about time you met one of the Pranns."

Eliza hurried to open the front door before her mother could answer. "Nathaniel, come in and meet my mother," she called out brightly.

Nathaniel tipped his hat and climbed down from the wagon. His face glowed with pleasure, no doubt at the friendly greeting. Eliza felt a twinge of guilt. He looked even younger than he was, now that Eliza saw him through her mother's eyes. He also looked completely unsophisticated.

"I've brought some fresh vegetables from my mother's garden," he said.

Introductions were made, and Nathaniel was invited to stay for tea. Eliza inwardly smiled at the way her mother appraised him. By New York standards, he looked like a common country boy—uneducated, with only the price of cows on his mind. In reality, Nathaniel was well-versed in Greek, Latin, and Bible study. Eliza watched the pair with amusement.

"Your father's been a farmer all his life, and his father before him?" her mother asked.

"Yes, ma'am. It's in our blood and has been even before my great-grandfather came across the ocean in 1620," Nathaniel explained and gulped down some tea.

"He farmed in England?"

Eliza could have pinched her mother. She acted as if no one respectable farmed.

"Yes, ma'am, in a village near Portsmouth."

Mrs. Robinson nodded as if she were familiar with the regions skirting London. "And you'll be a farmer too, I presume? Take over the family property?"

Nathaniel looked a bit uncomfortable at the direct question. "In our town, when the parents pass, the children divide up the inheritance equally. I'm not one for squabbling with my siblings over land. My father is set on me going to Cambridge and replacing the Reverend someday."

Mrs. Robinson's mouth rounded. "Cambridge? Well, who would have suspected?"

This was news to Eliza—he'd never talked about college before. Her mother's sting eluded Nathaniel, and he smiled in response.

"Would a reverend be able to care for a property such as this?" her mother asked.

Nathaniel's eyes widened, and he looked at Eliza. Her mother could hardly know what sort of ideas she was giving him.

Her mother continued with a few more questions, and by the time Nathaniel took his leave, Eliza saw that her mother was very satisfied with herself, thinking Nathaniel a potential buyer.

As the two women stood on the porch waving goodbye, Eliza turned and said, "Mother, you don't understand."

"What do you mean?" Her hand rose automatically to her hair, checking for flyaway strands.

"Nathaniel is only interested in this land for one reason."

Her mother's hand stopped mid-primping. She settled her steady gaze onto Eliza. "What reason is that, dear?"

"He's asked me to marry him." She watched the expression on her mother's face register her words.

"What did you say?" her mother asked faintly, her face draining of color.

"I told him we were too young."

Mrs. Robinson grabbed Eliza's arm and pulled her close. "You didn't make any promises, did you?"

"Of course not. You know my record of turning down proposals." She turned away and stared at the roof of the barn. She felt her mother's stare penetrating from behind her.

"Do you think the Pranns might purchase this land without you becoming Nathaniel's bride?"

Eliza bit her lip to keep from crying out. It was so typical of her mother to think only of money. "I don't think the Pranns know of their son's intentions towards me. I'm sure they'd be as horrified as you."

Mrs. Robinson began to protest, but Eliza went back into the kitchen and started clearing tea from the table.

⟡

Later that night, after her mother had retired for the evening, Eliza lit two candles at the kitchen table. With Helena's journal opened, she continued to read the turbulent events.

April 5, 1815. I've been locked in the high constable's barn for three days. Goodwife Wheyland has brought me quilts and food. I see pity in her eyes when she looks at me. I loathe that pity. When I asked Goodwife Wheyland what's to happen to me, she told me about the whipping post and the pillory. But she thought both punishments would be too harsh for a woman in my delicate condition.

Oh, I long for Jonathan and his warm brown eyes and strong embrace. He would take me away from this horrible place and care for me and our child. I would give anything to send word to him, to tell him what has happened. I know that he would leave his post immediately and come reinstate my honor by marrying me.

Why can't my mother be as compassionate? She has not been to see me yet, although my father comes twice a day.

Oh, God, I ask thee for forgiveness. How can something so beautiful be a sin? How long does thy punishment need to continue? I am in the depths of despair and feel like I'm already in hell.

Eliza's hand trembled as she turned the page—reading the words felt as if she were looking into the very soul of another. She felt unworthy to read such honest and tormented words. But she couldn't tear herself away.

April 9, 1815. Yesterday was my trial before the town magistrate. My sentence seemed too light to the brazen onlookers, but it was the worst I could have imagined. I am to live in seclusion in my parents' house until the birth—the most awful jail imaginable. No one is allowed to see my growing form, lest it be a bad example for the other girls. I've become a prisoner in my own house. My mother won't speak to me. Her silence pierces my heart.

May 1, 1815. I spend all day in bed, regardless of the sharp words my mother uses. Yes, she is talking to me again, but only to reprimand. I cannot exist without Jonathan's love any longer. Where is he? Why hasn't he come for me? I am leaving tonight and moving into the abandoned cottage by the old lighthouse—one owned by the O'Brien family, who left for England and haven't returned for years. I will leave a note for my parents, but I'm sure they won't persuade me to return. I hope they will leave me alone.

Eliza stared at the flickering candles for a moment. So that was how Helena came to live in her Aunt Maeve's cottage. Helena had run away from home, although not far, to escape her mother's relentless judgment. What a lonesome life Helena must have lived, carrying a child with no one to help.

⸎

The next morning, Eliza rose well before her mother to prepare breakfast. When her mother appeared, she looked surprised to see that Eliza had already laid the table with an appetizing spread.

"This is a nice final meal," Mrs. Robinson said.

"Are you going somewhere?" Eliza asked.

"We are returning to New York today. I thought about it last night, and I think it's for the best." She held up her hand when Eliza started to protest. "I know you wanted to stay longer and that you're fond of this place, but there's nothing here of value except the land. And you certainly don't have any promising future in this town. Once we reach New York, we'll hire someone to sell the place, and we'll put the money into a trust fund until you come of age."

Eliza looked at her mother in amazement. "What about the gossip columns? Are your friends ready to accept your wayward daughter?"

"Your status has undoubtedly been raised, Eliza. Remember, you are a woman of independent means now . . . Well, once we get this awful place sold and have something to show for it besides dirt."

How could her mother be so cold? Her mother sent her to this place to hide her from shame, yet now that she had inherited property, she was worthy to be among those whom her mother revered?

"I'm not coming with you," Eliza choked out.

"What did you say?" Her mother narrowed her eyes, daring Eliza to defy her.

"I'm not coming with you to live among those hypocrites."

Mrs. Robinson pointed a trembling finger at Eliza. "You're still under my care, young lady, and you will obey your mother."

"Just as I obeyed you and came to this place? You were embarrassed to have me around, and now that I own property, you are anxious to show me off." She folded her arms as angry tears slipped down her face.

Gripping the chair in front of her, Mrs. Robinson's knuckles turned white. "We'll be leaving in one hour."

⌒

Eliza loaded her mother's bags into the wagon and climbed into the driver's seat. Her mother's face was pale and drawn. Eliza settled next to her and urged the horse forward. Mile after mile they traveled in silence, until they reached the train station.

Mrs. Robinson alighted and called for the porter to unload her baggage. She turned and followed him into the station, without so much as a backward glance at her daughter.

Watching her mother disappear into the train station, Eliza had mixed feelings. She hated her mother's remonstrations, but it was better than hearing them constantly. Besides, Eliza wasn't ready to face New York City.

Did Helena have the same mixed feelings when she'd left her parents' home?

Fifteen

s soon as she reached the cottage after delivering her mother to the train station, Eliza walked into the hearth room and tossed her shawl onto the sofa. The past three days with her mother had left her drained and exhausted. She sank onto the sofa and closed her eyes. She'd have to write Jon again—she hadn't sent the journal with her mother after all. Eliza hadn't been able to finish reading it with her mother around, and she didn't trust that her mother wouldn't open the package out of curiosity.

The sound of footsteps on the porch startled her. When a knock came, she flinched. Opening the door, she saw the constable standing on the other side of the threshold.

"Good morrow, Miss," he said, tipping his hat.

Eliza nodded in greeting. "Can I help you?"

"I'm afraid I have bad news."

Eliza drew her breath in sharply. "Has something happened to my mother?"

"Not that I know of. I've come to inform thee that we are reopening the investigation into thy aunt's death."

"Why?" A gnawing began in her stomach.

"It appears that the man whom we thought guilty of her murder couldn't have done it," he said. "He happened to be in Hartford, Connecticut, committing a similar crime."

"Oh," was all she could say. She gripped the door frame, feeling her knees start to give.

The constable's mouth pulled into a tight line. "Thou hast better stay somewhere else for awhile."

"But why would someone want to kill my aunt?" she asked faintly.

"Perhaps they thought she had money or other valuables stashed somewhere, and when she awoke, they . . ." He stopped.

Tears burned in her eyes.

The constable's face softened with compassion. "Is there someone thou couldst stay with? I don't think it's safe for thee to be in this house alone until we've found the murderer."

In a daze, she nodded. "Yes, I can stay with someone. Thank you." Watching him leave, she walked out onto the porch and sank onto the steps. What did the murderer want? Money? Anyone familiar with Maeve would know of her simple life. Killing her for money didn't make sense. The closest neighbor was Ruth, surely the woman would welcome Eliza for the night. She decided it was time to pay Ruth a visit. She entered the barn and gathered some eggs to take with her and was surprised to hear another horse approaching.

Stepping out of the barn, she shielded her eyes against the sun to see who the rider was. "Nathaniel."

He climbed down from the horse and took off his hat. "Good afternoon, Eliza."

She squinted up at him. "What brings you here?"

"I've a business proposition for thee and thy mother," he said.

"Have you? You'll have to write my mother a letter then."

"Did she return to New York?"

"Yes, this very afternoon," she said, lowering her eyes. "We don't seem to agree on much."

"Does that mean thou are staying in Maybrook?"

Eliza chuckled. "Not exactly, Nathaniel. I don't belong to this way of life. I'll have to return home eventually."

But his eyes were still dancing with pleasure.

"All right." She put her hands on her hips. "Tell me the proposition."

Nathaniel glanced around the yard and twisted his hat in his hands. "Uh, I was hoping to present it to both thee and thy mother."

Eliza cocked her head to one side. "And why is that?"

Nathaniel reddened and kicked at the dirt.

"So that she could convince me to say yes to the proposition?"

He stared at her. "H-how didst thou know?"

Eliza shrugged and walked over to the porch. She sat on the top step and waited for Nathaniel to join her.

He stepped over and sat a comfortable distance from her. Finally he stole a glance in her direction and said, "Do you really want to hear it?" But her thoughts were far away. "Eliza?"

She turned and looked at him. "The constable stopped by today."

"What did he want?"

"The transient who they thought killed my aunt couldn't have possibly been in Maybrook on the night of her death."

Nathaniel reached across the step and took her hand, but Eliza gently pulled away.

He sighed. "Thou must come and stay at our house tonight. Thou aren't safe here."

"I know," she whispered, looking down at her feet. "But I already have a place to stay."

"Pray tell," he said.

"Ruth's."

"The spinster? It won't be any safer than here," Nathaniel protested.

"It's already been arranged." At least she hoped Ruth would take her in. Eliza rose and brushed imaginary dust off of her skirt. With her back to him she said, "Tell me about the proposition."

The air between them was silent for a moment. Then, "It doesn't seem right at a time like this to speak about business."

"Of course not. It can wait."

Nathaniel rose and walked over to her, grasping her hands. Eliza stiffened at the warm pressure of his palms and the scent of sweet hay in his clothes.

"I hope thou knowest my marriage proposal is still open," he said, leaning forward. "I love thee more each day."

Eliza moved away, and Nathaniel's hands dropped. She turned and stared into the distance, seeing nothing. Why did he have to be so persistent? "I'm sorry, Nathaniel," she said finally. "I'm not ready to make a commitment to anyone, especially someone as good as you."

"But—"

Eliza faced him, her tears brimming. "You deserve someone who loves you back."

Nathaniel stood still for a long time looking at her, as if memorizing every detail of her appearance, sadness in his gaze. Then he walked past her and mounted his horse.

Wrapping her arms about her, Eliza watched the dust billow behind him as he galloped away. She blinked until the stinging stopped.

✎

Eliza packed a small bundle of clothing and put the eggs on the seat next to her. The evening shadows were quickly enveloping the road as she drove the wagon to Ruth's house. Before leaving, she double-checked the locks and made sure the windows were secured.

A candle glimmered in Ruth's front window like a miniature beacon in a sea of descending darkness. Eliza had no doubt that she would be welcomed into the kind woman's home for the night.

Knocking on the door, Eliza glanced furtively about. She supposed that Ruth could also be a target, but it was quite well known within the Puritan community that Ruth wasn't any better off than Maeve had been. The door opened with a loud squeak, and the hunched woman appeared with a shawl clutched about her shoulders, her eyes as round as saucers.

"Hello, ma'am. It's Eliza," she said.

"What are thou doing out at this time of night?" Ruth asked.

"May I come in?"

The door opened wider, and Eliza stepped into the dim interior. The room felt quite different than the last time she'd been inside. Then it had seemed bright and cheerful in the morning light. "Are thou hungry?" the wizened woman asked.

Eliza shook her head. "I need a place to stay for a few nights."

"Thou are welcome to stay here, child."

"Thank you." She followed Ruth into the sitting room and settled next to the fire. Ruth picked up a ball of yarn and resumed her knitting. She remained silent, waiting for Eliza to speak.

"The constable came this afternoon," Eliza began.

Ruth nodded as her needles clicked.

Eliza watched the sparks crackle in the fire. "He's trying to find my aunt's murderer."

Ruth looked up from her knitting. "I thought the murderer was found."

"It turns out that it couldn't have been the person that was first accused."

"That's why thou hast come here then?" Ruth asked. "Don't worry about your safety here. We'll be fine."

Eliza nodded numbly and stared into the fire. Not until today did she want to leave Maybrook. The emotion from Maeve's death, funeral, and now the reopened investigation, had left her empty.

"Art thou feeling well?" Ruth asked.

Eliza sighed. "I'm wrung out."

"Perhaps you could read the letter I received from Jonny today," Ruth said.

Eliza raised her eyes suddenly.

"Ah, I thought that might interest thee. Thou can read it to me," Ruth said.

"Haven't you read it?" Eliza asked.

"Alas, no. I misplaced my spectacles." Ruth drew out a folded envelope from her apron pocket and handed it over.

Eliza took the envelope. The writing on it was now familiar to her—dark and bold, like the writer himself.

Withdrawing the letter, Eliza began to read. The words were common enough, asking about how Ruth was doing and offering monetary assistance. Halfway into it, she stopped reading.

"Continue, dear," Ruth instructed.

Eliza exhaled then began.

Apryl spent the weekend at Mr. Thomas Beesley's country estate, and I joined her there on my return. It was in a pleasant location, but unfortunately I wasn't able to enjoy the visit. Apryl and I traveled home together, and her parents rode in my carriage. It was nice to have some private time with my fiancée without her inquisitive parents. I can always feel Mr. Maughan itching to ask what my father's estate is worth.

Eliza's chest tightened. Jon had gone to Thomas Beesley's estate? Were they fast friends now? She groaned inwardly. What an unbelievable coincidence. Had they shared a good laugh about her at the Beesley estate—Jon, Thomas, the Maughans, and . . . his fiancée? Then the other part finally sank in.

He's engaged.

She looked at Ruth. "Who's Apryl?"

Ruth chuckled. "That's an interesting question with an interesting answer. Apryl Maughan is Jonny's fiancée. But from what I've heard of her, the pair couldn't be more ill-matched."

Eliza tried to ignore her tumultuous thoughts and focus on what Ruth was saying.

"I never thought I'd see Jonny get engaged so soon after law school," Ruth continued. "Aye, the boy has always had ambition, and he knows that to work underneath the public eye, things at home must be in order."

"What do you mean?" Eliza asked.

"He wants to enter politics . . . mayor, governor, congress, something like that. And a man who has a high-society wife and a strapping son or two will rise in leadership. Thou knowest that entertaining dignitaries and peers is an integral part of a public career. A bachelor can't accomplish that on his own."

"Are you saying it's to be a marriage of convenience?"

"I can't say exactly, child, since I've never met Apryl. Any girl in her right mind would fall for a handsome man such as my Jonny, right?" Her eyes gleamed.

Eliza smiled, feeling flushed. "Ruth, for living in Maybrook, you sure know a lot about the outside world."

Ruth placed the knitting needles into her lap and sighed. "When thou reaches my age, thou wilt realize that every society is governed by the same ideologies."

"And what are those?" Eliza asked.

"Money and religious persuasion."

Sixteen

Jon awoke well before sunrise. His eyelids felt heavy; the previous night he'd spent most of the time trying to fall asleep. Exasperated, he rose and donned a heavy robe and slippers. Padding down the stairs, he stoked the fire in the library until it was a roaring blaze, hoping the flames would push the gloom away from his mind.

The evening newspaper was still on the desk, and he picked it up, but nothing held his interest. Why was he so restless? Apryl had been more than contrite about the business with Thomas. His father's estate should be settled in a few weeks, and then wedding plans could begin. Thomas had left in a hurry last night, but not as an enemy. He'd sent the telegram to the constable in Maybrook, warning him about Maeve O'Brien's murderer. Everything was in order, and there should be nothing to worry about.

But something kept gnawing at him—nothing was under his control. He didn't know what had really transpired between Apryl and Thomas. She had sobbed when he accused her of kissing Thomas. The business with his father's estate could drag on for months. Thomas Beesley definitely had something planned against the Robinsons, and it couldn't be favorable. Maeve O'Brien's murderer was still at-large.

And Eliza was still in Maybrook.

There. He admitted that he was worried about the girl. Fool. Losing sleep over someone who had nothing to do with him was ridiculous. She had a family and an inheritance and a beautiful face . . .

"That's enough," he said aloud.

"Sorry," Sarah murmured.

Jon looked up and saw the maid leaving the room. "Wait, I didn't see you there."

Sarah turned around and faced him. "Would you like breakfast in the library this morning, sir?"

"Yes, that would be fine. I woke early and lit the fire myself. I apologize if I startled you," Jon said.

Sarah bobbed her head and left the room.

After breakfast was brought in and Jon had eaten his fill, he made a new resolve. He pulled out a sheet of paper, ink and a dip pen and began to write.

Dear Miss Robinson,

Thank you for your speedy reply. As you may know already, the transient who was thought to be your aunt's murderer has been proved innocent of that crime. I'm sorry that you continue to experience disappointments. But I assume you are returning to New York soon with your mother for safety purposes.

I look forward to having my mother's journal in my possession. It will be helpful to learn about her. If you would prefer me to fetch the journal from your place of residence, I'm happy to oblige.

Regards,

Jonathan Porter

He set the pen down. It was done. Now he could forget about her and attend to more important matters. He would begin the day with a trip to the flower shop and purchase a bouquet for Apryl.

Late in the morning, Jon emerged from the flower shop, a bouquet of white lilies for Apryl in his hand. A couple approached him, and he stepped to the side to let them pass.

"Good morning, Mr. Porter," the man said.

"Ah, Mr. Robinson," Jon said, noticing who it was for the first time. "What a pleasant surprise."

The woman at Mr. Robinson's side regarded him with interest. She was fair-haired and stately.

"This is my wife, Grace."

"Pleased to meet you ma'am." Jon briefly clasped her hand.

She seemed to radiate pleasure. In her smile, Jon recognized the likeness of her daughter, although Eliza's eyes and coloring came from her father.

"Haven't we met?" Mrs. Robinson asked.

Jon smiled. "I'm afraid not, ma'am."

"Grace, Mr. Porter is the young man whom I met on my journey to Maybrook," Mr. Robinson said.

She smiled politely, but distaste crossed her features. "A quaint town I must say. I returned from there yesterday."

A carriage rattled past, and Jon waited for the noise of it to fade before saying, "Did you enjoy your visit, ma'am?"

Mr. Robinson broke in. "Mr. Porter was raised in Maybrook. He was the one who helped Eliza get out of jail."

Mrs. Robinson brought a hand to her throat, as if she didn't want to be reminded of something so distasteful.

"Is your daughter quite recovered from her ordeal?" Jon asked.

Mr. Robinson chuckled, and Mrs. Robinson pursed her lips together.

"Our daughter is a stubborn one, but she will eventually come around to her mother's more civilized ways," Mr. Robinson said.

Jon looked from husband to wife. What was Eliza being stubborn about?

"She refused to return with her mother and remains in Maybrook for the time being," Mr. Robinson continued.

Jon gripped the bouquet tightly. "Do you think that's a good idea?"

Amusement leapt into Mr. Robinson's eyes. "Obviously you don't know my daughter well, Mr. Porter, or you would know that she doesn't concern herself with the conventional."

"Even when her life might be in danger?" Jon asked.

"What do you mean?" Mrs. Robinson's voice rose in pitch.

"You haven't heard?" Jon said. "The man who they thought killed Mrs. O'Brien turned out to be the wrong man, which means the real killer hasn't been caught."

Mrs. Robinson gasped and gripped her husband's arm.

"My humble apologies. I thought you knew," Jon said. "I sent a telegram to the constable in Maybrook so that he could reopen the investigation."

Mr. Robinson had grown pale.

"Let's find a place to sit down." Jon led the way a short distance past the row of shops, and they sat together on a bench. "Is your daughter still staying at the Pranns' house?"

"No," Mrs. Robinson whispered. "She's alone at Maeve's."

"That obstinate girl," Mr. Robinson said. "I'll drag her back here if that's what it takes."

"Perhaps the constable has already informed her, and she's taken protective measures," Jon suggested. But worry had already burrowed inside him.

"Let's hope." Mr. Robinson's jaw was set firm. "We should go, dear. I need to catch the afternoon train to Maybrook."

The couple rose from the bench and hastened away.

Jon stared after the Robinsons, thoughts of Eliza in danger tumbling through his mind. But what could he do? At least her father was on the way to Maybrook now. After several minutes, Jon finally walked back home. As he reached the doorstep, he realized that he still held the bouquet of flowers in his hand. A note from Apryl lay on the hall table—an invitation for dinner that night. Drained, Jon tossed the fresh flowers onto a table and scratched an acceptance reply.

∽

Hours later, Jon found himself seated at the grand table in the Maughan's massive dining room. Thomas Beesley and his sister, Jessa, were present, although they weren't seated next to him this time. It was like a recurring nightmare. Apryl sat on his left, resplendent in a scarlet dress trimmed in velvet. Jon thought of Thomas's words from the night with disdain, about being able to provide the lavish lifestyle Apryl was accustomed to.

Jon caught a glimpse of Thomas watching Apryl, and the familiar ill feeling returned. Last night's visit wasn't about representing Thomas in some legal matter against Mr. Robinson. Thomas was sizing up his competition. He'd probably laughed the whole way home. Jon's eyes narrowed in Thomas's direction.

May the best man win.

"You're awfully quiet tonight, my love," Apryl purred next to him.

Jon shrugged and took another sip of wine. He was feeling reckless, moody, and was on his third glass. The over-confident beast of a man across the table would soon be sorry he interfered. Jon had no intentions of representing Thomas against Mr. Robinson.

"Let's play charades," someone suggested.

"Oh, let's do," Apryl squealed and took Jon's arm. He followed her into the drawing room, where the guests chattered excitedly.

"Thomas should start us off," his sister said.

Thomas stepped forward, awesome in gaudy attire that would have made a king pale in comparison. Clapping greeted him, and he immediately delved into character. The charades had begun.

⌒✍⌒

Eliza gaped at the broken glass scattered across Maeve's floor.

"Is everything all right?" Ruth called from the porch.

"Someone . . . broke in. The side window is shattered." She and Ruth had come to check on Maeve's cottage. It was apparent that Eliza had made the right decision in not staying there the night before.

Ruth came in and stood next to Eliza, staring at the mayhem strewn about Maeve's hearth room. Ashes and torn pages from books covered the fireplace. The lighthouse picture had been ripped down, and a long gash punctured the front of the painting.

Arm in arm, the two women proceeded cautiously toward the kitchen. The sturdy table was upturned, and the drawers dangled open.

"What were they looking for?" Eliza whispered in dismay.

A cupboard door had been torn from its hinges. Others had been scarred with knife marks. Eliza felt frozen in place. Whoever it had been had given no mercy.

"We should check thine aunt's room."

Eliza exhaled. They walked to Maeve's room, where Ruth pushed open the door, which stood ajar. The bedding had been pulled off and lay in a crumpled heap on the floor.

"Whoever it was is not going to give up easily." Ruth pointed at the chest of disheveled drawers in Maeve's room. "It's a blessing you didn't stay here last night."

Eliza could hardly comprehend the destruction as fear iced through her. They moved back into the hallway. The stair-boards leading to the second level had been pried open.

Shivering at the thought of the intruder making another appearance, Eliza said, "Let's go. We must notify the constable immediately."

"Yes," Ruth agreed.

They left the house, and Eliza felt like she was stepping out of a dark hole into the light. But still she shivered. The women climbed into the wagon and headed for town.

༄

After the constable had finished his investigation of the house, he brought Ruth and Eliza inside. "Have a seat," he instructed.

Both women sat on the sofa, on top of the stuffing protruding from slashes.

"Did Maeve have anything in her possession that might be of value to someone else?" he asked.

"Nothing I know of," Eliza said.

"Everyone knows how simply Maeve and her husband lived," Ruth added. "Why, this land was the only thing of value they owned."

The constable looked past the ladies as if he was in deep thought. When he focused back on them, he said, "There must be something more to this. Thou must try to think of something Maeve might have had that someone else would desperately want."

"Secret recipes?" Ruth offered.

The constable's mouth pulled down. "Thou wilt have to try harder than that."

"If my aunt had a deposit of money, it would have been stated in her will, wouldn't it?" Eliza asked.

"I would assume so," the constable said. "But let's say it's not money. What else could Maeve have had that would be of value?"

"Eliza?" A male voice boomed from outside.

Her father. Her heart nearly burst at the sound of his voice. She hurried outside, having never before been so glad to see him in her life. It was truly him, in his dark suit, his hat askew. She rushed over and embraced him.

Her father held her tightly. "I've come to take you home," he said, then pulled away. "Are you all right?"

She took a steadying breath. "Someone broke in and destroyed everything."

"Were you hurt?" he asked.

"No, I stayed at Ruth's last night . . . she's the woman who raised Jon Porter."

Her father put his arm about her shoulders as Ruth and the constable appeared on the front porch.

The constable spoke first. "We'll board up the place until the murderer is found." He looked at Eliza's father. "I'd like to ask thee a few questions about thy sister. Come see what's been done to the place."

"Certainly," her father said and followed the constable inside.

Ruth moved to Eliza's side, grasping her hand. "Perhaps it's better to return to New York where it's safe."

Eliza nodded in agreement. Every bit of stubbornness inside her had fled. The gossip columns could do their worst, but Eliza couldn't remain in Maybrook any longer.

"Thou are both welcome to stay with me tonight."

Seventeen

*L*ong after Ruth and her father had retired for the night, Eliza lay in bed awake, thinking about Helena Talbot. She hadn't yet finished reading the journal, and tomorrow she would be on a train back to New York with her father. Then she'd have to return the book to Jon. Lighting a candle on the nightstand, she pulled the trunk from under her bed and removed the journal, deciding to finish reading it tonight. She climbed back into bed, pulling the covers high, and began to read.

December 5, 1815. Any day my child will be born. I have felt a few pains over the past days. As thou seest, my handwriting is somewhat shaky. I am weak and alone. But I am not afraid. This is a challenge from God, and I will meet it. Ruth said she would look in on me from time to time. I hope she takes it upon herself to come soon, for I feel my time growing nigh.

December 12, 1815. I can finally see the light. I gave birth to a healthy son on December 6th. Praise God. During the labor, a hurricane hit the coast and most of my windows were blown out. Ruth arrived just in time. She settled me into the room under the stairs, and Little Jonny was born. He is strong and perfect in every way. Ruth cleared the debris around the house and ordered new window panes. She showed me how to care for my baby. For a woman with no children of her own, she knows a lot.

January 2, 1816. I've written a letter to Jonathan telling him of his son's arrival. I pray he will receive it and come for me soon. I pray for the letter's safe journey across the ocean—the ocean that divides our hearts. The townspeople have left small gifts at the doorstep after learning of the birth. I am overawed by their kindness. Little Jonny changes every day. His eyes are bright and inquisitive. It's such a joy to have someone to love who doesn't judge me. At night I watch him sleep. His soft breaths are so trusting and innocent. Sometimes I can't hold him close enough, trying to ease the pain I feel in missing his father. Ruth is the only one whom I have seen, unless thou countest the lighthouse keeper, Gus. He is widowed with a young son. He's an odd sort, nice enough, but something in his eyes reminds me of a hunted fox.

Even my own mother will not come see her grandchild.

March 18, 1816. Gus has been helping me a lot lately in the evenings. On those nights, I fix him supper, and we sit together in the evenings and watch our sons. His company helps to pass the time. Little Gus is awkward and clumsy, but gentle and loving with my son, something I admire. Even though Gus doesn't go to Meeting, the townspeople seem to respect him.

I haven't received a reply from Jonathan. The wait is almost unbearable. I wonder if his reply was lost in its travels. I don't know how much longer I can wait.

The candlelight sputtered then dimmed. Eliza lit another and turned the page, surprised to see the next date—more than a year later.

July 23, 1817. I've decided to go to England. I'm raising chickens and selling eggs to anyone who will buy them, to raise money for the fare. I often attend market day, and some of the townspeople have been quite friendly. My father stopped by the other night and gawked at Jonny. When he picked up my son, he had tears in his eyes, and he held the baby for a long time. He promised that Mother would eventually visit. I doubt she ever will. I told Father I want to go to England, and he seemed concerned for my well-being. That made me sad, but I told him that at least I could hide my past there. After a quiet pause, he said that he would try to help with the fare.

September 1817. Gus comes over every night. I have been watching his son during the day while he's working. Little Gus is slow-witted, but sweet. Gus chops wood, keeps the house in good repair, and gives me money for food. I have found some comfort in his presence. I can't help but compare him to Jonathan. As the days pass, memories of Jonathan seem to grow ever more distant. As I watch little Jonny toddle about the house, I think of his father and wonder why he hasn't replied to my letters. Many nights I have soaked my pillow with tears.

October 12, 1817. My father came to the market today. He said he heard that Jonathan was married last summer. The anger in his eyes betrayed his concern for me. I turned away, trying to hide my tears. I think maybe my father, too, hoped that Jonathan would return and make an honorable woman out of me. I feel worthless and used. I bore and am rearing Jonathan's son, yet he has forgotten what we were to each other.

I have been so foolish letting my heart rule my head. I used to think the ocean was the only thing dividing our hearts; now I know that my heart has drowned in the deep waters.

Eliza wiped away a stray tear, feeling the pain in Helena's words.

October 28, 1817. My heart is heavy with grief. If only I could see Jonathan and know for myself whether he has married. Is his wife carrying his child? Gus came over last night, and I decided to tell him of my burden. He was sympathetic and comforted me. I found myself feeling secure and appreciated in his strong arms. I let him share my bed.

I awoke this morning and felt worse than ever for sharing my bed with Gus. When he left, I ran outside and vomited. What have I become? The very thing my mother called me. A whore.

November 2, 1817. I have sunk into the depths of misery. My heart is dead, but I continue to act as a mother and a mistress. After Gus leaves each morning, I pretend that Jonny and I are waiting for his father to come home after a hard day's work. It is only when I hear Gus's heavy step on the front porch that my dream is crushed yet again. It is as if I am trying to climb a cliff but keep sliding back.

The only one who knows about me and Gus is Ruth. But I'm not worried about her telling the townspeople, because she seems quite fond of both Gus and little Gus.

Eliza wondered if Jon remembered playing with little Gus, and of having the elder Gus staying at the house. What a strange twist of events.

February 13, 1818. I am leaving this hell I've created. I loathe Gus's touch, knowing it may be all I have for the rest of my life. His clumsy hands repulse me, and I can no longer pretend it is Jonathan caressing me. I've saved enough money for the fare to England. If Gus finds out, he'll be furious. I'll have to pack in secret for Jonny and me, and somehow get away. Maybe I could leave little Gus at Ruth's house and hope that I'm not found missing for a long time. I've gone into town to see about the train schedule and plan to leave in a few weeks.

February 20, 1818. Yesterday, Gus found the train ticket. When my lies didn't satisfy him, he hit me so hard, I fear my nose will never look the same. Sobbing, I confessed the whole plan. But my tears couldn't coax mercy from him. He stripped my clothes off and bruised me with his passion. I pretended to faint, and he finally climbed off of me and left the room. I stayed in bed for a long time, waiting for him to leave the house, but he didn't. Sometime in the middle of the night, he brought me tea and watched me drink it. Then he began to kiss me. I had to do everything possible not to retch. Finally this morning, he left. I am so bruised and sore that I can hardly walk. I don't know where he went, but I'm afraid of what he'll do next. He took little Gus with him, so maybe he'll stay in his own house from now on. Jonny lies in bed with me, stroking my face—my sweet angel.

Eliza fought back the tears. She turned the page with trembling hands and found page after page blank.

Helena Talbot never wrote in her journal again.

Eliza squeezed her eyes shut at the horrible images she'd read. Gus entering the house, and stomping into Helena's room, demanding her affection, angrily stripping her dignity away.

A breeze stirred the pages of the journal, and the hairs on her arm rose. "Ruth?" she called, peering into the darkness beyond the glow of the candle.

Silence.

"Father?"

A whisper sounded in her ear. *"Help Maeve."*

Eliza turned her head, her eyes searching frantically in the darkness. The voice was back. Eliza climbed out of bed. "Helena?" The beating of Eliza's heart was the only answer.

She stole out of Ruth's house, running blindly, stumbling over the uneven earth, until she collapsed onto the ground. Helena had been murdered. Eliza felt it. Her jealous lover, Gus Senior, must have done it. There was no other explanation, and it was up to Eliza to discover the truth.

Help Maeve, the voice had said.

A sudden thought dawned. Maeve's death had to be connected to Helena's. Did Helena know who killed Maeve?

"How can I *help* her?" Eliza called into the darkness.

She held her breath, listening to nothing. Slowly rising, Eliza brushed off her clothing. The early morning air was cold and damp, but she paid no attention to it. Her heart seemed to be pumping warmth through her veins. She pressed forward through the undergrowth until she finally came to the clearing with Maeve's home.

A faint light glowed from within. Eliza hesitated. Someone was there. Was Helena waiting for her? Could ghosts light candles? Eliza spun in a circle looking for any signs.

"Show me what to do," she said.

"Go to her." The voice was faint.

Eliza felt a shiver crawl up her back. She swallowed hard and walked to the door of Maeve's—Helena's—house. Even before she turned the door handle, Eliza knew it was Gus Junior inside. He sat on the rocking chair, staring at the ceiling, rocking slowly back and forth. When he saw her, he moved his head in surprise, blinking rapidly.

"Looking for something?" She was no longer afraid of the strange man, but she still stayed close to the door.

Gus's eyes narrowed. "What are thou doing 'ere?"

"This is my property now."

Gus rose from the chair. "Thou 'as it, doesn't thee?" He took a step forward.

Eliza held her ground. "Has what?"

"'Er journal."

"Helena's?"

Gus's face paled. "How dare thee speak 'er name? She'll hear thee."

Eliza stared at the man and realized that he believed Helena's ghost was present too. But she had something he didn't—Helena's support.

A draft of air stirred Eliza's hair, causing gooseflesh to rise on her neck. "Helena led me here."

Gus's face drained to white.

Eliza knew she had the advantage. "She can't rest until her murderer confesses."

"She drowned," he said matter-of-factly, as if trying to convince himself.

"I don't believe you."

He crossed to the sofa and sat heavily upon it. He buried his face in his hands, swaying back and forth. Eliza was taken by surprise—she hadn't expected this reaction.

Quiet sobs came from the surly man. "I didn't mean to tell. But father said he'd whip me if I told what happened. He tried to stop her, but she fought back too much. He couldn't let her get away. When he brought 'er back in the wagon, she wasn't moving. The town thought she'd drowned, and we let 'em believe it."

So it was true. Eliza sagged against the wall. "What did you do with Helena?"

Gus wiped his nose with his arm. "We hid 'er body."

She felt sick.

Raising his tearstained face, Gus went on. "I found the journal after my father's death and ne'er told anyone."

She actually felt sorry for the poor man. He was a child when this happened and wasn't to blame. "Your father can't hurt you anymore."

His shoulders stopped heaving, and his sobs quieted.

"Did you break into this house to find the journal?"

Gus lifted his head again, his eyes darkening with fury. "*Maeve* took it, and I know she was goin' to tell someone. And when you moved in, I knew I had to stop 'er."

Eliza steadied herself against the door. Had Gus just confessed to killing Maeve? She tried to conceal the panic in her eyes. "What did you do, Gus?" She inched her hand toward the door handle.

A shadow crossed his face as he rose. "Thou are goin' to tell 'em, aren't 'e? Thou are goin' to tell how my father killed 'er, that I had to take care of Maeve too."

Eliza reached the handle and spun around, pushing at the door with all her might. But it was too late. Gus lunged and grabbed her, dragging her to the floor. She gasped as she thudded against the ground. She was trapped beneath his weight. "Don't hurt me. I won't tell anyone."

He laughed like a wild animal. "I won't hurt thee, Helena. I love thee. Now stop moving so much."

Cold fingers of fear spread through Eliza. Gus was repeating words he must have heard his father say.

"I'm not Helena. Get off me!" she screamed.

He covered her mouth with his heavy hand and grinned, his breath sour. "I know thou still lovest me." Staring into Eliza's eyes, he brought both hands to her neck and started to squeeze. Gagging, she tried to scratch him, but it only made him squeeze harder.

"Helena!" she gasped. "Help me." A scraping sound came from the other side of the room.

Gus smiled. "It's the only way, m'love, that thou wilt stay mine forever."

Just before the darkness closed in, Eliza saw the rocking chair rise in the air and smash into Gus's head.

⁓

"Please find me."

Eliza opened her eyes as the voice faded from her mind. She was in a room with white-washed walls.

"Eliza?"

She turned her head and saw her father sitting next to her bed. He looked years older, his face darkened with whiskers and his eyes rimmed in red. Grimacing at the soreness in her neck, she tried to speak, but her voice was nothing but a croak.

"You're at Ruth's home," her father said. "You've had an accident."

Then it came flooding back to her—Gus, the journal, the attack. She closed her eyes against stinging tears. And now the voice was back.

Please find me, it had said.

Eliza wanted to get out of the bed, leave the house, and never return to Maybrook.

Her father took her hand. "You're safe now."

"What happened?" she whispered.

"We'll talk about it later," he soothed.

"Tell me now," she said, flinching at the pain in her neck.

Her father hesitated. "I heard you leave the house. At first I thought you had gone for a short walk and would return soon. When you didn't, I told Ruth, and she guessed that you had gone to Maeve's. So I rode over as quickly as I could; it was as if someone was guiding me in the dark."

Eliza swallowed painfully. She knew who was guiding her father.

He continued. "I heard a terrific racket and ran to the door, trying to push it open. Only it was blocked by something. Through the slit I saw a man pinning you down . . ." His voice cracked. "He was choking you."

She brought a hand to her throat.

"It was strange, but the rocking chair fell on top of him," her father said. "How that is possible, I do not know. But it made him release his grip on your neck."

Eliza remembered the rocking chair lifting—and knew that the only explanation for it was Helena.

"When the man saw me, he scrambled away from you and stood up," her father said. "I shot him with Ruth's pistol."

Eliza stared at her father's haunted face, shocked at her father's actions. With great effort she asked, "Is he . . . ?"

"The bullet hit him in the leg." Her father grimaced. "I've never been so scared in my life. The man's in jail now—he can no longer hurt anyone."

She brought her father's hand to her cheek, tears wetting his palm. "His father killed Helena."

Mr. Robinson stared at her. "Helena?"

"Jonathan Porter's mother." Eliza's throat throbbed, but she had to explain. "She used to live in Aunt Maeve's house. I found Helena's journal and suspected how the poor woman died. Gus was trying to protect his dead father's name. He thought Aunt Maeve had learned the secret of Helena's death."

Her father's jaw locked firm. Then he took Eliza into his arms and held her tightly. Even with the pain shooting through her neck, she clung to her father and let the tears fall.

"Please find me."

Eliza stiffened. "Did you hear that?" she whispered.

"Hear what?" her father said.

Eliza broke from her father, fear thundering through her. She'd discovered how Helena had died. She'd discovered who'd killed Maeve. Gus was in jail now. What more could Helena possibly want?

Leave me alone! she screamed inside.

"Father, I'm ready to go home," she said in a shaky voice. "Now."

Eighteen

ettling into the train compartment, Eliza allowed her father to fuss over her. He tucked blankets beneath her feet and placed a pillow behind her head.

"Thank you," she whispered.

Mr. Robinson offered a brief smile, temporarily masking the concern on his face. "Your mother will never forgive me." The crease on his forehead deepened. "It shouldn't have happened."

After Eliza had felt well enough to travel, she went with her father to the constable's office to make a sworn statement of all the facts she knew. She wrote her testimony about Gus's murder confession. Mr. Robinson was congratulated for his timely appearance, and none were saddened at the imprisonment of the strange man named Gus, now revealed as the murderer, who had apparently followed in his father's footsteps.

The bizarre event of how the rocking chair came to move across the room and fall upon Gus was explained by an open window and a strong gust of wind. But Eliza knew what had really happened. Helena had come to her aide. Still, Eliza was grateful that she was leaving Helena behind for good.

Now, Eliza's heart was heavy for a different reason. Her father would tell Jonathan what had transpired and present him with Helena's journal. Eliza's stomach churned as she thought about Jon reading his mother's words. Through her own close call with the younger Gus, she knew firsthand what Helena must have experienced. Then another question fleeted through her mind, but it was gone before she could answer it.

Why did Ruth own a pistol?

"Are you all right, dear? You look pale," her father said.

"Only tired," she whispered.

"Nothing will make me happier than to have you safe and sound at home."

When they arrived in New York, her father helped her off of the train and into a waiting carriage.

Eliza settled into the carriage seat with relief. Dismal clouds hung low in the sky, promising rain and dreary cold, but New York City had never looked so beautiful to her.

When they at last arrived home, her mother was waiting. She waved the maid away, followed Eliza into her room and helped her change from her traveling clothes.

"I was so worried when I received the telegram from your father. How are you feeling, dear?"

"Much better, Mother," Eliza whispered.

"I knew I shouldn't have left you—I should have dragged you home."

Eliza smiled at the thought of her mother physically dragging her. After all the tension that had been between them, it was good to know that her mother truly cared. When Eliza was settled beneath the down comforter and propped up with several pillows, she managed, "Are the papers full of my tale of woe?"

"Fancy that you are so interested in the local gossip on your first day back."

Eliza laughed. "I guess I've changed."

"The write-up was quite wonderful, actually," her mother said. "It outlined the death of poor Maeve and your fortunate discovery of the murderer."

"Really?"

"*Really*, Eliza. You're so cynical." She shook her head. "The earlier gossip was not brought up in today's paper, and neither was the reason you went to Maybrook in the first place."

"That's a relief," Eliza whispered.

Mrs. Robinson nodded. A knock sounded at the door. "Yes?" she called out.

"Mr. Porter is waiting downstairs," the maid, Bess, said through the door. "And Mr. Robinson requests your presence, ma'am."

Jon was here?

"I'm coming." Mrs. Robinson turned to Eliza. "Stay here. You'll be all right for a few moments?"

When her mother left, Eliza scanned the room, seeing it in a different light. Even though it had only been a couple of months, everything looked different, childish. Porcelain dolls lined one wall, and the curtains were a cheerful pink. A stuffed and ragged doll sat amongst the porcelain dolls—it was her childhood treasure. Her father had bought the doll for her when she was sick with the measles.

But now the ragged doll seemed unbefitting in the dainty room, as if she didn't belong in such a pretty world. Eliza turned to her side and hugged a pillow to her chest. She was like that doll, out of place in this sheltered house.

The door clicked open, and her mother entered. "What a persistent man. He practically tried to bowl over your father and come up the stairs to see you. Thank goodness he finally left." She frowned at Eliza. "Patience is a virtue in a person, you know."

He wants to see me. Eliza hid a smile as her mother fussed about the room. "He's engaged to the socialite Apryl Maughan. She's a trifle gregarious for my taste, and her figure shows her indulgent lifestyle. I don't understand how a mother could let her daughter become so overweight."

"Appearance isn't everything," Eliza croaked.

Her mother turned. "Of course not, dear. I wasn't suggesting such a thing. I was merely pointing out that there is always room for improvement."

Eliza stifled an exasperated sigh.

"You should get your rest," her mother said, adjusting the covers.

She waited until her mother left before letting out a moan into her pillow. Her mother was so judgmental—ironically, not unlike the Puritans who had ostracized Helena.

Warmth moved through her as she thought about Jon trying to push his way through the house to her room. Soon the warmth was replaced by exhaustion, and she fell into a deep sleep.

Eliza ran through the house, searching for Aunt Maeve. All of the doors were locked, and she began pounding then, one by one, until she finally started sobbing.

"Maeve, where are you?"

Then a knock sounded at the door, and she moved toward it, almost floating. It was Gus, and his face was lined with fury. "Let me in!"

Eliza braced herself against the door, but couldn't fend off his weight. The door swung open, she fell, and Gus was standing above her.

"It's time you joined Maeve." He grabbed her hair and pulled upward.

Eliza woke in her bed; the collar of her nightgown was damp. She tried to still her heaving chest. The candle on the nightstand was wallowing in a puddle of wax, since she hadn't blown it out before falling asleep. Eliza grabbed another candle, lighting it against the flame and placing it into a candleholder. She couldn't decide which was worse— the voice of Helena plaguing her, or nightmares about Gus.

She began to shiver, so she rose and grabbed the ragged doll. She climbed back into bed and held the tattered doll tightly, letting the flickering candle burn itself out. It was a long time before she fell asleep again.

In the morning, Eliza's voice was nearly recovered, only slightly hoarse. She stayed in bed long after breakfast, not ready to face the daily chatter of local events. Bess brought her a tray in bed, and Eliza was content with the quiet meal.

Before noon, her mother peeked in. "Are you ready to receive visitors?"

"I suppose."

Her mother smiled. "Wonderful. Mrs. Graydon will be coming at three."

Eliza hoped she was equal to the task. If Mrs. Graydon came, there would be no need for anyone else to visit. The seventy-year old woman was better than a newspaper at distributing news.

"I know what you're thinking, Eliza, but Mrs. Graydon has been one of the steadfast friends through all of this." Mrs. Robinson removed a letter from her pocket. "This was delivered this morning." She handed Eliza the small square envelope, her lips pursed.

"Thank you." Eliza wondered if it was another note from Nathaniel; she'd already received two. But there was no return address on the envelope. She pulled out the brief message.

"I hope you're feeling better."

There was no signature, but Eliza recognized the handwriting as Jon's. Eliza burrowed into her covers, thinking about the man who seemed to have plenty of compassion in him after all.

An hour later, Eliza was situated in the parlor, assailed with the jasmine aroma that preceded Mrs. Graydon's presence. Mrs. Graydon firmly believed in making an indelible impression on everyone she met, and although she was nearly seventy, Eliza thought the woman looked many years younger. Mrs. Graydon kept up with the latest fashions, showing them off with her still-trim figure.

Eliza smiled politely as the elegant woman sat next to her. With each movement, Eliza caught a whiff of perfume. But Eliza was glad for the visit—it made her feel normal. It made things like a ghostly voice seem unreal, existing only in her imagination.

"You look pale, my dear," Mrs. Graydon began. "And so thin." Her gaze flitted in Mrs. Robinson's direction.

Eliza's mother straightened in her chair. "Each day she grows stronger."

Mrs. Graydon placed a dry silky hand over Eliza's. "After what you've been through, it's a wonder you are out of bed at all. My granddaughter, Gina, would love to come and spend time with you. It will brighten your countenance to socialize again."

Eliza didn't know Gina well, but it would be nice to have a friend. All of her others had been silent since the Thomas Beesley incident. "I'd love to visit with Gina."

"What a dear," Mrs. Graydon crooned, her eyes watering. "I assure you, you've been at the top of my priorities. Just the other day, I went to see poor Miss Mable. She's still recovering from childbirth, you know. Some women aren't meant to bear children."

Mrs. Robinson threw Mrs. Graydon a piercing stare; the woman didn't seem to notice.

"You're normally a strong young thing," Mrs. Graydon continued. "When you marry, you'll have healthy children."

Eliza had to force herself not to laugh at her mother's shocked expression.

"Thomas Beesley has thankfully turned his attention elsewhere." It seemed Mrs. Graydon was not to be cowed. "As I told your mother, I support your decision completely. No one should feel pressured to marry, certainly in our modern world—"

"Well," Mrs. Robinson interrupted. "Should I call for refreshments?"

"Lovely," Mrs. Graydon said, then turned her attention back to Eliza. "Only a week ago, I ran into Mrs. Maughan. Have you met her?" Without giving Eliza a chance to reply, she continued, "Her daughter, Apryl, is engaged to a wealthy man—a Mr. Porter. Anyway, Mrs. Maughan thinks he's inherited quite a sum from his father's estate."

Yes, I know him.

As Mrs. Graydon filled her in on all the happenings in New York, Eliza's thoughts were far from the parlor.

Later that afternoon, with Mrs. Graydon gone, Eliza was exhausted and begged not to receive any more visitors. Her mother helped make her comfortable in the library by the fire.

"Your father and I have a dinner engagement tonight. Will you be all right without us?" her mother asked.

"Of course, Mother. I can ask Bess if I need anything."

Mrs. Robinson kissed Eliza's cheek and left the room. Half an hour later, Eliza heard them leave the house, and she was finally alone.

Dozing before the fireplace, she thought she heard the bell ring. Bess answered, and a male voice resonated through the hallway. There was some sort of discussion, and Eliza tried to make out what was being said and by whom. The library doors opened, and Jonathan Porter strode into the room.

Bess hurried after him, protesting, "Sir—"

Eliza stood a bit awkwardly at the sight of Jon. "It's all right, Bess."

The maid looked from Eliza to Jon, disapproval clear in her eyes. But in a professional manner, she nodded curtly and left, closing the doors behind her.

Jon stood there gazing at Eliza. She sat in her chair and motioned for him to do the same. He crossed the room and stopped in front of her. She offered him a faint smile, but he remained silent, his eyes searching hers.

"Hello, Mr. Porter," she said.

The sound of her strained voice brought him to his senses. A look of concern passed over his face as his gaze traced the dark bruises on her neck. "Are you all right?"

Eliza shifted, feeling her face heat up. "Each day is a little better."

"Tell me what happened, if it's not too . . . painful."

She looked down at her lap, tears beginning to fill her eyes. *Why am I crying? I haven't cried since returning home.*

Jon pulled a chair close to hers and sat down, grasping her hand. It was a tender gesture really, nothing more than any gentleman would do, yet it made Eliza's heart pound harder than it should have.

"I'm all right." She pulled her hand away from his.

"I should have been there," he said, rising to his feet. He shoved his hands in his pockets. "That man, Gus, is a strange one. I should have seen it from the beginning when he was bothering you in the lighthouse."

"How could you have known?"

Jon ignored her question and changed the subject. "I spent all day reading my mother's journal."

Eliza looked at him, searching his eyes—what had he thought? Had the news devastated him? He seemed more upset at Eliza's condition than reading about his mother's broken heart.

"Your aunt's murderer was the son of the man who murdered my mother . . . unbelievable. And," his voice softened as he looked at her, "he nearly killed you, too."

She swallowed hard. Before she knew it, Jon was kneeling in front of her, taking both of her hands in his.

"Why was he allowed to get away with it?" he asked.

Eliza looked at her hands enfolded by his. She didn't know if he was talking about Gus Senior or the one who had attacked her.

"Both of those men—Gus and my father—used her. How could anyone be so callous?" he said. "My father knew I had been conceived, yet he married another woman. Only later in life did he try to contact me." He snorted as he added, "to offer me money out of a guilty conscience."

She let him continue uninterrupted. She wanted to reach out to him, embrace him, but she didn't dare—for a number of reasons.

"My mother had the world against her. Even her parents acted like strangers, and they let her give birth alone and afraid. She waited years for my father to return, only to realize that he had betrayed her." His head lowered as he exhaled.

Eliza knew all of this, but she didn't want to tell him so. She didn't know what to think about Jon Porter now; she'd never seen him so vulnerable. So sorrowful. She caught a glimpse of the lonely boy he must have been in his youth.

Without thinking of what she was doing, she touched his cheek. He didn't move, didn't pull away, as she ran her fingers along his face then down his neck, stopping at his shoulder. "Jon," she whispered, "you can't change the past."

His bloodshot eyes seemed to burn through hers. He brought his hand to her neck and lightly touched the brutal markings. Eliza bit her lip, suppressing a gasp as his fingers brushed her skin, but she didn't move away. His touch was both painful and exhilarating at the same time. She closed her eyes, inhaling his nearness.

Then she felt his lips on hers, soft at first, hesitant. She couldn't say she was surprised that he'd kissed her—there had always been something tugging them together—but still, she felt like she was in a dream, that this wasn't really happening. *Couldn't* be happening.

Yet, it definitely was. As she ran her hands up his chest and behind his neck, kissing him in return, his hesitancy ended. She didn't know where she found her boldness, but right then, all she knew was that she wanted him closer. She didn't dare open her eyes, afraid Jon would snap out of whatever trance caused him to touch her, and the dream would end.

His hand moved along her jaw line, tracing its way to her hair. His kisses were deeper now, possessive, as if he couldn't get enough. The warmth between them turned hot, spreading to every part of her body. He pulled her upward until they were standing together, and she was fully in his arms. Every curve of hers seemed to fit perfectly against the length of his body.

"Eliza," he whispered, kissing her neck, the hollow at her throat, and then his mouth was back to hers. Her lips parted, and she welcomed them eagerly. It was as if she was a different person, not herself, but one with Jon, in another existence that was theirs alone.

Then as suddenly as the kiss had begun, it ended.

Jon released her and took a step away, his breathing ragged. "I'm sorry," he said, running his hands through his hair. But the way he was staring at her said he was anything but sorry. "I'd better stick to letter writing from now on."

"Jon—" She didn't want him to be sorry—but what had this meant? He was engaged, after all. What had they done?

He leaned toward her and brushed a stray tendril from her cheek. "Your face has haunted my dreams, Eliza," he said softly. Then he dropped his hand, as if he'd touched something hot.

Eliza lifted her face to his, wanting to kiss him again, wanting to hold him and not let go. His eyes searched her face, but sorrow had crept into them. He closed his eyes, exhaling. And at that moment, Eliza knew he was saying good-bye.

"But I don't believe in dreams," he said. "Forgive me. I've taken advantage of you, and I will not do so again."

Tears welled in her eyes; she turned away, not wanting to see him leave. She heard the library door open and shut softly. And then he was gone.

Nineteen

he following morning, Jon canceled all his
appointments and sent a note to Apryl,
inviting her to the matinee. He planned to
spend the day with her, and hopefully, erase the memory of
the previous evening. Maybe last night's after-dinner sherry
had affected him more than he'd realized. But today, sitting
in his library, Jon knew that alcohol was not responsible for
his behavior with Eliza. In fact, he would like nothing better
than to repeat it. And he believed she felt the same way.

Jon slammed his fist on the desk. *Damn her. Damn me.*
Pressing his fingers against his temples, he tried to massage
her out of his mind. Maybe he should move to England. Put
an ocean between them. He opened his eyes and stared
straight ahead. That was the answer. He and Apryl could
elope and honeymoon in Europe. Eliza would meet another
man, and eventually everyone would be happy. No promises
would be broken, no scandals would arise, and no political
career blackened.

He would not be like his father, abandoning the woman
he'd committed himself to.

He spent the rest of the morning taking care of correspondence. By noon, he was ready to leave and instructed Richards to prepare the carriage. As an extra touch, he brought wine and flowers. Arriving at the Maughans, he was surprised to see another carriage parked in front of their home—a sleek burgundy one—belonging to one Thomas Beesley.

Jon was led into the hall, and he insisted on waiting there. Merry voices floated from the drawing room, but he resisted the urge to inspect. Soon, Thomas, Apryl, and her parents appeared.

"Why, Jon, you've arrived." Apryl crossed over and kissed his cheek. "Thomas was just telling us that he has enlisted your help in a business matter concerning Mr. Robinson."

Jon shot a look at Thomas, who met his gaze smoothly. "We don't have the particulars worked out, but I'm sure the joint venture will be more than successful."

"If I know Mr. Beesley," Mr. Maughan said, patting Jon on the back, "You'll be generously compensated."

Jon kept his gaze on Thomas. "I've no doubt about that, sir."

"Well, then, it's settled," Apryl said brightly, then her face drew into a pout. "I asked Thomas if he would like to accompany us to the theater, but he said he didn't want to intrude."

Thomas smiled boldly at Jon, gallantly spreading his arms. "I'm a man who knows my place."

Everyone laughed except Jon.

Even after Apryl and Jon were seated in the carriage, Jon was still scowling.

"Oh, don't be so sour," Apryl said.

He turned to her. "I thought you weren't going to have anything more to do with that man."

Apryl's eyes widened. "He stopped over this morning to return something my mother left at his estate. When he started talking about doing business with you, I thought that all ill feelings had passed between you two, so there was no harm in keeping my friendship with him."

Jon didn't answer. On one hand, he couldn't stand Apryl's association with Thomas. On the other, if Apryl believed that Jon wanted to work for Thomas, it might make things easier between them. Apryl seemed to revere Thomas, and Jon didn't want that to come between them.

"Perhaps I've been too quick to judge," he said.

Apryl leaned over to kiss him. Jon met her lips, noticing the lack of warmth in her touch, as if their affection had become a formality.

Nothing about kissing Eliza the night before had been cold or remote, but he forced himself to clear her from his mind. "Let's make a toast to a day of nothing but frivolity." He brought out the wine and two flutes. Apryl giggled.

"My lady," he said nobly and poured a glass. Then the carriage hit a bump, and a few drops splashed across Apryl's chest.

She burst out laughing. "How am I going to explain already smelling like wine to my mother?"

Jon joined her laughter and realized he'd gone several seconds without thinking about Eliza.

Soon they arrived at the theater, which was already crowded. It seemed that everyone decided to see *Henry IV* that afternoon at the Bowery. Jon and Apryl greeted a few friends before they found their seats in the balcony. Moments later, excited chatter rose around them. Everyone was looking at the couple entering the main doors: President Martin Van Buren, his son Abraham, and daughter-in-law, Angelica.

Jon rose in respect and bowed as the presidential party passed their balcony entrance. President Van Buren nodded, and both Abraham and his wife smiled. When they had moved on, Apryl touched Jon's arm. "Did you see that? I think he recognized you."

"I don't think so, my dear," he said, amused with Apryl.

"I met him only briefly a year ago."

"You have something about you that draws people," Apryl said, her eyes shining.

He chuckled. "You're being overgenerous."

"Jon, I'm serious. They say the president's daughter-in-law now presides as the lady of the White House ever since his wife passed."

"Perhaps that's best."

They returned to their seats, and Apryl scanned the crowd beneath them, intermittently pointing out an acquaintance. Jon found himself nodding but not really listening.

"How odd," Apryl said rather loudly.

Jon glanced at her. "What is it?"

"Look there." She tilted her head toward the audience below. "Third row."

He saw Thomas Beesley squeezing his way through an aisle. A young woman, obviously not his sister, led the way. Soon they were settled, talking animatedly.

Apryl sniffed. "Well, he could at least have told me that he declined my invitation because he was already coming."

Jon looked sharply at Apryl, who continued to gaze at the lively couple. "It's none of our business."

"You're right. I don't know why I let it bother me." She tore her eyes away from the couple and focused on the rising curtain. The music started, quelling all audience conversation.

Each time Jon stole a glance at Apryl, he saw her glumly watching Thomas. Jon's neck grew hot beneath his collar. Thomas Beesley had probably planned this very incident to cause Apryl to grow envious. But why should Apryl be jealous, unless she had feelings for Thomas? That's what bothered Jon the most.

During the intermission, Jon remained in his seat. When Apryl left for the powder room, he found himself watching Thomas. To Jon's surprise, he saw Apryl approaching him. It appeared as if introductions were made, and then Apryl pointed to her seat in the balcony. Jon looked the other way to avoid being caught spying.

Moments later when Apryl returned, she was breathless with two bright spots on her cheeks. "I happened to see Thomas. He introduced me to his companion."

"Oh?"

"The woman is his next-door neighbor, and her escort became ill at the last minute. That's how Thomas happened to come with her."

Jon looked at Apryl. "And did he apologize for turning you down?"

"Most profusely," she said, smiling. "It's not like I care who he's courting; I just don't want him to have another awful experience like he did with Eliza Robinson."

He bit back a retort. "We only know one side of that story."

"You can't be taking her side." Apryl arched her brow.

"The people who gossip about her don't even know her." Jon glanced away, knowing he'd probably said too much. "Innocent until proven guilty."

Apryl scoffed. "One would think you knew her, Jon."

Jon didn't reply. He stared straight ahead, waiting for the next act to begin. He hadn't intended to argue with Apryl. It was only that he hated to hear Eliza being criticized by those who didn't even know her.

After the play ended, Apryl and Jon left together silently. Once outside, they greeted Thomas as if there had never been contention between them.

"Mr. Porter?" a man called out.

Jon turned and found Mr. and Mrs. Robinson standing before him. Behind them stood Eliza. She wore a large hat with a veil that concealed her eyes. The lace at her neckline was ruffled, obscuring any signs of discoloration on her neck.

"Good afternoon." Jon hadn't expected to see Eliza so soon . . . or ever again. His collar felt too tight, and he needed a good dose of cold air.

Apryl linked her arm through his, drawing close to him.

"Let me introduce Apryl Maughan," he said, recovering somewhat of his senses. "Apryl, this is Mr. and Mrs. Robinson and—"

"Our daughter, Eliza," Mr. Robinson interjected.

Jon was surprised that Apryl didn't faint on the spot. She put on her best smile and said in a honeyed voice, "Pleasure to meet you." She pressed against Jon's side, as if making it clear to Eliza that they were engaged. Which was ridiculous, because of course they were engaged, and Eliza knew it as well as anyone.

"It's our pleasure," Mrs. Robinson said. "I know your mother through the social engagements."

"I'll tell her we met you then." Apryl looked past the woman and openly appraised Eliza.

Jon cringed. He would hear about Apryl's opinion of Eliza soon enough. For now, he wanted to put needed distance between himself and Eliza. "Nice to see you again," Jon said as they left.

Once inside the carriage, Apryl wasted no time in delivering her pronouncement. "What a coincidence! She was prettier than I expected, but I couldn't exactly tell because of her veil. It's no wonder Thomas fell in love with her, but her personality was quite unremarkable. She hardly spoke a word. I'd think Thomas wouldn't have been happy with that for long. He needs someone who can equal him in conversation, keep him interested." She paused for only a second. "I wonder if Thomas saw her."

"I'm sure they would greet each other like civilized people," he said in a tight voice.

Apryl stared out the window for a few moments. "She was a dainty thing," she said. "Not a good match for a robust man such as Thomas."

Agreed, Jon thought. "I wish I'd gotten a better look at her, but I could tell she has an innocent-type beauty. She's surely used to being pampered."

"Pampered? How could you tell?" he asked.

She jabbed him in the ribs. "Oh, really, Jon. You say the funniest things sometimes. Did you not notice that porcelain doll skin and perfectly styled hair? She obviously has a half-dozen maids and spends every moment indoors with them at her beck and call."

"I didn't notice." He *had* noticed—particularly that she looked pale. Was it too early for her to be in public? Was she well?

"I wonder why she was dressed like an old maid," she said.

"She was nearly strangled to death, Apryl," Jon said. "The bruises on her neck are still visible."

"Oh?" She looked at him. "How do you know that?"

"I read the papers and . . . natural assumption, I suppose."

"I do feel sorry for her in that regard," Apryl said.

They rode the rest of the way in silence. When the carriage pulled to a stop in front of Apryl's house, she invited him to join her parents for dinner. Jon agreed and followed her inside.

Soon they were seated at the dinner table, steaming pumpkin soup before them. Apryl wasted no time in relaying the details about meeting Eliza at the theater. Mr. and Mrs. Maughan let their soup grow cold as they listened with great interest to Apryl's tale. When Apryl finished, she turned to Jon. "Tell us what she's really like beneath that awful veil."

Jon reluctantly set his spoon down, searching for words. He couldn't tell them about the way her hair fell onto her cheeks in silky strands. How it was the first time he'd seen her with such tight curls, because her hair had been wavy in Maybrook. Nor could he talk about the way she had stroked his cheek in his moment of weakness. He couldn't reveal how supple and inviting her lips were or the way she responded to his kiss as if there was no one else she desired but him. Or how torturous it was to meet her in public and not be able to talk to her or ask her how she was doing.

"She's quiet, but headstrong," he finally said.

"She'd have to be headstrong to turn down Thomas Beesley," Mrs. Maughan said.

Everyone around the table nodded in unison.

"Speaking of Thomas," Mr. Maughan said, "he's invited us to meet at his house for cocktails before the masquerade ball."

Although Jon didn't care for the topic of Thomas Beesley, he was grateful that the subject had left Eliza.

After dinner, Jon followed Mr. Maughan into the library. Cigars were lit and brandy poured. Wasting no time, Mr. Maughan said, "Tell me about the business between you and Thomas Beesley."

"I can't rightly say," Jon said.

"Client confidentiality?"

"Not exactly. We haven't gone over any specifics yet. I'm sure we'll meet soon to create an outline."

Mr. Maughan nodded and took a drag on his cigar. "How are things going with your father's estate?"

"Too slowly," Jon said, then, feeling it was the perfect opportunity, he added, "unfortunately there are some roadblocks I hadn't counted on."

Mr. Maughan leaned closer. "Such as?"

"Apparently I have a half-sister who wants a share of the estate," Jon said. Doughty had assured him there were no concerns, but he wanted to see Mr. Maughan's reaction. "I didn't know my father had married and had another family until I received notice in the will."

The man gave a little start, looking as if he were trying to keep his reactions under control. "I thought it was all left to you."

Just the reaction that Jon expected. "It was, but according to English law, wills can be contested by family members with probable claim."

Mr. Maughan sniffed, his mouth working against the cigar. "The property is rightfully yours, being his eldest and only son."

Jon remained silent.

After a few moments of companionable smoking, Mr. Maughan asked, "Out of curiosity, what would you say the estate was worth?"

Trying to keep his face somber, Jon casually shrugged. He'd decided to downplay the amount. The more time Apryl spent with Thomas Beesley, the less secure he became that she truly cared for him, and not his potential of earnings. "Perhaps only fifty thousand."

Mr. Maughan quickly recovered his shock at the small amount. "That will keep you comfortable."

Hiding a smile, Jon nodded in agreement. He knew the amount was not as much as the Maughans would have hoped for their daughter. But more importantly, what would Apryl think? The Maughans would find out soon enough that their future son-in-law was really to be a millionaire. Until then, Jon had business to take care of with Thomas Beesley, and that included discovering what Apryl's true intentions were toward the man.

Mr. Maughan checked his pocket watch. "It's getting late. I'm sure my wife is ready to retire."

Jon followed him out of the library. They found the women visiting in the drawing room.

"Ready dear?" Mr. Maughan asked.

Mrs. Maughan rose and took his arm. They left Jon and Apryl alone and went up the stairs.

Apryl smiled at Jon when her parents left. "I guess I'm rather tired too."

Jon helped her stand. Without letting go of her hand, he said, "Let's elope."

Her mouth dropped open. "Elope? You must be mad."

Perhaps he was mad. But he was also wondering if he wanted to spend the rest of his life married to this woman— did she really care about him? The way that he had felt that Eliza cared about him last night? "You're probably right," he said, "but wouldn't it be exciting?" *Wasn't exciting what Apryl wanted?*

She flushed. "I don't know what's gotten into you. My mother would be furious if I denied her the right to plan a wedding."

"But what if it made *me* happy?"

"Really, Jon. Why are you so interested in hurrying up things? I couldn't do that to my family."

Jon released Apryl's hand, both relieved and disappointed. Perhaps she wasn't as attached to him as she claimed to be. Was this what he wanted? A wife who wasn't in love with him?

"Very well," he said.

"Oh, don't be angry. It's because I'm their only child."

"I'm not angry," he said, trying to hide his annoyance with himself. He wasn't thinking straight. Kissing Eliza, then asking Apryl to elope—what had he been thinking? "Just impatient . . . Is an elaborate wedding necessary?"

"Of course—it's every girl's dream." She kissed his cheek. "Now be a good boy and let me get my beauty rest."

Jon studied her face, noting her too cheerful smile. He wanted to push one more time. "Think about it, Apryl."

She didn't answer for a moment. The only sound between them was the ticking of the grandfather clock in the corner. A slight frown crept to her brow. "Are you feeling well?"

"Nothing that will not soon pass." She was right. He wasn't feeling well—at least not in his heart. He showed himself out the door.

⌒✐⌒

The following morning he sent a note to Mr. Thomas Beesley, and that afternoon, they were seated across from each other in Jon's library.

Thomas smiled. "So you've come to your senses."

"If that's how you choose to look at it." Jon's eyes narrowed. "Let's begin. I want to know what legal action you have in mind."

"I want to terminate my partnership with Mr. Robinson. I have wanted to do so for some time, since his, er—"

"Since his daughter turned you down?" Jon finished.

Thomas dabbed his nose with a handkerchief. "It's difficult to work with someone on a daily basis when you don't respect them."

"Surely you wouldn't let a personal matter get in the way of honest business?" Jon countered.

Thomas grimaced. "I've lost important clients over the affair, and fear I'll lose even more. With his daughter back in New York, flaunting her inheritance and making people pity her for the attack that was made on her—"

"She was nearly killed, and you think she's seeking pity? You must really hate Eliza."

At the mention of her name, Thomas jerked his head up. "I don't hate Miss Robinson," he said evenly. "I hate the position she put me in. She flirted incessantly and made me believe she was very fond of me. There was never a dance or party in which she wasn't continually by my side."

Jon had a hard time imagining Eliza attaching herself to this irritating man. What did Thomas think about Apryl's behavior? "Don't you think it possible to put the incident behind you?

"I've tried. But the gossip columns continue, and my earnings are down this month. I can't afford the lost revenue."

"Have you tried speaking with Mr. Robinson about your concerns?"

Thomas chuckled. "According to our contract, we can't dissolve the partnership unless one of us participates in illegal action or can't hold up his end of the agreement."

"And Mr. Robinson has not violated any of the agreements?" Jon clarified.

"Not yet." Thomas shifted in his seat, his face reddening. "Are you going to help me or not?"

"That depends on what sort of help you need. So far I haven't seen any valid reason to end your partnership with Mr. Robinson, unless you are basing it on obstinate pride."

Thomas handed over a stack of papers, his hands trembling. "Read through the contract for any loopholes." He stood with effort. "If you can find one, I'll make it worth your while."

Jon took the papers as Thomas stormed out of the room.

Twenty

ach day, Eliza felt a little stronger, but each night Gus appeared again and again in her dreams. Helena's voice had fallen silent, but the nightmares only grew more detailed and frightening. Sometimes Gus chased her with a knife. Others, he cornered her in the lighthouse. And always, he called her Helena. Eliza's only comfort was to know that he was imprisoned.

Soon she took the medicine ordered by the doctor to help her sleep. It wasn't that she *couldn't* sleep, but she was afraid to dream. With the medicine, she woke feeling groggy, but at least not remembering the night.

But that proved equally frustrating. Too bad she couldn't take medicine to forget during the days. As it was, they were filled with thinking about Jon. His fiancée was certainly possessive enough, practically clinging to him when she'd met them, and didn't seem to be a woman to shy away from competition. But as the days went by, remembering Jon's kiss grew more difficult, and she was left with only the tortured events that followed it—Jon asking for forgiveness. Jon leaving. Jon's startled expression when they ran into each other at the theater.

And then one day, a letter came from him.

She took it to her room to read in private. The words were not what she had hoped for.

> *Dear Eliza,*
>
> *I sincerely apologize for the other week when I burst into your home and laid my problems on your shoulders. I've thought about my mother's words and realize I can't change the past. Nor can I change what happened between us. But I can apologize and hope that I did not embarrass you or hurt your feelings. I promise to be a complete gentleman in the future. I'm happily engaged and would not want something trivial to come between my fiancée and me. I trust you to be discreet.*

Eliza stared at the space where Jon should have included his signature, but it was blank. He hadn't even signed his apology. Maybe he feared someone would read it and guess what had happened. Her eyes burned as tears began to fall. Eliza let them drip onto the letter, blurring the inked words. *He* had kissed her. It was as if he was warning her not to create a scene and damage his reputation as a faithful fiancé.

At that moment, Eliza saw a little bit of Jon's father in the son. *What did I expect? He's engaged, and I knew he was engaged.*

She closed her eyes for a moment, willing rational thoughts to replace the wild ones in her mind. Then she felt composed enough to pen a reply.

> *Dear Sir,*
>
> *I'm more than happy to oblige you in your request. As it happens, it never occurred to me to*

make good on the affection you bestowed. I viewed
you as a distraught man, unsure of his feelings for
anyone, including his mother and his fiancée, let
alone myself. Now that you have everything
straightened out in your life and know what your
dreams are, I'll be the first to offer congratulations
and wish you all the best.

It is not often that a woman is saved more than
once by the same man. Perhaps it is your nature to
attract damsels in distress. And like your father, you
will always take the socially accepted path.
Whatever the case, you'll make a fine husband for
Apryl, and I wish both of you many happy years
together.

Best wishes,
A damsel no longer in distress

Eliza sorted through her closet. The masquerade ball
was in a few days, and she didn't have anything to wear.
She'd promised her new friend Gina that she'd attend the
ball with her. Eliza crossed to the dressing table and looked
into the mirror. The bruises on her neck were barely visible;
only yellow-tinged marks remained.

"Eliza," her mother called from outside the bedroom
door. "Gina is here."

"Send her in," Eliza said.

Gina entered the room and embraced her. They'd
become fast friends in only a couple of weeks, although
opposites in almost every way. Gina was tall with fiery red
hair and an infectious laugh. What she lacked in beauty, she
made up for in energy and enthusiasm.

"Have you talked to your parents yet about coming to
France with my family?" Gina asked.

Eliza smiled. With Gina, everything seemed so simple.
But hope had grown inside Eliza—hope that if she left the

States, the nightmares would stop, and Helena's voice would be left far behind. "I will mention the trip when they stop treating me like a glass vase."

"Don't stall too long; I'm dying for you to come." Gina grinned. "I'm so glad you'll be coming to the masquerade ball with me. I couldn't bear it if I had to stand by my parents the entire time. Or, heaven forbid, my grandmother."

Eliza laughed. "I'll probably be as tiresome."

Concern crossed Gina's sunny face. "Are you feeling up to the ball?"

"I suppose so." Eliza unconsciously touched her neck. "It will give me something else to think about." Going to the masquerade ball was so normal, so unlike what her days had become—hours when she was afraid to sleep, afraid to dream.

All smiles again, Gina said, "Show me what you're going to wear."

Eliza led her to the closet and pulled out a dress from the far corner. It was plain and simple, dark gray.

Gina wrinkled her nose. "You can't be serious."

"It was my aunt's—she was Puritan."

"You can't go as a Puritan!" Gina said, looking horrified. "The dress is dreadful and boring. No one will dare ask you to dance for fear of receiving a lashing at the whipping post."

Eliza pulled out another article from the closet—a white bonnet. "Don't you think this will complete the outfit perfectly?"

Gina braced herself against the doorframe. "If this is a trick—"

"Don't worry. Even *I* am not that brave. I want to blend in, not stand out."

Gina breathed a sigh of relief. "Finally, you've regained your good sense." After Eliza replaced the dress and bonnet, Gina asked, "What *are* you going to wear?"

"Mother says it's too late to have something made, so I guess I'll have to make do with what's in my closet."

Gina took a step back and surveyed her friend. "Hmmm," she said. "It will have to be something grand so all of the eligible bachelors will fight over you."

"I wouldn't want to take the attention away from your Queen Elizabeth costume," Eliza said.

Gina swept her hair back and twisted it into a bun. "Should I wear my hair like this?"

"Yes, but add a row of curls at the top."

Gina turned to the mirror, experimenting with several twists.

Eliza sat on the bed and watched her tall, graceful friend. Gina would make the perfect Queen Elizabeth. "Perhaps I'll wax my hairline like all the royal greats and be your half-sister, Queen Mary."

Gina twirled around and clapped her hands together. "That would be perfect. If you wear a scarlet dress, it will set off your complexion."

But Eliza waved her off. "Too elaborate for last minute."

Gina sat next to Eliza and grabbed her hands. "I have a dress you could wear, and we can make a crown for you out of beads."

"You're six inches taller than I am. It will be far too long for me."

"Emma will take in the hem." She tugged on Eliza's arm. "Come on, it will be fun."

Eliza hesitated. Perhaps dressing as Queen Mary would work. There were sure to be others dressed as royalty, so she would blend in. "All right. I suppose it couldn't hurt."

"Emma can redo the sleeves and lower the neckline . . ." Gina's face was radiant as she spoke.

Eliza covered her chest with her hands. "I don't think we need to be that authentic."

"If we don't, no one will even know who you are."

"But my parents—"

"Aren't going, and you can get dressed at my house," Gina said.

"What will *your* parents think?" Eliza asked.

"They'll realize you're a mature young woman. Besides, they will be tipsy before the first hour is gone and won't notice anyway." She burst into laughter. "You know that *Elizabeth* was the 'virgin queen,' not Mary, so you can be a little more daring."

The next few days were busy as Eliza and Gina spent time preparing their costumes. Gina's costume was nearly finished; they only had to add a lace ruff. Eliza's costume took the remainder of the time to create. After Emma's alterations, they began to embroider and sew on glittering beads. Gina insisted on attaching only a partial ruff, so Eliza's bosom wouldn't be completely hidden. Eliza discovered that she was enjoying the process and became absorbed in the plans for the ball.

Later that night, well after the twelve o'clock hour, she stole into the kitchen for a cup of warm milk. She was surprised to hear voices coming from the library. Tiptoeing to the closed door, she leaned forward and listened. Her father was discussing business with another man. Then she shrank back in horror as she recognized the high nasal pitch of Thomas Beesley.

"It's a breach of contract," her father said.

"My lawyer found that this clause applies to our situation," Thomas answered.

A pause, then her father said, "'An extraneous circumstance due to lack of cooperation?'"

Eliza held her breath. *Was this about Thomas asking her to marry him?*

Her father's voice came again. "You can't mean to apply this to what happened between you and my daughter? I know things have been strained lately, but I hoped that we could put it behind us—especially with all the details to work out on the new factory."

Thomas uttered a low chuckle. "You understand, Mr. Robinson, that I don't intend to open a new factory with you. And I mean to have my way."

She had to strain to hear her father's reply. "I thought we were men who could keep business separate from personal matters."

"It doesn't matter what we think, Mr. Robinson. It matters what our clients think—the ones canceling their orders and taking their business elsewhere."

"It's been a bad couple of months, but surely business will pick up again."

"I can't afford to wait for that," Thomas said. "Mr. Porter will draw up an agreement this week, and I'll have it sent over."

Eliza gasped at the mention of Mr. Porter—*Jon*?

"I know the relationship between your family and Mr. Porter," Thomas said. "I thought it might make my job a little easier, as Porter apparently knows the character of your daughter."

Her father's next comment was sharp with anger. "How dare you insinuate that my daughter's character is questionable? She's merely too young to be serious about a marriage proposal from any man, including you."

Thomas's voice matched the anger. "I know plenty of young women her age who would be more than happy to accept such an offer."

Tension seeped through the doors and wrapped its grip around her.

"Some women are ready for matrimony sooner than others," her father said in a low voice. "But this is not the case with Eliza, and no one should force her to marry. I have never been insulted such as this in all my life."

"Now you know how I feel," Thomas replied bitterly.

Eliza heard the scrape of a chair; Thomas was preparing to leave. She fled down the hallway and hid behind the curved arch of the staircase. A moment later the library doors flew open, and Thomas strode through the opening. Eliza caught a glimpse of his scarlet face as he stormed through the front door.

She remained crouched for a long time behind the stairway, trembling. Even after her father had ascended the stairs to retire for the night, Eliza couldn't bring herself to leave her hiding place. A deep hole had formed in her soul.

Jonathan Porter had betrayed her family.

Twenty-one

*E*liza woke early on the day of the masquerade ball. She hadn't dreamed last night—no Gus, no Helena. She exhaled in relief. Maybe burying herself in dance preparations had replaced the nightmares. She was looking forward to the ball, although she was nervous for it. The Queen Mary costume was complete, down to the last details on the ruff and overskirt. She spent the morning bathing and washing her hair. Emma had provided an ointment that was supposed to make her hair look redder. But after it had been applied, Eliza couldn't see much difference.

After lunch, her mother bustled into the room. "Let's see the costume."

"It's at Gina's," Eliza said.

Her mother's lips moved disapprovingly. "Why didn't you bring it home?"

"We're getting ready together at her house tonight."

Hesitating, her mother said, "I suppose that's all right. I did want to see you dressed up though."Mrs. Robinson kissed Eliza's forehead. "Be sure to wake me, dear, when you return home, so that I can see your costume." And with that she left the room.

Eliza breathed a sigh of relief. She didn't want her mother fussing over her tonight. It was time for her to face reality now. Discovering that Jonathan Porter was Thomas Beesley's lawyer was a revelation. The world was full of people who only had their interests in mind, not caring who their grand agendas affected.

She was glad that the ball was a masquerade, so she'd remain anonymous until midnight, although she planned to be waiting in Gina's carriage by then. She knew there was a chance Jon would be there with Apryl, and she couldn't endure another falsely cheerful introduction, followed by scrutiny.

By mid-afternoon, Eliza decided to approach her father and talk to him about her aunt's estate. She could go to Maybrook for a couple of weeks and distance herself from Jon.

Mr. Robinson was in the library, writing letters. He looked up as she entered and smiled wearily. "Come in. What can I do for you?"

She settled into a chair near his desk. "Have you given any more thought to what we'll do with Aunt Maeve's property?"

A faint look of surprise crossed her father's face. "The property is listed for sale. Once that's complete, the money will go into a trust until you're twenty-one. I thought we'd already discussed this."

"Oh, I know. I just wondered if I decided to take a trip, could I use some of the money for the expenses."

Her father leaned back in his chair and folded his arms. "You want to travel at a time like this?"

"Only to Europe, and not for long. Gina Graydon's family is leaving in a couple of weeks for France. I've never been outside the States, and I thought it might be a good opportunity before . . ."

"Before what?" Her father prompted.

"Before I marry and have my own household to run." *I want to get away for a while and stop the nightmares for good.* Her father frowned. "I didn't know you had been thinking of marriage."

"Not in the immediate future, of course—another few years at least."

"Perhaps we could plan a family trip sometime. But I don't think your mother would want you to leave until you're fully recovered."

Eliza hesitated then said, "All right." She left the room feeling disappointed. She had to find a way to convince her father to let her travel with Gina.

When it was time to leave for Gina's house, she bid her parents goodbye and climbed into the carriage alone, nervous and excited at the same time. It would be her first dance since leaving New York to stay with her aunt. Undoubtedly Thomas Beesley's large figure would be a dead giveaway if he was to attend the ball, so it would be easy for her to avoid him.

The evening air was brisk as Eliza settled into her carriage. Gina lived in the more fashionable part of town, and Eliza marveled at the size of the homes she passed. One of them was Apryl Maughan's.

When Eliza arrived at Gina's, her friend flung the front door open before Eliza could ring the bell.

"I've been watching for you," Gina said breathlessly. The girls embraced and hurried up the stairs to Gina's room.

They spent the next hour primping and preening until each was satisfied with the outcome. Then they tried on their masks. Looking at each other, they burst into a fit of giggles.

"No one will ever guess who you really are," Eliza said.

Gina strode about the room. She held her head regally and spoke in a low voice. "I'm the stately Queen Elizabeth."

Then she stopped and surveyed Eliza. "Your hair might give you away."

Eliza lowered her mask. "How so?"

"No one has thick wavy locks like Eliza Robinson."

Eliza patted her head. "That's not true."

Gina laughed. "In your costume, only the most astute will recognize you."

Eliza gazed in the mirror, raising and lowering the mask. She wondered how astute Thomas Beesley and Jonathan Porter were. Her gaze fell to her swollen cleavage, pushed up by the costume so that she looked like she might rival the likes of Apryl Maughan . . . not that she was trying to rival anyone. Her face flushed a deep red.

"You look very alluring," Gina said.

"What if I attract the scoundrels?"

"Don't worry. I'll fend them off with my ice-cold queen look." Gina laughed. "By the way, did you ask your parents about going to France with us?"

Eliza sighed, replacing her mask. "Oh, that. I talked to my father, but he thinks my mother will object—which really means he objects."

"It will be so dreary without you. Following my parents around will be the death of me," Gina said with a moan.

Eliza rolled her eyes. "How horrible to be traveling in Europe. I'm sure everyone will pity you."

"Ha." Gina swiped at Eliza, who easily dodged her.

A voice from the outside of the door called out, "Girls, are you ready?"

"One more minute." She grabbed Eliza's free hand. "Are you ready?"

Eliza swallowed and looked into her excited friend's eyes. "You tell me."

Gina grinned. "You look perfect."

⟨✑⟩

A line of carriages had formed in front of the City Hotel. Gina's mother let out an audible sigh. "It's bad enough that we have to wait to get in the door. Why can't they hurry things up?" She adjusted the folds on her Roman tunic. Her face was an exact replica of her daughter's, only older. Her hair was a more faded red. Mrs. Graydon had the same stately height and infectious laughter, although tonight she was quite impatient.

Gina's father smiled as he smoothed his own tunic and straightened the wreath of leaves on his head. "We'll be inside soon enough, dear." He licked his lips as if he could already taste the wine.

While they waited their turn, Eliza watched the elegant carriages lining up one behind the other. She didn't recognize any of the people who climbed out of them. Maybe decoding each other's disguises would be harder than she thought.

Gina pointed intermittently at arriving guests, trying to guess who their costumes represented. "There's Marie Antoinette, and look, that must be Caesar Augustus, just like Father."

Finally they were next in line, and it was their turn to exit the carriage and enter the grand hotel. A full orchestra played at one end of the ballroom, and a table stood close to the entrance, set up with drinks. Gina's parents stopped at the table. Mrs. Graydon said, "We'll meet you right here after midnight. Look for the Romans." A high laugh escaped her lips.

Gina tugged Eliza through the maze of costumes until they had reached the far wall, where chairs had been set up. Eliza scanned the room. Cloth streamers billowed from the ceiling, and paper flower arrangements adorned each table. She pulled away from Gina. "I don't want to sit there."

"That's how the men know we're waiting to be asked to dance."

Eliza grimaced beneath her mask. "Let's walk around for a moment to look at all the costumes. I don't want to seem desperate for a dance partner so early in the night."

Gina laughed, and they began to mill through the crowd. They stared at the numerous guests who looked curiously back. Nearing the entrance they saw Gina's parents still standing next to the wine table, caught up in animated conversation with another couple.

"Look," Gina said, grabbing Eliza's arm. "There's Mr. and Mrs. Gelding."

The stooped shoulders and slow gait of the elderly couple made it obvious who they were. Eliza remembered them from drawing-room gatherings. "Who do you think they are chaperoning?"

"Maybe no one." Gina shrugged. "Maybe they're here for the free spirits. Come on, let's find a seat. I can't wait to dance."

Eliza followed her friend into the mass again. They pulled two chairs together and sat down. It wasn't long before a couple of men approached and asked for a dance.

Gina rose immediately and accepted for both of them. Eliza stood and was led to the floor by a man half a foot shorter than she, who wore white trousers and a military-style jacket. The dancing was a bit awkward at first until Eliza grew used to her partner's jerky movements.

"Are vous from around here?" His accent was thick.

"Yes, I live in the city," Eliza said. "Where are you from?"

"Paris," the man said, accentuating the second syllable.

"*Bon*," Eliza replied.

The man grinned. "Ah! *Parlez-vous Française?*"

"*Un petite peu.*"

"*Trés bien.*" He quickened his pace. "What is your name?"

"I cannot tell you," she said.

"Because of the mask?" He stared at her quite intently. "Are you Queen Mary tonight?"

"*Oui.*"

The man pulled her a little closer, so that Eliza caught a full whiff of his cologne. "I'm here for one week only," the man said. "Tell me your name, Mary, so that I may remember this dance on the voyage home."

What was the harm? She'd never see this foreigner again. "Eliza."

"Ah. So vous *are* related to Elizabeth. How very clever."

"And what's your name, sir?" she countered.

"Alfred . . . Bonaparte."

"Bonaparte? Isn't that your costume tonight?"

"Yes, clever, no?"

The dance number came to an end, and Alfred escorted Eliza back to her seat, where Gina was waiting. She thanked him, and he left after giving her a dramatic bow.

"How was the dance?" Gina asked, stifling a laugh.

Eliza settled next to her. "It was . . . interesting. How about your dance partner?"

"Oh, he was wonderful. He asked me a lot of questions though," Gina said.

Eliza turned to look at her. "Did you answer them?"

"Most, but I didn't tell him my name," Gina said.

"I told my dance partner mine," Eliza said nonchalantly, looking at the dancing crowd.

"But why?"

Eliza shrugged. "He's from Paris and said he was leaving soon."

"Look over there," Gina said, nudging her. "Isn't that the man you danced with?"

Eliza followed Gina's direction and saw Alfred Bonaparte surrounded by a group of people. His short arms were flailing as if to emphasize a very important point he was making. Before she realized it, a member of the group had broken off and crossed over to her.

"May I have this dance?"

Eliza's tongue froze. The man before her was none other than Thomas Beesley. Did he know who she was? It would be frightfully rude to turn him down at a public ball, so she nodded, and the man led her to the dance floor for a waltz. She swallowed the revulsion that had risen in her throat, hoping Thomas didn't know who she really was.

"How are you, Eliza?" he asked.

Eliza felt sick. "How did you know it was me?"

"I sent a scout."

"The Frenchman?" she asked.

Thomas chuckled until other couples surrounding them looked over. "He's a loyal friend trying to help me out."

Heat rose in her face; she was glad the mask concealed her embarrassment. "That was a cutting move, Thomas."

"We need to settle some things between us," Thomas said in a low voice. His hold tightened. "I've heard that you're trying to taint my reputation."

"I've done no such thing," she said, stepping back and trying to put more distance between them.

But Thomas held her firm. "A reliable source has informed me that you have threatened to sue me for breaking the partnership with your father."

Eliza tried not to panic. "Your reliable source is a meddling liar," she retorted in a low voice. "If you and your shoddy lawyer, Jonathan Porter, want to believe such filth, go right ahead. The fact is, you've tainted your own reputation because of the way you've come after my father to cover your wounded ego." With effort, she pulled away from him. "Never come near me again, sir."

Eliza held back her tears until she'd left the dance floor. It was too cold to stand outside so she turned to the left and walked down a dark hallway until she found a bench to collapse on.

Twenty-two

*J*on watched the entire interchange between Thomas and Eliza. No costume could disguise Thomas, and it took only a moment longer to realize that the partner was Eliza. The unmistakable hair and translucent skin gave her away.

When they had first arrived at the ball, Apryl pointed out Thomas almost immediately. Since then, Jon had kept an occasional eye on the man, wondering when they would cross paths. He'd heard about the exchange between Thomas and Mr. Robinson, and was sorry he'd ever gotten involved. Eliza would undoubtedly discover the connection.

Apryl had been dancing with a tall gentleman dressed as William Shakespeare. Jon had watched her for a moment, before moving through the crowd to find the wine table. It was then that he saw Thomas with Eliza. They were talking rapidly, and Jon wondered if they were catching up on old times. Before the number ended, Eliza withdrew from Thomas and left the dance floor, her mouth set in a firm line.

When Jon looked to find Thomas again, the man had already joined his friends, talking and laughing as if nothing untoward had just happened. Perhaps the exchange with Eliza hadn't been anything more than a regular conversation. What would a normal conversation between them look like?

She was clearly upset, and it had to do with Thomas. Without another thought, Jon scanned the room. She was nowhere to be seen. As he passed the wine table, he took a glass and continued, walking outside. The night was quiet, and the first snow of the season had started to gently fall.

Walking back inside, Jon stopped and scanned the foyer. A darkened hallway extended on both sides. At the end of one stood a couple, their masks removed. They were busily engaged in kissing. Jon opted for the other hallway. The sound of his shoes against the polished floor echoed on the walls. He was about to turn around when he heard a sniffle around a corner.

He walked in the direction of the sound. As he grew closer, he could make out the form of a person sitting on a bench and the faint glitter of a costume.

"Eliza?" he whispered. He heard a sharp intake of breath, and he removed his mask.

The voice that answered was cold. "What do you want?"

"It's me, Jon," he said.

"Please leave me alone. You've done enough damage."

Jon crossed her, trying to read her expression concealed by the shadows. "I sent you an apology."

"That's not what I'm talking about." Her voice steely, cold.

Jon didn't let that stop him, although he probably should have. Ignoring himself, he sat beside her. "What is it?"

"You know very well." Eliza gathered her heavy skirts around her and scooted to the far end of the bench.

"You'll fall off," Jon said.

The humor was lost on Eliza.

"Does this have something to do with Mr. Beesley?" he asked.

With that, fresh tears cascaded down Eliza cheeks. She turned her face away from Jon. "Don't men like you have anything better to do with your time than destroy a man and his family?"

Jon sighed and wished he could reach out and console her. "Your father will walk away from the lawsuit with only minor setbacks, nothing compared to what Thomas will face. Thomas is no decent man—"

Eliza turned and faced him. "That didn't stop you from becoming his lawyer and trying to ruin my father." Without giving him a chance to answer, she stood and began to walk away.

He jumped to block her and placed both hands on her shoulders. "I don't know what you've been told, but I'm not Thomas's lawyer." He lowered his voice. "Please believe me."

Eliza blinked back tears and met his eyes with defiance. "Why should I?"

Slowly, he lowered his hands. A thousand words floated through his mind, all disjointed and unattainable. If he could only tell her how he really felt. The faint glimmer of hope in her eyes pierced his heart. He reached for her hand, but she drew back. "I can't bear to think that I'm the cause of your misery," he finally managed.

Her eyes grew cold and hard again. "Don't flatter yourself." She pushed past him.

Jon stared after her, aching to follow and take her in his arms. The sorrow in her eyes would remain with him forever.

Eliza hurried down the hallway, not knowing where she was going. A staircase rose in front of her, but she didn't want to climb it. She sat on the lower stair and tried to calm her rapid breathing. The pressure of Jon's hands on her shoulders had sent daggers of heat through her arms. She rubbed them furiously, trying to erase his touch. She couldn't deny the conversation she'd overheard between her father and Thomas. Was Jon brash enough to lie straight to her face?

"*Tell him.*"

A cold chill spread through Eliza's body. It was Helena's voice again. It hadn't stayed behind in Maybrook after all. Frustration crashed through Eliza. Looking around in the dim light she said, "Tell him *what*? Tell him that his mother is haunting me?"

No one—or nothing—answered. Only the distant sound of the orchestra could be heard.

"Why have you followed me here?" Her voice grew hysterical. "Why can't you leave me alone?" She buried her face in her hands, trembling. How could Helena still want something from her? Maybe the voice was in her head— maybe it had always been in her head, and she was going mad.

Eliza rose and put on her mask. She retraced her steps down the now-empty corridor to the front entrance of the ballroom. The wine table had never been so inviting. She crossed over to it and helped herself to a glass, then another. A few feet away, she spotted Thomas surrounded by his friends, including the supposed Frenchman.

She felt nauseated. She put down the wineglass and went to find Gina. Pushing through the throng of elaborately dressed people, she finally spotted her friend.

"Where have you been?" Gina asked as soon as she saw her.

"I don't feel well," Eliza said.

Gina studied her. "Do you need to sit down for a while?"

"I want to leave."

"I'll go with you then," Gina offered.

"No, enjoy the evening. It's not even ten yet. I'll be fine." Eliza turned and hurried to the front entrance before Gina could protest further.

Outside several public carriages were waiting. She climbed into the first one and gave the driver directions to take her home.

⌒✐⌒

Eliza ran up the stairs to her room and was half undressed when her mother entered.

"You're home early."

Eliza nodded as she began to pull the pins out of her hair. Her mother crossed the room. "Here, let me help you."

Eliza lowered her arms and allowed her mother to undo the apparatus on her head.

"Are you feeling all right?" her mother asked.

"I think it was too early to go out," Eliza said. "I'll feel better in the morning."

Her mother kissed the top of her head. "Sleep well then. I'll hear more about it tomorrow."

When her mother was gone, Eliza's brave exterior began to crumble. She climbed between the cool sheets and hugged her pillow to her chest. She eventually fell asleep on her tear-stained pillow.

Helena packed her bags as little Gus watched her. "I'm going on a trip, sweetie, and will be back soon. Tell thy papa not to worry." The little boy nodded with trusting eyes. She patted his head as she passed. "Be a good boy."

She left him and climbed on her horse, with Jonny strapped in front of her in the saddle, sleeping. She could barely keep the horse on the road and was tempted to take the shortcut. But she didn't want any neighbors to notice her. She had to appear as if she were simply going to market, and she hoped the bundle tied to the back of the saddle wasn't too suspicious. Then the accident happened. The horse tripped on a root and threw her and Jonny from the saddle. Jonny woke with a start and began to wail. She untied him from the horse and tried to help the horse to its feet, but it was lame.

Helena hobbled along the road as quickly as she could, carrying her bag and child. She couldn't afford to be late to the train station. She hoped the townspeople wouldn't be alerted by her dirty appearance.

Her heart sank when she heard a rider approach behind her. One fearful look over her shoulder, and she knew it was Gus. She turned sharply and ran into the trees, hoping to lose him. But he was gaining, and she finally put Jonny down, kissed him through her tears, and ran in the opposite direction. Someone would find Jonny. Gus could have his way with her, but she wouldn't let her child witness it.

It wasn't long before her strength ran out and Gus was on top of her. His eyes were burning, his chest heaving. It was only when she saw the glittering blade in his hands that she realized she would never see daylight again. She'd never see her son again. She heard someone shouting Gus's name, but it was too late. As the blade began its trail across her neck, her last words were, "God forgive me."

Eliza woke from her dream with a start, her pulse racing.

"Tell him how I died."

The voice seemed to penetrate her skin, sending goose pimples up her back. She sat up and gripped the pillow tightly.

"Go away!" she said into the darkness, and then she succumbed to the shaking sobs.

Sometime later, with her eyes still squeezed shut, the voice whispered again, *"Tell him how I died."*

This time, Eliza felt a calm pass over her. The voice had

been clear. Helena wanted her to tell Jon about the horrible dream. The clock downstairs chimed once.

Perhaps the only way to stop Helena's haunting her dreams was to tell Jon about them. Her breathing came rapidly as she thought about seeing Jon again. Panic rose in her throat. How could she tell him that she dreamed about his mother's death? That his mother spoke to her? He'd think she was insane.

She'd tell him right before leaving New York—it was the only way to escape the voice and to forget Jon. And going to Maybrook wasn't an option, even though Gus was in jail. She didn't want to be reminded of all that had happened there. Surely the voice would grow more demanding and the nightmares would get worse. The more she thought about it the more she realized that Europe was the answer. She had to convince her parents to let her go.

The following day an opportunity arose that Eliza couldn't pass up. After telling her mother the details about the ball, omitting the part about dancing with Thomas and being cornered by Jon, her mother mentioned that the Graydon family was traveling to France soon.

Eliza saw her chance. "I've been meaning to tell you that they've invited me to go along."

Mrs. Robinson's painted lips parted. "Have they, now? When did this happen?"

"A few days ago." Eliza pressed forward. "I'd like to see another country, and the Graydons would like company for Gina."

Mrs. Robinson stared at her. "Eliza. You can't be serious. You barely escaped for your life a matter of weeks ago."

"I'm in the way here—you and father are so busy right now with all the changes in the business."

"How do you know about any changes?" her mother

asked.

Eliza looked at the floor, avoiding her mother's gaze.

"I don't think you're strong enough to travel. You couldn't even stay at the ball for more than an hour last night."

"I'm better each day, Mother. It will do me good to have a break from all the people who know all about what happened to me. And I can't go back to Maybrook."

"No, you can't," her mother said firmly.

Eliza waited for more, but her mother had fallen silent.

"Should I speak to Father about it?" she asked.

Mrs. Robinson appraised Eliza for a moment. "No, I will."

Eliza's heart leapt. That meant her mother was considering it.

⌒⟋⌒

After supper that night, Mr. Robinson called his family into the library. He looked at his wife and daughter, his face etched with concern. "Things aren't going so well with the company right now."

Eliza flushed, knowing it was the fault of Thomas Beesley and his sidekick, Jon Porter.

Mrs. Robinson asked, "Will we keep the estate?"

"It's not as serious as that, dear," Mr. Robinson said. "But we're going to have to close a factory instead of opening one, if we are to stay profitable." He looked at Eliza. "The reason I'm including you in this bad news is that I have decided that I feel that the strain of our family, and what you went through in Maybrook, is hurting your health. It might do you good to travel for a bit—get away from everything. I've decided that you shall travel to Europe with Gina's family."

Eliza stared at him, not knowing whether or not to be overjoyed or dismayed. She was desperate to leave her nightmares and Helena's voice behind, but not if it would hurt her family. "But you'll need all resources for your company. The money from Maeve's place could help the business."

Her father smiled tenderly at her. "You are generous, but the cost of traveling with the Graydon family will be minimal. You'll share their rooms and meals. Besides, I received notice today that Maeve's property has been sold. I'll withhold a portion of it from your trust so you can enjoy yourself in Europe."

"I don't want to go if you and mother are struggling," Eliza said. "Take the money for your company. I don't need it."

Mr. Robinson shook his head. "The business will soon improve, and your mother and I will be fine. The balmy weather in southern France will improve your health."

With her parents' minds made up, Eliza began to prepare for the trip, wishing her father wasn't going through such a difficult time, but relieved that she'd finally be able to get away from Helena's voice. Surely a ghost couldn't travel across the ocean.

Twenty-three

I t was two days before she was scheduled to leave for France when Eliza woke in the middle of the night, her forehead perspiring, her mouth dry—the image of Gus Senior strangling Helena fresh in her mind. Gasping, Eliza tried to calm her nerves. She lit the lamp at her bedside and with trembling hands began to write down the dream. When she was finished she knew she had to mail it to Jon. Either that or tell him in person.

She stared at the flickering flame dancing in the lamp a long time before she began a letter to him.

> *Jon,*
>
> *It is not my wish to write you this letter. It is your mother's. I know that must sound strange to you, but ever since I lived with my aunt in Maybrook, I've felt someone close by and have heard a voice—your mother's. Each night I've dreamed of her death and have been tormented by the details.*

Are they true? Is my dream what really happened? I don't know, but I've decided to record the nightmare and give it to you. You'll find it enclosed with this letter.

I hope the news is not too shocking. I don't know what to believe myself anymore. But I hope that once I complete this task, your mother will rest in peace. Please do not contact me or try to contact my family. I will be away for some time.

Eliza

Without rereading the letter, Eliza sealed it in an envelope. As soon as the hour was decent to leave the house, she went out and posted the letter herself. She wouldn't take any chances with her mother seeing to whom the envelope was addressed.

Preparations for the journey were made more complex by her mother's fussiness. "You'll need at least seven hats. The sun can be quite brutal in that part of the world," Mrs. Robinson said, examining their hatboxes.

"I'm not going to be gone for more than a couple of months. I think I can get away with four."

"Four day hats—and three evening ones."

Eliza sighed, watching as her mother arranged them on the bed. She placed each hat next to a respective outfit. When she reached the final one, she held up the plain gray dress. "What's this shabby thing?"

"It was Aunt Maeve's. I wore it while helping her in the garden."

Her mother stared at her. "You are *not* taking this."

"I thought if I left it behind, you'd throw it out."

"You're probably right." Her mother wrinkled her nose. "But you can't be serious about taking something so ghastly."

Eliza folded her arms. "I won't if you promise not to get rid of it."

Mrs. Robinson carried it to the closet and hung it up. "It will stay there until you return."

Eliza looked back at the bed, then rolled her eyes when she saw what her mother had added. "Mother, I won't need three parasols. It's not as if we are going to be in one neighborhood and run into the same people each day."

"You can never been too prepared." Her mother's mouth was firm. "I'll call Bess to organize your things into the trunks."

Before Bess arrived, Eliza removed two parasols, two hats and three dresses from the bed. She stuffed them in the back of her closet, hoping her mother wouldn't notice.

Bess entered and embraced her. "I'll miss you."

"It's only for a short while." Eliza squeezed back. "I'll be back before you know it."

"You'll be grown up, I say, travelin' abroad an' all."

"I'll miss you too."

Bess wiped her eyes, and then both women turned to the bed and began to pack silently.

The following morning, Eliza woke early. Energy hummed through her body, and she realized she was looking forward to the trip more than she'd thought. Surely Helena couldn't follow her to Europe. Eliza would leave the woman's voice and nightmares behind.

Descending the stairs, Eliza was surprised to see both of her parents already at the breakfast table. Her mother's eyes were moist, and Eliza thought back to the day when they had departed in anger at the Maybrook train station.

Now, there was only tenderness in her mother's eyes. "Eat a good breakfast, darling."

"I don't feel hungry," Eliza said. "But I'll try to eat something."

Mr. Robinson watched as Eliza picked at her food. "Remember to only eat things that are *cooked* over there."

"What about *escargot*?" she asked, only to see what her mother would say.

Her mother blanched, and Eliza hid a smile.

"Only if the restaurant is reputable," her father said.

"And only stay at hotels with indoor plumbing," her mother cautioned.

A tap sounded from the front door.

"The carriage must be ready," her father said.

Her mother rose. "Always show good manners, and don't speak to strangers."

"Everyone will be a stranger, Mother." Eliza pushed away the breakfast plate and stood.

"If Gina's family is speaking to someone then it will be all right to speak too. Just don't leave their side."

Eliza nodded. She embraced her mother, then her father. They walked her out to the carriage. After hugging her parents, she climbed in, hardly believing she was actually leaving.

The carriage traveled to Gina's home, where Eliza waited until they were loaded and ready to go. Gina climbed in beside her. Her face glowed with excitement, and she squeezed Eliza's hands. "I'm so glad you're coming with us. It would have been so dull—"

"I know, I know. You'd die of boredom in dreary France."

Gina grinned as the carriage set off for the harbor. Eliza stared out the window, half listening to Gina's chatter, and soaked in the details of the passing scenery as she wondered what the streets of Europe would look like. They moved through the quiet, still slumbering neighborhoods, past the rows of shops and then through lesser neighborhoods.

Eliza spotted a young boy who was barefoot, sitting on the corner, selling the morning paper. His youthful face was streaked with dirt, but his countenance was happy. She wondered how a boy who had practically nothing could look so content.

Soon they arrived at the harbor. Eliza climbed out of the carriage and stared at the massive ship that would take them across the Atlantic. Sailors moved furiously about the harbor, loading crates and other cargo.

Gina tugged at her elbow. "Let's go on deck."

Eliza linked her arm through Gina's, and they walked up the ramp together, Gina's parents following close behind. Other passengers surrounded them, waving to those on shore.

"It'll be another thirty minutes before we leave. Let's go see our quarters," Mr. Graydon said.

Eliza and Gina followed them into the main lobby. Down a flight of stairs, they arrived on the first floor below deck, where their cabins were. Gina and Eliza shared one adjacent to Mr. and Mrs. Graydon. At first, Eliza was surprised to see how small the cabins were, but they were immaculately decorated.

Two narrow beds were positioned against the sloping wall. A single dresser and a closet were the only places for their clothing. Their trunks had already been brought in.

Gina plopped on one of the beds. "Which side do you want?"

Eliza shrugged and crossed over to the porthole. It was hard to make out any details beyond a fuzzy image of the harbor.

Mr. Graydon stepped into the doorway. "Ready, girls?"

Gina rose. "Let's go say goodbye to America."

Together they exited the cabin and followed the Graydons up the stairs to the deck.

The number of passengers had increased. They moved through the crowds until they reached the rail, where Eliza stood by the family and waved to the people on shore. Many shouted their goodbyes around her, and she saw a few passengers had tears in their eyes.

A small commotion on the ramp caught Eliza's attention. A man was being turned away. Eliza squinted at the figure and caught a glimpse of the man's profile. For an instant, she thought he resembled Jonathan Porter. She stared at the man, but then shook her head to rid the foolish assumption as he retreated down the ramp. After all, what would he be doing trying to board a ship bound for Europe?

Supper would be served at one o'clock. Gina had spread out her clothes on the bed, and for several minutes she deliberated what to wear. Eliza had decided to wear the same dress she had arrived in then change for the evening meal.

"I thought your mother brought a lot of luggage," Eliza said dryly.

Gina frowned in concentration. "How long is this voyage?"

"Fourteen days."

Gina pulled a cream colored dress from the pile and held it up. She turned toward the mirror hanging on the wall. "Why does the mirror have to be so small?"

"I'll be your mirror. You'd better get dressed, or we'll be late and draw unwanted attention," Eliza said. "Unless, of course, that's what you wish."

Gina smiled.

Once they were finally ready, they waited for the Graydons to join them before entering the dining hall. Eliza stared at the opulent dining room. Pale blue brocade drapes hung against the narrow windows. The wallpaper was blue and white in an Italian cherub pattern, and fine crystal glasses and china adorned the tables. The atmosphere was quiet as people politely milled about, greeting fellow passengers.

Anytime Eliza saw a tall man with dark hair, she thought of Jon. *But he's in New York, not here. Don't be foolish.*

The Graydons were led to their assigned table and found themselves joined by another family. A man and his wife were already seated. The man rose and made introductions. "I am Monsieur Bonne, and this is my wife, Madam Bonne. Our son will be joining us shortly." He was plainly French, but unlike the man she'd met at the dance, Mr. Bonne's English was excellent.

Mr. Graydon introduced his wife and Gina, then their guest, Eliza. The waiter took their orders, and Mr. Bonne ordered for his absent son. He then turned to the Graydons. "What takes you to Europe?"

"Pleasure," Mr. Graydon said.

Mr. Bonne flicked open a snuff box. "Ah, and where will you visit?"

Eliza listened politely as Mr. Graydon outlined the cities and sites they planned to tour. Then her attention was diverted elsewhere. Approaching the table was a boy of fourteen or fifteen.

Mr. Bonne turned his head and saw the young man. "Ah, here's our son now. André, we'd like you to meet Mr. and Mrs. Graydon, their daughter Gina, and their family friend, Eliza."

André gave an adorable bow then greeted them in perfect English. "Pleased to meet you," he said, then took his seat.

As the Bonnes talked about their homeland, Eliza's thoughts wandered again to Jon. Had he received her letter yet? What did he think of her dream?

"Have you young ladies been to France before?" Mrs. Bonne asked, paying particular attention to Gina.

"I've been once," Gina answered. "But Eliza hasn't yet."

Eliza smiled politely and let the two of them discuss various sites and people that they knew. She thought again of Jon and whether it could have possibly been him trying to get on the ship.

"Are you ready?" Gina was saying to her.

Snapping back into focus, Eliza looked down at her barely touched dinner. "Yes."

They excused themselves from the table, and on the way back to their cabin, Gina linked arms with Eliza. "What's wrong? You hardly said a word in there."

Eliza glanced over at Gina. She really had been a good friend. Perhaps she could share part of her worries. "I didn't tell you the whole story of what happened at the masquerade ball. Meeting the French family reminded me of the Frenchman who asked me to dance."

"I remember."

"But I didn't tell you about the next man who asked me to dance—Thomas. He accused me of planning to bring a suit against him. We argued, and I escaped the dance floor."

They'd reached the cabin door, and Gina opened it, ushering Eliza inside. The women sat on their beds, facing each other.

"I walked down a corridor," Eliza said, "but someone followed me. Jonathan Porter."

Gina's eyes widened. "The man you met in Maybrook?"

"He's Thomas's lawyer now." Eliza exhaled. "Why do I have to keep running into vile men?"

Later that night, Eliza lay in bed listening to Gina's even breathing. It had been nice to confess to Gina, but Eliza still hadn't told her everything. Gina would think her mad if she knew about the voice. Eliza closed her eyes and tried to sleep, but she couldn't stop wondering what Jon had thought her letter describing her nightmares about his mother. Thankfully, last night she hadn't dreamed at all. She hoped that tonight she wouldn't either. Maybe Helena was pacified now that the truth of her death was in her son's hands. Maybe crossing the ocean was the answer.

Eliza finally fell asleep to the gentle rocking of the great ship.

Jon stood before her. "Eliza? It's Jon."

"I know who you are," she said, glancing at his Shake-spearean costume. She lowered her mask.

216

But she knew that the darkness couldn't conceal her tear-brimmed eyes.

He knelt before her, as he had once before. "Eliza," he whispered, "Please trust me." He pulled her into his arms.

She didn't resist him. She couldn't. Her body felt powerless as he kissed her. It was the kiss she'd been yearning for. The words she'd been hoping for.

Eliza opened her eyes. Her body was completely warm and relaxed, as if the dream had continued into reality. She pulled her pillow from behind her head and squeezed it tightly against her chest. The kiss was still hot on her mouth. Then her mind began to focus—Jon was not holding her in his arms. She was in bed, on a ship, heading for Europe. But the contentment from the dream would not leave, no matter how much she scolded herself.

Finally drifting off to sleep again, Eliza realized that in running to Europe, she was doing what Helena had tried to do—and lost her life over—all those years ago.

Twenty-four

J on read the letter from Eliza for the umpteenth time. Her words chilled him. He couldn't explain it, but he believed her—his mother had been somehow communicating with the girl.

It was late in the morning when he had first opened his correspondence and read the letter. At first he was angry at the presumption Eliza had taken, assuming intimate details about his mother. What right had she?

He had gone to her home immediately, only to find that she had departed for Europe. The ship was still in the harbor when he'd leapt from the carriage and ran up the loading ramp. "No ticket, no entrance," he was told. He turned away, deflated, not knowing what he was going to say to her, but also not ready to see the last link to his mother disappear.

It was with dejection that he headed home and spent the next several hours in seclusion, reading and rereading the letter Eliza wrote about her dreams.

When Thomas Beesley arrived at four, Jon had nearly forgotten they had an appointment. As the man was led into the library by Mr. Richards, Jon stood and cordially greeted Thomas. "You've gone over my notes on the contract, I presume?"

"Yes," Thomas said, settling into the opposite chair. "But I have another concern I'd like to discuss with you. It has to do with Mr. Robinson's daughter. I've heard through reliable sources that she is planning to sue me for slander," Thomas said.

Jon almost choked. He couldn't imagine Eliza suing this man. "On what basis?"

"That I fed malicious gossip to the newspapers."

Jon stared at the heavy jowls on Thomas's face. "Are the allegations true?"

Thomas chuckled. "Spoken like a true lawyer. Perhaps there's an inkling of truth to them, but there's no evidence or witnesses."

Fed up with the man, Jon decided to get straight to the point. "I can no longer represent you."

Thomas's face reddened. "Why in the hell not?"

Jon pushed a piece of paper across his desk. "Here are two references you might look up."

Thomas ignored the paper.

"I cannot represent a case in which I do not believe."

"You've grown soft," Thomas spat out.

"I know both sides of the case, yes, and perhaps I am biased because of recent events."

Thomas clenched his hands together. "I saw you follow her."

Jon's heart jolted. "You what?"

"At the masquerade ball. You followed Eliza out."

Jon leaned forward. "What's your point?"

"That you are interested in the girl—"

Jon stood and pointed his finger at Thomas. "Don't you dare say what I think you—"

"You're a philandering scoundrel who's not good enough for Apryl!" He stood and faced Jon, his face scarlet. "I'll see that she never marries you." He grabbed his hat from the end table and tugged it onto his head. Seconds later, he was across the room, making his exit.

It was several seconds before Jon realized what had transpired. He sank heavily into his chair and pressed his palms against his temples, squeezing his eyes shut. A voice inside his head kept saying *Thomas is right*, but he couldn't allow the thought to progress any further.

A sickening feeling rose inside him, and the grisly events began to play before his eyes: Thomas arriving at Apryl's with lavish gifts, convincing her that her fiancé was in love with another woman, spreading gossip throughout the city until all chance of him running for public office was ruined.

It was well into the night before Jon climbed the stairs to his bedroom. And even then, lying in bed, he couldn't sleep. He knew that Thomas had nothing to base his implications on, but the words had struck Jon dead center. As he finally fell asleep, a single question haunted his mind.

How could he marry one woman when he was in love with another?

When the dull gray morning light woke him, Jon rose and dressed. Looking in the mirror, he saw a gaunt face staring back at him. He'd lost weight, and his features had taken on a gray tinge. Something Ruth had said once to him came back to his mind. *If you really want something, you'll find a way to get it.* She had encouraged him to leave Maybrook and take the money from his father for college. Education was everything, she had told him.

The dark eyes reflected in the mirror were haunted, confused and lonely. It was time to make up his mind—to leave his parents in the past and look to the future. He needed to begin the steps to achieve his goals. Marrying Apryl would introduce him to the proper circle of society to jump into the political confidences. Letting Eliza crowd his thoughts was a dangerous deterrent. She was in Europe, and according to his newest resolve, she may as well no longer exist.

Yet less than an hour later, Jon found himself drafting a letter to Mr. Robinson, father of the non-existent Eliza. He explained that he was no longer representing the opposing party and wished the man the best of luck. Reading over the letter, Jon shook his head at his own foolishness. Then he shredded the page and dropped it into the fire. All ties needed to be broken with the Robinsons—even ones that might provide some recompense.

That same morning, Jon received a note from Mr. Doughty. His father's estate was now in order, and he was required to sign the paperwork. Jon breathed a sigh of relief. It was a sign. Time to move forward with the wedding plans and begin his life as a gentleman and politician.

With anticipating steps, he made his way to the solicitor's office. Entering, he brushed past the oily-haired clerk and bounded up the stairs two at a time.

Mr. Doughty raised his head in surprise as Jon entered. "Good morning, Mr. Porter. I see you received my note."

"Indeed." Jon sat in the nearest chair and looked about the office with pleasure. It was now organized, removed of excess books.

Mr. Doughty slid a folder across his desk. "I trust you'll find everything in order."

Grabbing the folder, Jon leafed through the pages. Then he returned to the first and swallowed hard.

"You're a wealthy man," Mr. Doughty said softly.

Jon looked at the lawyer, a slow smile spread across his face. "It's more than I expected . . . I thought there would be debt to pay, my half-sister's family to support—"

"The number you see is the amount after all business obligations have been settled."

Jon blinked and refocused on the page before him. He was a millionaire many times over.

"There are three places for you to sign," Mr. Doughty said, handing over a pen.

"What happens next?" Jon took the pen.

"In two to three months the money will be funded to your bank. After the bank receives the funds and these documents, estate taxes will be paid, the property consolidated. And then the holdings will be transferred to your name. From there it's up to you. You may choose to visit England or decide to sell the property right away, or a portion of it." At the surprised look he received from Jon, he chuckled."Who knows? Maybe you'll fall in love with the place and decide to become a citizen."

"I doubt that, sir," Jon said with a smile. He leafed through the pages again, and with an unwavering hand, he signed his name three times. Returning to the first page, he stared at the numbers again until they went out of focus. He closed the folder and passed it back to Mr. Doughty.

The solicitor came around the desk and extended his hand. "Congratulations, Mr. Porter. I hope we can do business again in the future."

In a sudden movement, Jon embraced the man and clapped him on the back. "Thank you," he said in a thick voice. His future was about to change.

The walk back to his home was not quick and light as it had been on the way over. Now it was the slow, deliberate steps of a man who had the weight of power and fortune upon his shoulders, and many questions about the future.

In bed that night, Jon lay awake for a long time thinking about whether or not he should make a trip to England. By viewing his newly acquired property, he'd be able to make responsible decisions about them. Explaining the matter to Apryl might prove quite difficult. Undoubtedly she already knew from her father that Jon's holdings were supposedly insignificant. In the quiet darkness, he decided to invite her to travel with him. It would be good for their relationship to get out from under the scrutiny of her parents and the ever-present Thomas Beesley. She could bring one of her aunts or a friend as a chaperone.

Then in England, after showing her the estate, he'd reveal the true amount of his inheritance. It would be a surprise she'd never forget.

The following evening, Jon arrived at the Maughan household as a guest for yet another dinner. He was relieved, but not surprised, to discover that Mr. Beesley and his sister would not be in attendance. After dinner, Jon had a chance to speak to Mr. Maughan in the library about the possibility of taking Apryl to England.

"Her mother would never allow her to accompany you un-chaperoned," Mr. Maughan said, lighting a cigar for Jon.

Jon accepted it. "Of course Apryl will bring along one of her aunts or a friend. I can assure you, sir, that she will be well taken care of."

Mr. Maughan nodded. "I trust you, Jon. But Apryl can be overcome with flights of fancy from time to time."

"What do you mean?" Jon asked.

Hesitating, Mr. Maughan finally said, "I probably shouldn't mention this, but when you were in Massachusetts, both Mrs. Maughan and I grew quite concerned about her." He rushed on. "Nothing to worry about now, though. She's seemed to come back to herself since your return."

"Did it have anything to do with Thomas Beesley?" Jon asked.

Mr. Maughan's face remained impassive. "Looking back, it all seems quite ridiculous to have ever worried, doesn't it?"

"Worried about what exactly?"

"Oh, just that Apryl can have flights of fancy."

Jon took another puff on his cigar. Were her flights of fancy over with now?

It was another hour before the guests went home, and Jon had a secluded moment with Apryl. He found her in the drawing room, gazing absently at a painting. "Tired, my dear?"

She looked at him, her eyes unusually dull. "Yes. Has everyone left?"

"They have." Jon sat beside her. "My inheritance has been settled."

Apryl's eyes shifted to him curiously.

"I need to travel to England on related business."

Her attention went back to the painting.

Jon grasped her hand. "I want you to come with me. We'll get away from all this for a while. It will be the two of us . . . except for a chaperone."

Apryl offered a small smile, yet her eyes didn't hold promise. "My mother would never allow it."

Chuckling, Jon said, "That's what your father said."

"You already asked him?" She turned her head to really look at him.

"Of course. Apryl, let's get married right away, and we'll go to England on our honeymoon." He stopped speaking when he saw her eyes fill with tears.

"You don't understand, Jon. It's not about a marriage certificate that I want. It's the engagement dinner and the perfect wedding dress and all that accompanies it."

Jon leaned back and sighed. "Is that what you want, or what your mother wants?"

"I want everything I've dreamed of since I was a young girl," she said, her voice trembling. "I want the white dress with the long train and the flower girls walking before me. I want my father to give me away, and for you to be standing at the end of the aisle, dressed in a fine black suit. I want thousands of flowers and a cake no one will ever forget—" Her words were choked off by her sobs.

Jon put his arm around her shoulders and brought her cheek to his. "You shall have all of that and more. I promise."

The next thirteen days were the most peaceful Eliza could remember having in a long time, perhaps as far back as before meeting Thomas Beesley.

She didn't dream, she didn't hear voices, she didn't have any conversations with eligible men. Jon was never far from her mind, but she decided that that would soon change too. She and Gina spent a lot of time on deck, in the fresh air, talking about nothing. Which was divine.

When the ship docked outside of the Bordeaux harbor, Eliza and Gina were on the deck, watching the approach anxiously. Once ashore, they found themselves a little unsteady on their legs, and they clung together, laughing.

Mr. Graydon hired a carriage to take them to a hotel. Young boys ran after them, shouting things in French.

"I wonder what they're they're saying," Gina said.

"They want to see the Americans," Eliza said, staring out the window.

"You understand them?" Gina asked.

Eliza nodded. "Doesn't everyone know a little French?"

"She was never proficient in the languages," Mrs. Graydon said.

Gina ignored her mother's comment and pointed at a passing sign. "What does that say?"

Eliza squinted into the growing darkness. *"La Petite Café,"* she read.

"What does it mean?"

"The Little Café," Eliza said with a laugh. "They probably have refreshments there." She hoped the Graydons would take the hint.

"Oh, how quaint," Mrs. Graydon said, peering out her window. "But we'll be at the hotel soon enough. Then we'll have tea."

Eliza settled back into her seat for the journey. There would be plenty of time tomorrow to explore the area. For now, she was exhausted and looked forward to sleeping in a bed that didn't sway.

Their hotel was small but elegant. Eliza marveled at all of the artwork on the walls. The employees were cordial but reluctant to speak English. Eliza tried her best to use French and received warm smiles in return.

In the morning, she accompanied the Graydons on a stroll through the surrounding village. Many children waved and watched them with curiosity. Upon returning to the hotel, the manager informed them that a special reception would be held that night for all visiting foreigners.

Gina clapped her hands. "Maybe we'll meet a handsome foreigner," she whispered to Eliza.

Eliza smirked. "*We* are the foreigners here."

"Oh, of course," Gina said, but continued to smile.

It didn't take long for Eliza to fall in love with the French countryside. A couple of weeks in Bordeaux had her fully converted, and now they were on their way to Marseilles. Though the velvety darkness now enveloped the landscape, Eliza felt the charged atmosphere of romance that France was famous for.

They were in a sleeper compartment on a night train, Mr. and Mrs. Graydon on one, and Eliza and Gina in the other. Gina was sleeping, but it wasn't late yet, and Eliza pressed her forehead against the window, trying to make out any shapes in the darkness. The moon, darkened by passing clouds, didn't offer much light.

The train slowed as it approached an upcoming station, and Eliza watched as a lone person climbed on board. No one exited. Soon the train pulled away and gathered momentum.

Just then Eliza remembered the letters stowed away in her baggage, two envelopes that had arrived for her that afternoon. She had asked the porter how they happened to arrive so quickly.

"They were sent on a smaller, much faster cargo ship," he had replied.

She rose and stretched over Gina's sleeping form and brought down her bag from overhead. With the rush of repacking, Eliza hadn't had the time to read them. One was from her mother, the other from Nathaniel.

Deciding to read her mother's first, she opened the envelope. The news was general and a trifle sentimental. But the postscript caught her attention.

P. S. Soon after your carriage left, Mr. Porter appeared at our doorstep. He was in a rush to speak with you. What ever could he have wanted?

Eliza wondered what he thought when he'd received the letter outlining her dream. Was he angry? Her mother's letter stated only that he'd been in a rush.

Finally, Eliza opened the letter from Nathaniel. She wasn't surprised he'd written her again. She'd received two letters since leaving Maybrook.

Dearest Eliza,
I'm writing in hopes that thy recovery hast been full. I am leaving Massachusetts soon and hope to visit thee before I go. I'll be attending Cambridge

overseas for a period of four years. Knowing that I'll likely live my life in Maybrook, going to England now may be the only chance I have to see any of the world before becoming a reverend. Of course, I will continue to work my own land and provide for a future family, but God may have other plans for me.

The town will help pay for my schooling, provided that I commit to return to them in due time and take over Reverend Clement's position.

Please reply and let me know how thou fares. May the Lord be with thee always.

Thy truest and ever hopeful friend,
Nathaniel Prann

Eliza let the letter fall into her lap. Wouldn't her parents be surprised to see a Puritan show up on their doorstep?

She picked up his letter and scanned the words again. It was easy to say what one really meant in writing. Deciding to write him back in the morning, she closed her eyes and soon fell asleep to the rhythmic motion of the train.

The following morning, Eliza and the Graydons descended from the train at the Marseilles station. Eliza found herself relieved to have the long journey over with. Once they were settled into their hotel, Gina asked Eliza to explore with her.

As they walked along the boardwalks with their parasols, Eliza enjoyed being away from everything she knew. She felt free. Helena had been quiet; perhaps ghosts couldn't transcend oceans.

That first evening in the hotel, Gina fell asleep almost immediately. Eliza took the opportunity to reply to Nathaniel's letter. She made it brief.

Dear Nathaniel,

I was pleased to hear that you are leaving for college. As you may know by now, I have left New York and am currently traveling in France with a friend and her family. The change of scenery has done me good. I feel stronger already, and it seems that the events surrounding my aunt's death are far removed.

I wish only the best for you.

Regards,

Eliza

Twenty-five

*J*on gazed at the diminishing New York harbor. He could no longer make out Apryl's violet-clad figure, nor her hand waving animatedly to him. Holding up his for one final farewell, he found that he was one of the last passengers on deck. Most had gone to their cabins to settle in for the voyage.

Ironically, he'd been at this same harbor four weeks before, trying to find Eliza. But that was in the past, and now he was headed to his future. When he returned, he'd surprise Apryl with the news of his true wealth, and he'd give her the lavish wedding she'd always dreamed of.

When Apryl had first discovered that he was going to England, with or without her, she had been disappointed. That was when he'd committed to a wedding date, and after that, she didn't seem to mind his impending departure.

With the absence of Thomas Beesley in their lives, Jon found that he had become more rational about his feelings toward Apryl. Once in awhile, he even fancied that he loved her. During his youth, he'd never witnessed a marriage firsthand. Only the Puritan couples at Meeting provided a limited example. He'd seen deep lines etched upon faithful faces and never doubted that they held a great love for their way of life. Although life had been hard in Maybrook, husbands and wives worked together as one.

That was the most important thing in marriage, Jon determined—a willingness to work together toward a common goal. The romantic frills of love were for the less ambitious. He needed practicality, social standing, and good morals surrounding him. Apryl would provide them.

Jon scanned the eastern horizon. It was still early in the day, and the sun was new in the sky. A bird landed not too far from Jon, and he watched as it hopped about the deck, scouring the planks for any sign of nourishment. The immaculately swabbed floor didn't offer a single morsel, and eventually the disappointed gull flew away.

A few deckhands scrambled about, going about their business. Jon walked into the lobby and found the stairs. Descending them, he passed a few passengers and was greeted in French or English.

His cabin was small but respectable—two beds stood side by side. He began to unpack his baggage. He'd brought several books to read on the voyage, including a volume of poetry by William Bryant.

With two hours until the midday meal, he made himself comfortable across the beds and started reading "The Constellations."

The next couple of weeks were uneventful. A squall arose, but nothing the capable crew couldn't handle. Jon spent most of his time playing card games with other gentlemen who were content to pass the lazy hours in such a way. One evening he attended the ship's jubilee dance, but then left soon after it started. He wasn't in the mood to keep frivolous conversation with ever-flirtatious ladies.

At last, England's coast came into sight. They passed through the English Channel, and after stops at Portsmouth and Dover, arrived at Norfolk.

Stepping onto land, Jon felt as if he were entering another world. The mist hung heavy with potential rain, and instead of expanses of untamed land, Norfolk was a neat and tidy province. Once his baggage was unloaded, he hailed a carriage. He climbed inside and stretched his cramped legs before him. The carriage was smaller than he was used to in New York, but it would do. His overcoat did little to prevent the damp air from reaching his skin, causing him to feel chilled to the core.

At last they reached Norwich, the capital of Norfolk, and the carriage slowed. Jon peered through the windows at the drizzling scene before him. Few people were in the shop-lined streets, braving the moist weather. Jon watched as a group of bawdy men stepped out of the pub, turned up their collars, and scattered in different directions. The supper hour was over.

Once he'd gone over Bishop's Bridge and across the river Wensum, the scenery began to change. The cramped buildings thinned and the foliage grew denser. Soon they were traveling on a lonely road, with only an occasional farmhouse coming into view. Presently the carriage driver stopped at a massive hedge. Jon leaned forward and looked beyond the hedge at an even more massive gate: Porter Estate.

The driver stepped out of the carriage and into the thick mud which surrounded the wheels. He pushed the heavy gate open then climbed back onto the seat. Jon had expected some sort of security at such a pretentious gate, but the place was quiet.

The lane leading to the house wound through a dense grove of trees. The rain had stopped, but the winter leaves above were still dripping with water. The ground was littered with small branches and leaves that seemed to groan underneath the weight of the passing carriage.

As they rounded the final bend, the dismal clouds parted above, offering a peek at the waning sun. The Porter House came into view at last, the sun shedding a more favorable view than the rain would have. Windows lined the stoic rock exterior of the two-story mansion. The house looked forlorn, as if awaiting its master's arrival.

The carriage circled the driveway and pulled to a stop by the front entrance. An older gentleman appeared at the doorway, his face as gray as his suit. The man made no move to step down and greet the visitor. Instead Jon climbed out of the carriage and ascended the porch steps.

"Jonathan Porter," he said, holding out his hand. "I'm here to see Mrs. Mary Reine."

The man shook Jon's hand limply. If he was surprised at the visitor's name, he did not show it. "Mr. March, head butler."

Jon nodded and motioned for the driver to bring his luggage.

Entering the massive hall behind Mr. March, Jon noticed the lack of decoration. A bronze bust sat upon a side table and a rather soiled rug lined the floor.

"Mrs. Reine is expecting you, sir. She's waiting in the library."

Jon told the driver to place his luggage in the entryway then paid the fare. "Lead the way," he said to Mr. March.

The butler opened the first doors on the right. There was no forewarning knock; his half-sister had probably watched his arrival.

She was older than he'd expected, maybe only a couple years younger than he. Her dress was as drab as the room she stood in, and her black hair was pulled into a severe bun, her expression matching her style.

The coldness of the room was the second thing Jon noticed. *Doesn't anyone build fires in England?* The hearth behind the woman was merely a gaping hole with a few smoking logs.

Mrs. Reine looked at Jon for several moments, as if she was unsure what to say. Her mouth worked almost imperceptibly until Jon wondered if she had a nervous habit. "I didn't expect you to look so much like him," she said at last.

"I wouldn't know. I never met my father."

Mrs. Reine gave a curt nod. "You've had a pleasant journey?"

"Yes, thank you." He crossed to her and gave her a peck on the cheek, which was received with genuine surprise.

A faint color spread to the woman's cheeks—the formal atmosphere had been cracked. "Sit down, please, and tell me about yourself."

Jon found a chair near the one Mrs. Reine stood in front of. "There's not much to tell. I grew up an orphan, raised by a Puritan woman who knew my mother. When Mr. Porter made his relation to me known, I attended Cambridge on his contribution."

Mrs. Reine's eyes rounded as if she was surprised at his honesty, but didn't want to show it. "Our family learned of your existence only after my father's death." She took out a handkerchief and dabbed her eyes. "You can well imagine our shock."

Jon lowered his gaze. He could imagine it indeed, especially since he'd been named heir.

The woman continued. "As you may know, I was the eldest daughter. Father always lamented that I wasn't a son, but after a while he seemed to grow content with having a daughter. Now I know that his lament wasn't as genuine as he led us to believe."

"A son by his wife would have been ideal for him, I suppose."

Mrs. Reine nodded. "Of course. I was grateful that my mother did not live to learn of his secret."

Jon shifted in his seat. "And I'm grateful my mother never learned that he married and had a new family."

The woman paled and looked away.

"I know we have different loyalties, Mrs. Reine . . ."

"Call me Mary. After all, we're brother and sister," she said in a strained voice.

"All right, *Mary*. My mother was a Puritan—a young, innocent girl of seventeen when she met our father."

Mary clutched the edge of her chair. "Really, I don't think the details are necessary."

"I do," Jon said, raising his voice. "You asked me to tell about myself, and that begins when my mother met my father."

Staring past him, Mary's eyes began to cloud. "Let's leave the past alone."

Jon felt frustration building in his chest. "No. The past has been buried long enough. I want you to understand that I'm not here just to go over financial matters. I came to discover why my father seduced my mother then abandoned her to live a life as an outcast among a people who would reject her."

Mary placed her hands on her knees, looking at the carpet.

Jon continued the story he had wanted to tell for so long. "My mother knew she was with child before he left but didn't want to tell him, making him feel obligated toward her. She wanted him to return for love. *Love.* Can you imagine that?

"Her family disowned her, and then she gave birth to me, alone in the world. For the next three years, she saved every penny so she could purchase a fare to England. She wrote letter after letter to my father, but never once received a reply."

Mary looked up at Jon, her watery gaze riveted to his face.

"When she finally had enough money saved, she was ready to leave behind everything she had built for her life. But as she was leaving, she was stopped by another man— one who thought he owned her and could do what he willed to her. Instead of letting her go, he killed her."

Mary suppressed a gasp with her thin fingers.

"I was about three years old at the time. A neighbor took me in and raised me as her own. At what point your father learned of my mother's death, I do not know. But the inheritance left to me by our father is small compared to the pain my mother endured." Jon stared into the gloomy fireplace and presently heard Mary sniffle.

Moments later, she finally spoke. "I'll have Mr. March show you to your rooms. The solicitor will arrive in the morning. Supper is at eight."

Jon snapped his head around and looked at his half-sister. Hadn't she heard a word he'd said? Maybe she would rather keep cobwebs on the past, but he intended to find answers to his questions before leaving England. He left the room and found Mr. March in the hall, apparently waiting to show him the way.

Following Mr. March up the main staircase, Jon once again noticed the plainness of the décor. It was as if his father had been a bachelor all his life—perhaps he had been one in his heart. The hallway was dimly lit. Jon quickened his pace to keep up with the old man. Portraits lined the paneled walls, undoubtedly ancestors dating back several centuries.

"Your room, sir." Mr. March stopped and opened a door near the end of the corridor.

Jon ducked his head and passed through the doorway. A stately room greeted him, and although musty, it looked clean. The furnishings were dark, the coverlet on the bed a deep blue. Crossing to the large windows, Jon gazed at the backside of the estate. The sprawling lawns were dotted with trees and cut in half by a river.

"Anything else, sir?" Mr. March asked.

Jon shook his head and thanked him.

"Very well. Until supper then."

After the butler left, Jon started unpacking when a soft knock sounded on the door.

Mary was on the other side, her eyes rimmed in red. She held a book up. "You might be interested in our father's journal. I found it a short time ago."

He stared at the brown leather binding, then took it from Mary. "Thank you," he said in a voice thick with emotion.

"You're welcome," she whispered, then turned and walked down the hall.

Left to himself, he moved toward the narrow windows, and opened to the first page and began reading. He'd read his mother's writings, and now he held his father's in his hands.

April 15, 1815

I arrived in Norwich yesterday. My father gave me a grand welcome home, but I can see from his complexion that he is very anxious. His health is failing, and he wants me married and settled so he can die in peace.

Lord, how I miss Helena. I should have thrown away all caution and brought her with me. We could have been married as soon as we reached English soil. Then my father wouldn't have been able to object.

There is already talk of my marrying Shannon Worth. She is the perfect match, they say—wealthy, from a proper family, pleasant to look upon—as if these attributes could guarantee a marriage of love.

Helena, if I could reach across the ocean and pull you toward me, I would.

Jon scanned the next few pages. Most of the writing was similar, telling of how much he missed Helena. Then one entry stopped Jon.

June 1, 1815
Tomorrow I marry Shannon Worth. It is sudden. Father asked me when I intended on proposing. It wasn't a request, but a command. My inheritance and the future of the Porter family depended on the union, he said. It's been two months since I've seen Helena's angelic face, and I am beginning to think she was a dream, not real at all.

Shannon is real, even though she doesn't hold my heart.

As soon as my first son is born, I will burn this journal, and my second son will be forgotten.

The next entries were spaced weeks apart, with less and less mention of Helena. One entry documented the birth of his daughter, Mary.

The light was fading outside, so Jon lit a candle and continued leafing through the journal. Pressed between two pages, he found a letter. He opened the brittle, yellowed paper carefully. It was a letter from his mother. The writing was faded, but familiar. It told of his birth and her hopeful waiting for his return to Maybrook. His father had kept the letter through the years and hadn't been fearful enough to burn it. Why? Nevertheless, the secret had been well-kept until his death.

Jon leaned back in the chair, gazing through the windows at the descending darkness.

Had Shannon Worth ever known of her husband's divided heart?

Twenty-six

*J*on entered the dining room at eight and found Mary seated at the table with her husband and two children. They were somber and formal when introduced.

Throughout dinner, Mr. Reine made an attempt at light conversation, but Jon found it superficial and pointless. Jon answered politely, but finally the man fell silent. With the formalities of their first meal over, Mary requested Jon join them in the library.

The children were shuffled off by a maid, and Jon followed his hosts to the library. Once seated, Mary began. "We're ready to vacate the home upon your request."

Of course matters had to come to this. "I haven't finalized my decision, but will do so tomorrow, after meeting with the solicitors."

"Of course," she said. "My husband and I have overseen the care of the estate for several years as Father's health declined and he continually put more and more responsibility upon us. It was our assumption that we would be the permanent caretakers of the place. That is, until the will was read."

Jon winced at the familiar territory. "No doubt I was left the property out of guilt."

Mary's face grew pale, and her husband's face reddened. "We don't envy your inheritance, Mr. Porter," Mr. Reine said.

"Of course you don't," Jon said in a careful voice. "The old man must have left you something."

Mr. and Mrs. Reine glanced at each other.

"Well?" Jon prompted.

"He did leave some property which provides a modest income," Mary said quietly.

"But not what you feel you deserved, I assume?" Jon asked.

Mary shifted in her seat and looked at her tightly clenched hands.

"Let's meet tomorrow evening after dinner," Jon said.

Mr. and Mrs. Reine stared at Jon, apprehension in their eyes.

⸺

Jon rose early the next morning and walked the misty grounds. Delicate dew clung to the leaves as the sun began to warm the earth. He kept his pace brisk to fend off the morning chill and to prepare his mind for the decisions ahead. Whatever bounty he bestowed on his half-sister and her husband must be a single, final act. He didn't want this to drag on.

When he entered the massive front doors, Mr. March was waiting for him. "A letter has arrived for you, sir."

Jon took the letter and saw Apryl's familiar handwriting. He walked into the library and settled next to the cold hearth. It would be good to hear news from home.

Jonathan,

Although it's only been two weeks since you left, it seems ages ago that I waved goodbye to you at the New York harbor. Since I don't know when to expect your return, I thought I'd write this letter explaining recent events. The day after you left, Thomas Beesley visited our home. He explained what had really happened between the two of you. I don't blame you, Jon, for I know that you only had the best interest of the Robinson family in mind, but I had to agree with Thomas. He laid the details out, and I realized that you had been far too critical of him.

Thomas confessed that he has loved me since our first encounter. In our first encounters, I thought he was teasing, but he began to tell me things that only the most ardent suitor could notice. At first, I was overwhelmed with a man expressing such sincere devotion and undying love, but soon I began to believe him. I couldn't help but compare him to you. Perhaps it was wrong of me to compare the two of you, but I couldn't help see what was lacking in our relationship when I compared you to Thomas.

My parents and I had quite a row about my change of mind, but eventually they began to see what I saw in Thomas. It breaks my heart to have to write this to you, but I've accepted a proposal of marriage from him.

You might wonder how that is possible, as I am yet engaged to you. But Thomas says you viewed our engagement as a business opportunity, as your inheritance amounts to so little. That knowledge helped me make my decision. I love Thomas, and now I know that what I felt for you was but deep affection and regard.

*We have set the date for the first of June, and
you will, of course, be an honored guest. I hope we
can remain civil and on friendly terms. Perhaps,
Jon, one day you'll find someone you'll truly love.*

Sincerest regards,

Apryl Maughan

Jon let the letter drop onto his lap. Disbelief shot
through him—disbelief and disgust for Thomas Beesley.
Disgust for the entire Maughan family, who had allowed
themselves to be tricked by a greedy man. Thomas didn't
love Apryl any more than . . . well . . . any more than Jon
himself did. That's what hurt the most—the fact that Thomas
had told Apryl that her engagement to Jon was only a
business arrangement, when Thomas was the one obsessed
with money.

He opened the letter again and stared at the words until
they jumbled together illegibly. Jon stood and began to pace
the room. "I'll be damned," he muttered under his breath, "if
I let Thomas Beesley have Apryl."

He sank onto a chair. He was thousands of miles away.
What could he do? Take the next ship back and arrive in two
weeks' time—after the ring had been chosen and the cake
ordered? Pledge his love to Apryl then? Would she change
her mind if he did?

A knock sounded at the door. "The solicitors have
arrived, sir," Mr. March said.

"I'll be down shortly," Jon replied. He placed the letter
in his waistcoat pocket and straightened his collar. It was
time to sign the final documents.

Two gentlemen were waiting in the library. They both
stood when Jon entered. Extending his hand, Jon greeted
them.

"I'm Mr. Rush, and this is Mr. Penchant," said the taller
man.

Jon sat opposite them at the head of the credenza and nodded for them to begin.

Mr. Rush opened his satchel and withdrew a stack of papers. "There are several documents that need to be signed. At the end of today, everything will be transferred to your name." He proceeded to issue one document at a time, explaining the fundamentals of each.

Jon leaned forward, feeling the sharp corner of the folded letter in his pocket. It made him realize that his fortune would be his alone now, with no bride to share it with. After signing his name on the first document, he blotted the ink dry. His signature was added to the official papers, making him a multi-millionaire in a single morning.

With the paperwork done, Jon poured his guests a drink. They toasted to the successful transaction, and then Mr. Rush and Mr. Penchant were on their way. When Jon bid the men goodbye, he saw Mary hovering at the top of the stairs. He didn't call her down yet. After the letter from Apryl, his decision about the Reines would be changing.

At nine that evening, Mary and her husband were seated in the library where Jon had stoked the fire into a roaring blaze. The place was entirely his now, and he wanted it warm.

Jon turned to his expectant audience. "I've made a decision on the house."

Mary and her husband both watched him warily.

"For the time being, I do not plan to reside in England. And I do not plan to sell the estate. Thus, I need to hire an estate manager, someone who can be trusted to look after all of the details."

Mr. Reine glanced surreptitiously at his wife.

"Perhaps the two of you wish to take on the task." Jon looked back and forth between them.

Mr. Reine raised his eyebrows. Clearly, he hadn't expected this development. "Wonderful! What would it entail?"

Jon smiled and folded his hands behind his back. "The offer will be more generous than if I were hiring a stranger. I think even the old man himself would be pleased." He glanced upward. "You'll live in the house and care for it as your own. A regular salary will be paid and all estate expenses covered. We'll go over those details tomorrow. Your children's educations will also be paid for."

Mary's eyes were shining.

"I expect a quarterly report on all the happenings, expenditures and events surrounding the estate," Jon continued.

Mr. Reine nodded his head vigorously.

"If I decide to relocate to England, then you'll be asked to move. So there is some risk involved. But for now, you'll have a comfortable income and your childhood home in which to raise your children," he said, looking at Mary.

Tears formed in her eyes. "We're so grateful for your generosity."

"I'm not as generous as you think. I expect a well-run estate in return. Also, I will be selling the other property."

"Of course," Mr. Reine said.

Mr. and Mrs. Reine stood and came forward to thank him. Jon received Mary's kiss and her husband's enthusiastic handshake.

Jon spent the next few weeks riding about the property with Mr. Reine, meeting the surrounding neighbors, and learning about how the estate functioned. With each day that passed, Apryl grew further from his mind. At night he slept fitfully, only to be awakened early in the morning with disturbing dreams about his parents and visions of things that had never happened. He saw his mother traveling on the ship to England, arriving and finding her love married to another woman. In a way, he was repeating his mother's history—although this time, he was the one who had been rejected.

Mr. Reine offered to take him to visit some of the surrounding towns, then finally to London, where he'd take the ship back to New York. The night before leaving Norwich, Jon fell asleep easily, but his dreams took a different turn.

She stood before him, dressed in a white nightgown. The same one she'd worn the night he found her struggling through the mud. The gown was clean now, falling in soft folds about her body. He reached out to touch her, but she smiled and turned away, her hair cascading down her back, gently swaying in the breeze. She started to run, looking back at him, laughing. He ran after her as she zigzagged through the fields. Where was she heading? He tried to call out, but he had no voice.

The lighthouse loomed ahead. She ran into it and shut the door. He hurried to the door and tried to push it open, but it was stuck. Kicking with all his might, he finally forced the lock. She was lying on the floor, her nightgown spread out from her body, her hair a halo about her face. But something was wrong—she was writhing in pain and clutching her throat—eyes wide and staring.

He ran to her and lifted her head, cradling it.

"Eliza! Eliza!" He tried to yell her name, but no sound came.

Sitting up in bed, Jon wiped the dampness on his forehead. Even after the letter from Apryl, he hadn't allowed himself to think of Eliza again. She was somewhere in Europe, only a ghost of his past now.

He knew he couldn't change what had happened to her or what had happened between them, but he could try to forget. Pressing his temples against the throbbing pain, he sighed. Why was Eliza entering his dreams now? It was as if he had really seen her, had really chased her laughing figure, and had really cradled her head in his arms.

Jon crossed his arms over his chest, trying to squeeze away the aching sensation that had formed inside him. He lay back in bed, placing his hands behind his head. The sky outside was still black, and he knew there were many hours until dawn. He would stay awake all night, if only to not fall prey to such dreams again.

Eliza was in his room, standing over him. He wanted to ask why she'd come to Norwich. He couldn't form the words. She smiled at him and reached for him, saying nothing. He didn't intend to let her come into his heart, but Apryl wasn't in the way anymore. Why was he holding back?

He felt her lips on his, and soon she was nestled next to him. It was as if they'd been together their whole lives.

Jon opened his eyes. He had allowed himself to fall asleep again. Pulling the covers to his chin, he concentrated on the coolness of the fabric. Eventually, the warmth of his dream faded, and he began to laugh at himself.

He made a sorry, rich bachelor.

"I'm in the lighthouse."

Jon bolted straight up. "Who's there?" He looked around.

The room was quiet. No one was in his room. Letting out a sigh, he settled beneath the covers again. Not only was he dreaming about someone he'd probably never see again, he was hearing voices . . . like Eliza did.

Twenty-seven

"We're leaving for London tomorrow," Gina said, entering the room with a bright smile. She carried the paper in her hand. "Father has a bit of business there. I've always wanted to see London. We'll be staying at his cousin's townhouse, right in the city.

Eliza smiled absently and browsed through the paper for any news that might be of New York.

One item in particular stood out—an announcement for the wedding of Mr. Jonathan Porter to his fiancée Miss Apryl Maughan. The wedding date had been set.

The following day, Eliza stepped out of the carriage at a London townhouse. "It's not much, but it's cheerful," Mrs. Graydon announced.

Eliza and Gina started up the stairs, leaving the driver to bring their baggage. They entered the front hallway together. The wooden floor shone in the sunlight, and the place smelled of lemon. "It's beautiful," Eliza said.

"Follow me." Gina led Eliza up a set of narrow stairs. They entered one of the bedrooms. "It looks like this one's ours. Two beds and a dresser."

Eliza crossed the room and peered out the window. Below the bustle of the city street reminded her of New York. With the official wedding announcement of Jonathan Porter to Apryl, Eliza realized that she'd been waiting to hear about it. Now that she had, it brought finality to her thoughts of Jon. It was time to put him completely and utterly in the past.

"What do you think?" Gina asked.

She turned and smiled. "Perfect. I'll take it."

"Like we have a choice." Gina laughed. "Let's go have some tea."

They descended the stairs together and the housekeeper, Rochelle, brought in tea.

Mr. and Mrs. Graydon only stayed a few moments before going off to meet friends. Gina pled a headache, so Eliza stayed behind with her. A cozy fire glimmered in the fireplace, and Eliza was content to sit and watch it while sipping her hot drink.

"I feel so grown-up traveling Europe," Gina said.

"Somehow you look older."

"I hope that is a compliment."

Eliza laughed. "So, what are you going to do with all of your freedom tonight?"

"I don't know. Perhaps freedom is overrated. I'll just do what you do." She let out a sigh. "Cambridge is quite close, and surely there are plenty of eligible bachelors there. Maybe we can visit."

Eliza took another sip of her tea. "I already know one of those eager bachelors at Cambridge."

"Oh?" Gina asked, leaning forward. "Do tell."

"Nathaniel Prann."

"The one from Maybrook who proposed to you?" Gina asked.

"One and the same."

"You know, love isn't everything in a marriage," Gina teased. "But since you're obviously not in love with Nathaniel . . . who comes to mind when you think of love?"

Immediately the image of Jon's dark eyes and unruly hair appeared in Eliza's mind.

"Why, you're blushing. Tell me his name. Is it another mysterious Puritan?"

"I—It's no one," she stammered. "Just an ideal every woman carries, I suppose."

"Very well, keep your mystery man to yourself," Gina said. "As for me, I'm going to scour the bookcases and find the most scandalous novel to read."

The following morning, the sun was high in the sky by the time Eliza awoke. Stretching, she realized that it had been months since she'd slept so well, and without dreaming. She looked over at the other bed and saw that Gina had already risen.

After wrapping her robe about her, Eliza went into the adjoining bathroom to brush her teeth. She gazed at her image in the mirror and fancied that she seemed older as well—perhaps twenty or twenty-one. She certainly felt wiser. After washing her face, she went downstairs in search of breakfast. Mr. and Mrs. Graydon were already gone, and Gina was reading in the parlor. Apparently she'd found quite a good gothic novel.

"Oh, there you are," Gina said. "Eggs and toast are in the kitchen. When you've finished come sit with me."

Eliza found the breakfast covered with a lid and still warm. She ate then joined Gina, who asked, "Did you sleep well?"

"Like a dream." Eliza stifled a yawn.

Gina closed her book. "I have some good news. The funniest thing happened last night when my parents went to dinner." A small smile crept to Gina's lips. "They told me all about it this morning over breakfast. Last night, they were eating at the new restaurant down the street and couldn't help but overhear what was being said at the table next to them." She paused.

"And . . .?" Eliza prompted.

"It was a group of college students from Cambridge," Gina continued. "My parents heard someone speaking like a Puritan."

"No," Eliza said.

"Yes. My parents were curious and got to talking to them. A young man at the table was none other than Nathaniel Prann.'"

"You're teasing."

"No." Gina's eyes danced with amusement. "My parents asked if he knew your family, and he pulled his chair over to their table and joined them for dinner. My mother said she thinks his *thee's* and *thou's* are simply charming."

Eliza was speechless. But there was no mistaking that it was Nathaniel whom Gina's parents had spoken about. Her friend continued to talk; all Eliza heard was a faint murmur. What were the odds of this encounter? What did Nathaniel think when learning that she was in town? Had he received her letter?

". . . and he said he'd stop by this afternoon."

Eliza's mouth fell open. "Here?"

"Don't look so surprised. Of course he wants to see you. I'm sure only as a friend, though," Gina said, her voice teasing.

Eliza began to feel lightheaded. Maybe Nathaniel hadn't received her letter. "Did he say something about me?"

Gina laughed. "He didn't need to. My mother said it was written all over his face."

By afternoon, Eliza was pacing the floor of the bedroom, ignoring the fact Gina watched from the bed with amusement. Eliza wore a pale green dress, and her hair was piled on top of her head. What could she possibly say to Nathaniel?

"Let me put a few ribbons in your hair," Gina said.

"No. I don't want to look like I primped too much."

"Men don't notice those things," Gina said.

"Then why do it?" Eliza faced her friend. "Look, there's something you don't know."

Gina clasped her hands together in eagerness. "Do tell."

"Nathaniel has proposed to me twice." Eliza sighed and sank on the bed. "I've told him over and over that we are not meant for each other, but he won't give up. Meeting him will encourage him further." She groaned and covered her face with her hands.

"Simply be honest with him," Gina suggested, patting Eliza's shoulder.

"I have been, but he won't take no for an answer," Eliza said.

"You must admit," Gina said, "this all seems so romantic."

Eliza moaned.

"Was that the doorbell? I think he's here."

Eliza dropped her hands and reached for Gina's arm. "What am I to say?"

"Talk about the weather; that always works for me." She flashed a smile.

"This is the last time I'm ever going to see him." Eliza left the room and descended the stairs. *Take deep breaths.*

In the entryway stood Nathaniel, handing his overcoat and hat to Rochelle.

He was just as she remembered—a little taller perhaps. His regular clothing made him look older than the young man who had wooed her on the countryside of Maybrook.

"Eliza," he said simply.

She crossed the hallway, and he took her hands and kissed her cheek.

"Thou are beautiful."

"I see you haven't changed your opinion of me," she said.

Nathaniel laughed. "Never."

Eliza offered a nervous smile and led the way into the parlor, where they sat across from each other. "What a coincidence that you met the Graydons last night."

For a moment, Nathaniel didn't say anything—so intent he was on studying her. "'Tis a miracle."

Eliza flushed. "Nonsense. Just a . . . coincidence."

"The Lord works in mysterious ways."

Her neck grew hot. "You're very presumptuous."

He grinned. "I've made some changes that I know thou wilt be pleased with."

"Oh?" Eliza shifted uncomfortably in her seat. She didn't want him making any changes with her in mind.

"I've decided not to return to Maybrook as a farmer."

"I know. I received your letter while we were in France."

Nathaniel continued, his eyes bright. "And I received your reply." If he had, he certainly didn't seem upset over her answer.

"I plan to repay Reverend Clement the money for the first year of school, then procure a scholarship to help pay for the rest." He leaned forward. "I'm going to start my own religious branch—a more modern form of Puritanism."

"Is there such a thing? I thought that Puritanism was a reformation in itself."

"Don't you see, Eliza?" he said. "Thou wilt not have to settle for being a farmer's wife. I'll have my own congregation, and I've already started writing a book about my ideas. Once people become converted to my true doctrines, I'll make a living on the proceeds on my book."

Eliza shrank back in her chair, glancing desperately at the door, wishing that Gina would come in.

"I'll build thee a beautiful home, and our daughters will wear dresses with petticoats and ruffles—"

"Please stop, Nathaniel Prann." Eliza's throat constricted, and her cheeks flamed. She stood abruptly. "I'm so very sorry. I spoke the absolute truth in my last letter—I still feel the same. You must stop hoping that it will change."

Nathaniel's smile faded. "But I thought that was what thou wanted, and if I provided, thou wouldst change thy mind."

Eliza crossed her arms. "No, I won't change my mind." The look on his face made her want to cry. She moved to the door, holding it open for his exit.

She avoided his gaze as he walked out of the door. She shut it firmly and leaned against it, realizing that she was shaking. She heard Nathaniel's quiet thanks to Rochelle as he gathered his coat and hat. Despite her words to him, he was still the gentleman to the maid. Finally the outside door shut.

Moments later, Gina burst into the parlor. Taking one look at Eliza's pale features, she asked, "What happened?"

Eliza sank into a chair. "I think he finally received the message."

Gina's eyes strayed to the window. "I wouldn't be too sure about that. He's coming back."

Eliza turned her head and saw Nathaniel ascending the porch steps. "Tell him I'm busy." She ran out of the room and up the stairs. There she hovered, listening to the voices coming from below.

Soon the door shut, and Gina came upstairs. She entered the room, holding an envelope. "He gave this to me and asked me to assure you that he's only inviting you as a friend."

Eliza took the envelope and opened it—inside was an invitation to a formal ball sponsored by the university. She looked at Gina. "Odd. He's inviting me to a ball—he doesn't dance."

"Puritan restrictions?" Gina took the invitation from Eliza and read the details.

"This man has a lot of nerve," Eliza mused. She lay back on her bed and stared at the ceiling. "This doesn't sound innocent."

"It's harmless. After all, there will be plenty of interesting men there. I'll go with you."

"Just what I need . . . you coming so that you can pick out my future husband," Eliza said and threw a pillow at Gina.

Gina ducked and started laughing.

❦

The next two weeks the weather was blustery. Gina and Eliza got out when they could, but mostly they stayed inside by the fire, visiting with whatever distant relation of the Graydons happened to stop in. Letters kept coming from Nathaniel.

"A letter for you, Miss Eliza," Rochelle announced one morning.

"Thank you," she said and glanced at the address. She placed the envelope on the side table, upon a growing stack of unopened letters.

Gina watched with amusement. "Are you ever going to read them?"

"Not unless I grow desperate." Eliza stood before the fire to warm her hands.

"What about the ball?" Gina asked.

Eliza shrugged. "I'm not going."

"Poor Nathaniel."

"Don't pity him. Pity *me*," Eliza said.

"I would never pity you, Eliza Robinson." Gina sat on a chair. "Men fall at your feet wherever you go, and you don't appreciate any of them."

Eliza remained silent.

Rising, Gina joined Eliza at the hearth. "Are you going to tell me his name?" she asked quietly.

"Whose?"

"The man you think about when your thoughts are far away."

"I don't have the slightest notion what you are talking about," Eliza said. "Don't you have a scandalous novel to read?"

"That I do," Gina said with a smile. She touched Eliza's arm. "Don't worry. I'm sure he feels the same way about you."

Eliza opened her mouth to protest, but Gina flounced out of the room and up the stairs.

Taking a deep breath, Eliza knew she could never tell her friend that the man who occupied her dreams was about to marry another woman. She pulled a chair close to the fire and sat down, wrapping her arms about her. Clouds crowded the sky outside, making the light from the window dim.

"I'm in the lighthouse."

Eliza froze at the sound of the voice. She'd thought Helena had left her alone for good. "What do you mean?" she asked the empty room. The fire sputtered, and a log crackled as if to answer. Eliza shivered despite the warmth. The journal had been found and Maeve's murder solved. She'd even written to Jon about her dream.

"Please," she whispered. "Please tell me what you want me to do."

Twenty-eight

Eliza slept little, her mind wracked with why Helena continued to haunt her—even in England. There was nothing Eliza could do for Helena here. She didn't dream, didn't have nightmares, but maybe that was because she couldn't sleep. When morning finally arrived, it dawned gray. When Eliza went down for breakfast, Mrs. Graydon met her at the bottom of the steps, a letter in hand.

"Another letter from Mr. Prann," she said. "I think you should read it."

Eliza took the envelope. Would she never be able to free herself of Maybrook? First Helena was speaking to her again, and now another letter from Nathaniel. She walked into the parlor and tore open the letter.

> *Dearest Eliza,*
> *Tomorrow night is the university ball, which I would love to attend with thee. I hope all is well. Know that I'm praying for thy forgiveness for my*

*bold assumptions. As stated in my other letters that
you have not replied to, I am truly sorry for my
behavior.*

I only want thy friendship.

*I'll be on thy doorstep tomorrow night at eight.
Answer my knock if thou wants to join me. If not,
I'll walk away and never contact thee again.*

Sincerely,
Nathaniel

Eliza closed her eyes for a moment. Had Nathaniel
finally accepted the inevitable and only wanted a companion
for the ball? Eliza had two choices: Cower in the townhouse,
dreading Helena's voice, or go out and forget Helena's
torments for an evening.

She walked upstairs to the bedroom and sifted through
the closet. There was one dress that she hadn't worn yet since
leaving New York, which might work. She pulled out the
lavender gown and held it up to her figure. It would have to
do.

That evening, Eliza and Gina were ready by seven-
thirty. She paced nervously in the parlor while Gina sat
engrossed in her book.

Eliza began doubting her decision. What if Nathaniel
was trapping her into another long tirade about the
alterations he was making in his life so that they could be
married? She sighed at the thought. She had never asked him
to make changes in the first place, and she'd told him that
she wouldn't marry him even if he did.

The minutes ticked by, agonizingly slow, but finally she
heard a carriage arrive. Gina looked up expectantly. Eliza
went to the door and opened it before he could knock.

Nathaniel stood on the porch, his hand raised. When he
saw Eliza, his eyes widened. "Thou hast forgiven me," he
said, smiling. "I mean . . . you have forgiven me."

Was he changing his manner of speech too? For some reason, it sounded unnatural coming from him. "We're only friends?" she asked.

"Yes." He agreed. "But I have to tell thee that you look heavenly."

Gina laughed behind them, and the two of them followed Nathaniel to the waiting carriage.

The ball was in full swing when they arrived. Carriages lined the streets, unloading passengers. Nathaniel could barely contain his excitement and spoke non-stop about all of the friends he planned to introduce them to. "I've told them all about you."

Eliza held in a groan. "What have you told them?"

"That thou are a wonderful young lady and maybe someday . . . I mean, your friendship is valuable, and I want them to meet you."

Eliza smiled politely, but inside she was nervous—what exactly had he told his friends about her? Gina elbowed her, stifling a giggle. The carriage came to a stop, and Nathaniel helped her down.

They had arrived at a stately building, with dozens of stairs leading to the entrance. Nathaniel offered his arm to Eliza, and together they walked up the steps. The music grew louder as they approached. Soon after they entered the great hall, Nathaniel was greeted by another couple, then another. It seemed he knew almost everyone at the ball. Introductions were made and smiles shared. Gina was asked to dance almost immediately. By the time Nathaniel led Eliza to the dance floor, she was relieved to be away from introductions.

He wrapped one arm about her and held her other hand in his—his palm was perspiring.

"Are you all right?" she asked.

"This is my first real dance," he confessed.

Eliza pulled away. "I don't want you to do something against your religion."

"No, you don't understand." He drew her back into position, his brow creased. "I've been practicing for weeks; I wanted my first dance to be with you."

Eliza's neck grew warm as Nathaniel led her around the floor. His steps were awkward, but accurate. No one seemed to notice that a Puritan had joined their ranks. "Relax," she said. "You're doing fine."

He smiled, sweat beading on his forehead. Glancing around, he whispered, "Do you think people are watching us?"

"No one is." Eliza couldn't help but smile. "And if they are, they won't notice anything different."

Nathaniel's steps grew more fluid, and his shoulders straightened. Eliza found herself enjoying the evening, perhaps she was capable of maintaining a friendship with this ever-changing man.

Time passed quickly. Eliza danced with several of Nathaniel's friends. Each of them had amusing stories to tell about him, and she found herself laughing along with them. She started to see Nathaniel in a different light, although that didn't change her resolve.

When she danced with Nathaniel again, he glowed from physical exertion and the occasion of dancing with numerous girls.

"I've met so many delightful women here," he sputtered. "All of them have been patient with my questions."

Eliza smiled. "I'm happy for you. I'm sure you'll discover that I pale in comparison to the women of London."

He looked at her fondly. "You'll always shine in my eyes, Eliza, no matter what happens."

Glancing away, Eliza felt a lump form in her throat. Nathaniel drew her close. He began to hum softly in her ear, but Eliza remained stiff in his arms.

"Another thing that has changed me," he whispered, sending shivers down her neck, "is that I can show my affection for the woman of my choosing."

The music came to an end, and before another waltz number started up, Eliza disengaged. But Nathaniel held her fast and continued to hum. "If you ever do change your mind," he said. "I'll be waiting."

"Nathaniel, you said we were friends," Eliza said.

"Friendship is a wonderful basis to build a marriage on."

The spell had been broken, and Eliza pulled away. "Excuse me. I must find the powder room."

Nathaniel released her, reluctance in his eyes. "I'll be here when you return."

She turned and moved through the crowd. She knew her cheeks were flaming, but she didn't care who noticed. Once inside the powder room, she found an empty chair and sank into it. She squeezed her eyes shut. Coming had been a mistake. Nathaniel would never change.

After several minutes, she felt composed enough to reenter the ball. She'd find Gina and tell her she had to leave, and to pass the message to Nathaniel so he couldn't stop her from leaving.

Standing on the outskirts of the dance floor, she scanned the faces. No one looked familiar—yet everyone looked familiar. Amid the swirling skirts, she couldn't find Gina.

Eliza sighed, gazing at the churning mass of colors before her. One separated from the rest, and Eliza stared in disbelief at the man coming toward her.

It was *him*. Blood rushed to her head. She reached out and steadied herself on a marble column. Jon had seen her— the man who had haunted her dreams for months.

She glanced around, trying to spot Gina, who was nowhere in sight. Gazing forward again, she looked for *him*, but he'd disappeared also—maybe it hadn't been him after all.

"Eliza?"

He stood next to her, those same dark eyes that she'd seen in her dreams a thousand times, absorbing her features. His hair was blacker than she remembered, his shoulders broad under a well-cut suit. But it was his countenance that seemed the most changed. He was a man with hope in his eyes.

"Hello, Jon," she managed to say.

"You look as if you've seen a ghost," he said.

"I think I have."Her voice sounded tinny to her ears, as if someone else spoke the hollow words.

Jon's eyes clouded. "You mean my mother?"

Shaking her head, Eliza took a step backward. He must be on his honeymoon—but so soon? Maybe they moved up their wedding date. "Are you here with your wife?"

A look of amusement crossed his face. "I'm not married."

Not married? Her mind raced as she tried to comprehend. "But I thought . . ." Her face flushed. "Your fiancée then, of course."

Jon took a step closer. "If you can believe it, Apryl left me for Thomas Beesley."

Eliza covered her mouth. She didn't know whether to laugh or offer sympathy. *Thomas and Apryl? Of all the odd things to happen . . .*

Jon seemed to read her thoughts. "I've no hard feelings anymore. It's rather amusing when you think about it."

Not married. Eliza tried to organize her thoughts. "Quite amusing." His eyes stayed on her, quite unnerving her in fact. "What brings you to England?"

"I came to settle my late father's estate in Norwich. I'm in London with his son-in-law, a Cambridge graduate."

She nodded, hardly daring to believe that Jon was standing before her.

"I've a confession to make," he said.

The music around them grew dim, and the people faded into the background. Eliza looked at him, her heart pounding, trying to remember what he'd said.

"The morning after I received the letter from you about my mother," Jon said, "I hurried to your house and . . . finding you gone, I decided to try to catch you at the ship harbor. But I wasn't allowed on board."

Eliza stared at him. *So it was him.*

"And," he paused, "I need to explain that I'm not Thomas Beesley's lawyer, nor have I ever represented him." He tilted his head, capturing her gaze. "I want you to know that when I return to New York, I'll be in a position to help your father if he needs it."

Thomas Beesley lied. All of this time, she'd believed him. Of course Thomas had lied—she knew his character better than anyone. What a fool she'd been.

"You never represented Thomas Beesley?" Eliza asked.

"No. I have a very little opinion of the man, and even less so now, if that's possible," Jon said.

She opened her mouth to inquire further, but Jon cocked his head to one side and said, "Now tell me what you are doing in London."

"I'm . . ." She hesitated and glanced away, hoping Nathaniel was nowhere in sight. "Mr. Graydon has business in London for several days."

Just then, Nathaniel appeared. "Hello, Mr. Porter," he said, his greeting sounding more like a question.

The warmth faded from Eliza's face, but she managed to keep a pleasant expression. She didn't know what Jon would think of her being at the dance with Nathaniel.

"All the way from Maybrook? What a coincidence," Nathaniel said.

Jon looked from him to Eliza, curiosity in his eyes. "Quite."

"What brings you here, sir?" Nathaniel asked.

"I'm here with a relative who happens to be an alumnus," Jon explained. "But even more surprising is seeing *you* here, Mr. Prann . . . at a dance."

Nathaniel gave a curt nod. "I'm attending Cambridge."

Jon remained silent, waiting for his question to be answered.

"And I've had a change of conviction," Nathaniel said with a smile. "When I return to home, I will found my own sect based on the Puritan laws I was brought up on, but it will have a more modern understanding and flexibility."

"As in an understanding of the art of dance?" Jon asked.

A flush crept onto Nathaniel's face. "Among other things," he said stiffly.

Jon nodded. "It's a pleasure to meet you again, and I wish both of you all the best."

Eliza touched Jon's arm. "You'll be in England long?"

"I depart tomorrow, as a matter of fact." He glanced at Nathaniel, then Eliza. "Good luck with your plans." Jon spun on his heels and walked away.

Nathaniel took Eliza's hand. "What a queer fellow. So moody—"

"Excuse me for a moment," Eliza said, tugging her hand away.

She turned away and zigzagged across the room, hoping that Nathaniel wouldn't see that she was following Jon. As he reached the entrance of the hall, Eliza caught up with him.

"Jon," she said.

He turned, puzzlement crossing his face when he saw her.

"Please wait." She covered the last few steps, glancing furtively behind her.

"We can talk outside, if you don't want him to see us," Jon said.

Eliza hesitated for a moment then followed him. The sky was clear, with a bright moon, but the air chilly. She wrapped her arms about her with a shiver. "I wanted to explain."

"You don't owe me an explanation," Jon said. "Would you like my jacket?"

"I'm fine." Eliza lowered her gaze, searching for her next words.

"I think it's wonderful that you and Nathaniel are together. His regard for you has been obvious all along." Jon spoke the generous words, but his voice was empty. "He's a good man, in addition to the fact that he's changed his Puritan ways for you—a true statement of devotion."

"I'm not marrying him," Eliza blurted.

Jon's expression was as flat as his tone. "He appears to think otherwise."

Glancing away, Eliza bit her lip. "Not for lack of trying to convince him on my part."

He was silent for a moment. "I should go."

Eliza brought her gaze back to Jon, not wanting him to leave yet. "You received my letter?"

He nodded. "It must have been quite horrific for you to dream about her death," he said gently.

"It still is."

"You're still dreaming about her?"

Eliza hesitated. "Among other things." She felt Jon's hand on hers, and her pulse quickened.

"Like what?" he asked.

His touch was warm and comforting somehow, but Eliza wondered whether she should tell him any more. This might be her only chance. "Your mother speaks to me, and she told me that she's in the lighthouse. But I don't know why she tells me that or what she wants me to do."

Jon's eyes flickered, but his face remained grave. "I'm sorry," he said finally. "I suppose it's her way of letting us know what happened to her."

Her tears began to fall, and Eliza wiped them away. "What happened to her was awful. I only wish she was able to board that ship to England."

Jon dropped his hand and looked past her. "She might not have liked what she found."

"What do you mean?" she asked.

"I've been in England to settle my father's estate, among other things," he said. "Apparently, my father married soon after I was born. If my mother had arrived in England, she would have found him with a wife and child."

"But she knew about his marriage." A sigh escaped Eliza's lips. She'd read it in the journal.

"Seeing it would have been hard."

"Perhaps it was better that she never came over to England."

"Perhaps." Jon brought his gaze back to focus on her.

Eliza tried to think of something else to say that wouldn't be unpleasant. But the only topics the two of them had in common seemed melancholy—Apryl and Thomas Beesley, Nathaniel Prann, or Helena. Feeling deflated, she said, "I should get back to—"

"To your future," Jon finished.

"No, I don't—"

Suddenly, Jon took both of her hands and held them to his chest.

Eliza's breath hitched at his touch.

"It was a great surprise to see you again, Eliza," he said. "And . . . finding you in good health, enjoying the social scene, was more than I expected. I hope you'll be able to put the nightmare of my family tragedy behind you."

She nodded blindly, her eyes stinging. "But meeting you was a blessing, not a nightmare."

Jon held her hands tightly for another moment before he reached out and stroked her cheek. "Perhaps dreams do come true."

Eliza searched for the words to say—words to keep him from going away. But he turned and left, disappearing into the night.

She stood there for several moments, staring after him, oblivious of the twinkling stars above. Finally the cold air made her to return to the dance hall, where she found a chair to sit on. She was relieved that no one asked her to dance, for she was trembling and sure her eyes were bloodshot. Closing her eyes, she tried to calm her breathing.

Perhaps dreams do come true. Just not mine.

Twenty-nine

The rest of the evening was a blur. When Eliza saw Gina, she hurried to her side.

"I'm not feeling well," she said, hoping she wouldn't have to explain.

Gina took one look at her and said, "I'll fetch Nathaniel. Meet us at the entrance."

The ride home was quiet after Eliza assured both Gina and Nathaniel that she was only tired and needed rest. Once they arrived at the townhouse, Nathaniel escorted both women inside.

After Gina disappeared upstairs, Eliza endured a clumsy goodbye in the form of a stiff hug with Nathaniel. Tonight had been nothing like she expected. She walked slowly up the stairs to her room, where she changed into her nightgown. Gina stayed downstairs, talking to her parents. Eliza fell into bed, clutching her pillow close, still feeling Jon's warm touch on her cheek. Her tears could finally come, and she let them flow.

Eliza lay awake into the morning hours, afraid to sleep and dream. It wasn't until after the sun had risen that she fell asleep, exhausted.

Soon after midday, Eliza woke with a start. When the events from the night before came into focus, she touched her cheek. Would she ever see Jon again? She rose and peered out the curtains. The normal business of the day seemed to be going on below, without her.

By the time the afternoon post arrived, the Graydons had left on errands. Eliza was dressed and sitting in the parlor, writing a letter home. Rochelle brought in the post on a tray and placed the letters next to her.

There was one from her parents, and another from . . . Eliza's eyes widened at seeing Jon's handwriting. She tore open the envelope and scanned to the end of the page. Nervously she began to read from the beginning.

> *Dear Eliza,*
> *This letter may come at an inopportune time, but I have spent the whole of the night since leaving you, awake. Your connection with my mother is more remarkable than anything that I can express at this time. I tell myself over and over that I should be grateful for meeting you and Nathaniel in London. I offer my sincerest congratulations and know that you will be a strong and devoted couple.*
> *I confess that seeing the two of you together made me anything but happy. I wasn't prepared to feel this way upon seeing you again. Having said that, you probably don't have the slightest idea what I am talking about.*
> *When I received the letter from Apryl telling me that she'd fallen in love with Thomas Beesley, I was, in fact, envious. Not because she loved another,*

*but because she knew what she wanted and had the
courage to partake of it.*

*I did not think that I could look upon another
woman and think of marriage—until I saw you at
the dance.*

Forgive me for my intrusion.

Sincerely,

Jonathan Porter

Eliza read the letter again and then a third time. Was
Jon saying what she thought he was? That he truly cared for
her? She dropped the letter onto the sofa and ran out of the
parlor. "Rochelle, bring me my cloak."

The maid appeared, a worried look on her face. "Where
are you going?"

"To the harbor."

"But a storm is approaching," Rochelle protested.

"Call the carriage."

"The Graydons took the carriage."

"Then the wagon."

Once the wagon was prepared, Eliza climbed in. She
leaned forward, watching the passing scenery impatiently.
She'd told the driver to make all haste, but he seemed to be
driving unusually slow. Eliza retied the scarf about her head
against the increasing wind. With luck, the weather would be
too turbulent for Jon's ship to depart today, and it would still
be docked.

Even before they rounded the last bend, Eliza knew it
was gone. Although she argued against the sinking feeling
she had, when the harbor came into view, she couldn't deny
the fact that there was no ship in the harbor. Jon was gone.

Vendors were cleaning up their wares amidst howling
gusts. She signaled for the carriage to stop and climbed out.
Wrapping her arms about her, a fruitless effort to stave off
the biting wind, she walked to the edge of the dock. Two

ships were on the horizon, although it was difficult to tell whether they were departing or arriving. They might as well have been a thousand miles away, for all the good it would do her. Jon had left.

Head down, Eliza returned to the waiting wagon. The ride back to the townhouse was swift and cold. The single blanket did little to protect her from the icy draft.

Once inside the house, she went straight to the parlor and found the letter, unmoved, and took it to the hearth. Rochelle had lit a fire, and Eliza sat next to it, reading the letter over and over. Finally, she folded the pages and tucked them into her bodice.

Eliza had to tell Nathaniel the truth. He'd have to know she was in love with another man or Nathaniel would never give up. Even if she lived out her days as a spinster, she'd be more content on her own than marrying Nathaniel out of pity.

༚

In the early evening, someone knocked at the door. Eliza sensed Nathaniel's presence before she heard Rochelle greet him.

The Graydons were sitting in the parlor as well, and they all decided to go upstairs at once. By the time Nathaniel entered, Eliza was the only one in the room.

"Thou—I mean—*you* look tired," Nathaniel said, taking her hands and gazing at her face.

Eliza lowered her eyes. "I didn't sleep well last night." *Or at all.* She gently removed her hands from his and directed him to sit down.

Nathaniel smiled brightly. "Well, I have good news that might help. I received a letter from home, and my parents have reconciled themselves to my change of plans."

"That's wonderful for you," Eliza said in a polite tone.

"I thought it would be wonderful for us."

"Oh, Nathaniel. Please don't do this." Eliza rose and crossed to the darkened window.

Nathaniel came up behind her and placed his hands on her shoulders. "I awoke this morning with a feeling of dread. Please, tell me you've changed your mind and that you'll marry me."

She turned and faced him. "I'm sorry. I can't."

His face paled. "Then it's true. How I envy Jonathan Porter." His shoulders sagged, and his composure began to crumble.

"What are you talking about?"

"The man who has your love will be blessed for life." He turned and paced the room. "I should have seen it in Maybrook, from that first moment I saw the both of you at the lighthouse."

"I hardly know him—" Eliza began.

"Love isn't knowledge." He stopped and looked at her, his eyes flaming. "It comes from here," he said, bringing his fist to his chest. "Thou wilt never know, Eliza, how thy rejection has wounded me."

"It hurts me, too, Nathaniel—"

"I've been a fool." His voice rose. "A fool to fall in love with a woman who makes rejecting suitors a daily habit."

She stared at him, his hurtful words burrowing deep. "I've always been honest with you. How dare you think I've been heartless."

Nathaniel's countenance fell. "I'm sorry. That's not what I meant." He sank into a chair. "All of my plans have been dashed."

Seeing him crestfallen, Eliza's throat swelled. She crossed to him and placed a hand on his shoulder. "I've no doubt you'll find someone who will return your love. Give yourself the freedom to search for it."

He raised his head and looked at her, his eyes bloodshot. "Perhaps thou are right. I gave up everything for thee. Love shouldn't have to be that way, should it?"

She shook her head.

"I've seen reason and will no longer fall prey to foolish dreams." He stood.

Eliza watched as Nathaniel picked up his coat and hat and strode out of the room, out of the house, and out of her life.

❧

It had been weeks since Eliza's return to New York, but she remained restless. The nightmares continued, although the voice had been silent. The daily tasks of shopping with her mother and writing thank-you notes for the welcome home visits she had received seemed pointless. And furthermore, she had no desire to attend social gatherings or parties—especially if it meant encountering Jonathan Porter without any privacy.

But she was afraid to go to his home and confess her feelings. So she waited and wondered if he'd contact her. He must know she was back in New York and wasn't engaged to Nathaniel . . . Jon had probably taken precautions to avoid her, and she didn't blame him. After all, he didn't know how she felt. She kept his last letter hidden in her jewelry box. No one would ever see his words, though she doubted he meant them anymore.

Yet the words of his letter had given her the courage to return to New York and help her family face the business problems. There had been a complete split between Beesley and her father, but her father had secured a large investor making the rebuilding of the business possible.

She knew Nathaniel would have no trouble finding a young woman who would find happiness in his sun-kissed hair and bright blue eyes—a happiness she could never envision for herself.

During the daylight hours she listened to her mother prattle about who was doing what. But it was during the darkest moments of the night when her nightmares returned.

Each night she dreamt about Helena, and each morning she woke to her voice repeating, *"I'm in the lighthouse."*

Soon, Eliza's mother noticed the circles under her eyes.

"Are you ill?" Her mother placed a cool hand on Eliza's forehead. "Maybe you should rest today."

Eliza found herself agreeing, and as days passed, she spent more and more time secluded in her room. Even Gina had stopped visiting very often.

Spring arrived, and Eliza confined herself to her room, pleading a persistent headache. As brilliant greens emerged outside her window, a dark curtain had fallen over her heart.

One mid-April night, Eliza awoke from her sleep. She stared into the darkness—trying to remember her dream— then realized there hadn't been one.

"Are you finally gone?" she whispered.

"Go to the lighthouse."

A jolt passed through Eliza's body. The voice was not giving up.

She knew that she had to go look in the lighthouse—if not for Helena's sake, then for her own. She lit the candle by her bedside and rose. Packing took very little time, and writing a note to her parents even less. She hoped that they would not come after her, at least before she had a chance to discover the truth about the lighthouse. She needed to do whatever it took to get rid of the voice once and for all.

Stepping off the train at the Maybrook station, Eliza squinted into the bright sun. Nothing had changed about the sleepy town, and few people gave her a second glance. She hired a buckboard and horse, and loaded her single bag into the back. As she drove along the familiar rutted road, memories of Maeve flooded through her, and she found herself smiling.

Shortly after turning onto Main Street, she arrived at the constable's office. She knocked at the door, and after a moment, it opened.

"Good morrow, Miss," the constable said, surprise registering on his face. "Come in."

Eliza followed him into the inner office and helped herself to a chair. "I've come to speak with Gus."

The constable blanched. "Whatever for?"

She hesitated, eyeing the constable carefully. "I believe he knows where Helena Talbot's body is buried."

The constable's face was a mask of stone. "Gus is not here."

"Has he been moved to a different jail? Where can I find him?"

Averting his eyes, the constable spoke quietly. "He was released last month. Haven't seen or heard from him since."

Eliza gripped the edge of her seat, half-rising. "How could you release a murderer?"

The constable held up his hand, his eyes hard. "It's cruel to imprison a slow wit, and he never confessed to the crime."

Sinking back into her chair, Eliza let out a small cry. "He confessed his father's murder of Helena to me. Gus wanted to avenge his father, and he tried to kill me. Isn't that enough to hold him?" Her head began to spin, or was it the room? Before she knew it, she had pitched forward, and all went dark.

When she awoke, the first thing she saw was the constable's ruddy face staring at her. "Canst thou stand, Miss?"

Eliza grimaced and rose to her elbows.

"Easy," the constable said.

She let the constable help her to her feet.

"I'll bring thee some water," he offered.

Eliza nodded, her head aching from the fall. She ran her fingers along her forehead and discovered a growing bump. The constable brought a cup, and she gingerly took a couple of sips.

"Where art thou staying?"

Eliza looked at him in surprise. She hadn't expected such a consideration from the constable. "I don't know."

"Ruth has been ill and hasn't been seen in town much, but Goodwife Temple has a room she lets out," he said.

"That sounds fine," Eliza said.

"She lives above the bakery. Wouldst thou like me to walk with thee?"

Eliza shook her head and handed back the cup. "I think I'll be all right. I've hired a buckboard." She rose to go. "Thank you all the same."

As she rode along Main Street, Eliza marveled at how everything looked as it had the year before—yet different, too. The people hurried along the boardwalk, their clothing ever conservative, their gazes respectfully lowered. She stopped in front of the bakery and entered the warm shop. Shelves were lined with freshly baked goods. The smell reminded her of Aunt Maeve's home.

A stooped man stood behind the counter, dressed in a clean white apron. His watery gray eyes surveyed her with surprising steadiness.

"I'm looking for Goodwife Temple," she told him.

The man nodded and rang a bell. Soon a woman appeared from the back room, looking as aged as the man behind the counter. "Yes?"

"My name is Eliza Robinson. The constable said I could find a room for the night here."

Goodwife Temple appraised her then nodded. "I'll show thee the way."

Eliza followed the woman's slow step up the back stairs. Two rooms were at the top of the landing, one occupied with personal belongings, the other bare except for a washbasin and bed.

The goodwife motioned her to follow. "This will be thy room. Master Temple and I are next door if thou needest anything."

Eliza crossed to the window and looked out across the street. "Have you lived above the bakery long?"

"Many years now. After Mistress Talbot passed, we bought the place and turned the downstairs into a bakery."

Eliza spun around and stared at the elderly lady. "Mistress Talbot?" So this was where Helena grew up. This might be her bedroom.

"Aye." The woman looked at her with curiosity. "We didn't need all of the room and didn't want any space to fall into idleness."

Eliza sank onto the bed, lost in thought. Downstairs was where Helena had probably first noticed Jonathan Senior watching her. The walls looked recently whitewashed and the floor polished. She traced the quilt beneath her and wondered if this was the same bed Helena had grieved for her lost lover. Goodwife Temple left the room, shutting the door softly behind her.

Thirty

The absolute silence woke her.

Stillness surrounded her like the soft quilts Aunt Maeve used to stitch. Eliza closed her eyes and tried to imagine Maeve's home. The sturdy clapboards formed a square, and the second story sat upon the first like a well-designed birthday cake. Then the walls changed and stretched upward, narrowing toward the top.

The lighthouse.

Eliza sat up in bed. *Helena is in the lighthouse.* Eliza thought back to the last conversation she'd had with Gus. What had he said about where they hid the body? He *hadn't* said.

If Helena's body was somewhere in the lighthouse, then it hadn't been buried.

"Now I understand," she whispered into the gray light of dawn. "You want your body to be properly buried."

The sun had yet to rise, but Eliza couldn't waste another moment. She rose and dressed quietly, trying not to disturb her slumbering hosts in the next room.

Once outside, she saddled the hired horse Master Temple had tied behind the bakery for her. The mount stepped cautiously along Main Street, as if he knew it was prudent to be quiet. When they reached the end of the buildings on the road, Eliza urged the horse faster. Soon they were galloping along the way leading to Maeve's property.

Only when the lighthouse came into view did Eliza rein the horse in. She panted as hard as the animal. Heart beating wildly, she climbed down and tied the horse to a nearby tree then she let herself into the lighthouse.

It took a moment for her eyes to adjust to the dimness inside. She wished for a candle. She took a deep breath. "I'm here, Helena. What do I do now?"

After waiting several moments in silence, Eliza felt foolish. Here she was, just before dawn, standing alone in a lighthouse, talking to herself. Not to mention she was still wearing her nightdress. Eliza turned and reached for the door. Then a shuffling sound above made her stop cold in her tracks.

She groped for the door handle in the dark then she saw the knob, suddenly illuminated in an orange glow. A deep shiver ran through her entire body as she realized with horror that a candle had been lit behind her.

"Thou hast returned," a guttural voice said.

Eliza turned, terror filling her. Two large eyes peered from the shadows, grotesquely illuminated by the flickering flame of the candle Gus held in front of him. She covered her mouth, stifling a scream.

"Don't be afraid, my dear," a woman's voice spoke behind him. "We've been expecting thee."

Eliza stared as a slight figure stepped from behind Gus.

"Ruth?" Eliza managed to whisper. She was confused. "What are you doing here?"

Chuckling, Ruth took the candle from Gus. Her thin gray hair hung in strands about her wrinkled face, and the nightgown she wore was crumpled and soiled. "We might ask the same question of thee."

Something cold and dark seeped into Eliza's heart. Had Ruth been hiding Gus? Is that why no one had seen him in town?

"I heard thou was in Maybrook. I knew it was only a matter of time before Helena led thee here." Ruth moved closer, eyes glinting in the candlelight. "She speaks to me, too," Ruth said, linking her arm through Gus's.

Eliza felt a sense of relief flood through her. Ruth wanted the same answers she did. But why would Ruth care for Gus now? Why would she harbor a criminal? "Then you know Helena wants a proper burial."

A laugh erupted from Ruth's small frame. As the pitch rose, Gus joined in.

Eliza looked from one to the other. "Am I mistaken, then?"

When Ruth's body stopped shaking, she said, "No, my dear. Thou are correct—almost. Helena doesn't plead with me as she must you. She *threatens* me."

Cold shuddered through Eliza. "What about?"

A smile spread on Ruth's wrinkled face, looking grotesque in the candlelight. "She wants her revenge. She's an angry spirit, but I think I know what will silence her."

Eliza's breath caught, and she took a step back until her back touched the wall. Had Ruth already found the body and buried it? "She wants a proper burial," she said again.

Ruth barked out a laugh and shuffled forward, holding the candle higher and casting her face into a deeper shadow. "Helena doesn't deserve a proper burial. She was evil. She tried to hurt my brother—"

"My father," Gus interrupted. "She tried to leave him and bring disgrace to his name."

Eliza stared at Ruth. "Gus Senior was your brother?" she whispered.

The smile returned to Ruth's face, and Eliza shuddered. Her mind spun as she remembered the words in the journal. Ruth wouldn't have been happy if Helena had abandoned her brother.

"A sister will do anything to protect her brother and nephew from being abandoned." Ruth took a step forward.

Of course . . . Dread filled Eliza's stomach. "What did you do to Helena?"

Ruth chuckled. The sound turned into an eerie high pitch. "We gave her what she deserved—it wasn't right that she leave my brother. So I helped him get rid of her, as we will now do with thee."

Eliza gulped, and her hands automatically flew to her throat. She glanced wildly about the floor and along the walls for some kind of weapon, but there was nothing.

"Helena will never have a proper burial, but I'm sure she'll enjoy thy company. She'll see that she can't haunt us anymore, for she'll know it will only bring more death." Ruth's eyes narrowed as she held the candle high in the air.

Gus tapped the floorboards with his foot. "Under here is where thou'll rest thy pretty head." He sank to his knees and pressed his cheek to the floorboards. "It's a secret," he said, stroking the wooden planks beneath him. "I won't tell . . ."

"She's under the floor?" Eliza asked, her voice thin.

Gus raised his head, eyes smoldering. "Never tell—*I said never tell.*" He stood and began to move towards Eliza again.

"No," she said. "I'll never tell."

Ruth held a pistol aimed at Eliza. "Revenge is always sweet, my dear."

Eliza shrank against the door, grasping for the latch. She turned and pulled with all her strength.

"Move out of the way, Gus!" Ruth shouted.

Eliza felt his greedy arms encircle her and squeeze. She gasped for air, and it was as if her lungs couldn't get enough. Just as she felt she would faint, the door crashed open.

A cloaked figure yanked Gus away by his hair. A shot from the pistol rang out, and Eliza screamed. Gus howled in pain and wriggled free from the figure, then staggered out of the lighthouse.

The stranger turned to Ruth, who switched her aim from Eliza to his head. With one swift lunge, the man had the pistol wrested away from her. Ruth screamed and sank to the floor, sobbing.

The stranger ran out of the lighthouse, in pursuit of Gus.

Ruth was crying in hysterics on the floor. "My gun!" she called out. She struggled to her feet, desperate eyes focused on Eliza. "Thou hast ruined everything!"

Eliza braced herself as Ruth dove against her. She fought off the old woman's clawing hands and kicking feet. Then Eliza was able to deliver a strong blow to Ruth's torso, which sent her sprawling backwards.

For a moment, Ruth looked dazed, and then she crawled to the door. Grabbing onto the handle, she pulled herself to a standing position. "I must save Gus," she hissed. She stumbled out the door and ran in the direction of the ocean.

Eliza wrapped her arms around her quivering body. Several minutes passed before she felt steady enough to leave the lighthouse. Against the brightening horizon, she saw a lone figure returning. Panic caught in her throat. Was it Gus? She ran to her horse then started to untie it with shaking fingers.

"Wait!"

Eliza froze. She knew that voice. "Jon?" she whispered in disbelief, letting the reins drop from her hands.

Then she was in his arms.

The trembling came first, then the sobs. He only held her tighter and stroked her hair, murmuring, "It's over."

When she couldn't cry any more, she raised her face and gazed at him. "Are you really here?"

Jon touched her cheek, wiping tears from them. "I thought I was too late . . . when I saw the horse and the light inside . . . I could only hope you were all right."

"But how did you know?" Eliza asked.

"Your father came to me for help when he found your note. Said you'd come to Maybrook, that you hadn't been well . . . We came as soon as we could; your father went to alert the constable." He paused, gazing at her long and hard. "And my mother told me you were in the lighthouse."

Tears filled Eliza's eyes again. "Her body is beneath the floorboards."

Jon released his hold and took her hands, hanging his head for a moment. When he raised his eyes, they were moist. "We'll have her properly buried so that she can rest in peace at last."

Eliza nodded numbly. Jon led her to a tree and spread his cloak on the ground, but Eliza pulled back.

"They'll return soon," Eliza said, fear rising in her voice.

"No . . . Gus jumped."

Eliza stared at him. "What?"

"Gus ran straight for the cliff. Didn't even slow down," Jon said quietly. "Ruth is out calling for him. I can't believe the woman who cared for me all those years could do such a thing . . ." He sank onto the cloak, staring in the distance.

Eliza settled next to him. "I don't think any woman with half a heart could turn away an innocent little boy." She did wonder why Ruth raised little Jon, but perhaps the woman had compassion buried deep inside. Perhaps she couldn't reject a little boy who had already been rejected by the town, even though she was angry at his mother.

They sat together as the sun began its ascent in the east. Its rays sparkled against the blue-green sea, and it was difficult for Eliza to comprehend the beauty of the morning after the horror of what had happened. Several moments passed before Jon spoke again. "Eliza," he said then stopped, looking away. "I cannot abide what you must think of me . . . I was a coward to send that letter. I should have told you in person."

She swallowed over the lump in her throat, not knowing what to say.

"I should have come to see you, but I was afraid," he said. "Afraid of what I had revealed in the letter." He looked at her expectantly.

For a moment, she remained silent. "Was it true?"

"At the time it was. I was confused, thinking you would be marrying Nathaniel," he said, looking away.

Shaking her head, she whispered, "Oh, Jon, I told you—"

"I know. But I couldn't believe it then, not after the way he looked at you."

Eliza hung her head. He'd said he was *confused*. He probably hadn't meant the words in his letter.

"You took my heart with you when you went to France," Jon said. "I tried to make the relationship with Apryl work anyway. When she broke it off, I was angry because of the sacrifices I had made. I knew I was falling in love with you, but I was still willing to marry Apryl. I didn't want to be like my father, abandoning my commitments. It wasn't until you left that I realized exactly what I'd lost."

Eliza raised her eyes, not daring to believe his words.

"My mother knew that I loved you before I did. She trusted you with the truth, and for that you paid a heavy price," he said.

Biting her lip, Eliza felt tears begin to form.

"This belongs to you," Jon said, removing a well-worn handkerchief from his waistcoat. The initials *E.M.R.* were embroidered in the corner. "I found it in your aunt's house last year, and I've kept it all this time."

She took the handkerchief, amazed that he'd held onto it.

Jon continued. "Until I met you, I was a self-serving man who cared little for anyone else. My only happiness was found in ambition. But I have changed." He reached out and took her hand in his. "Being engaged to Apryl, I sacrificed my love for you, Eliza." He took her other hand and stood, pulling her up with him. "But that has all altered. You have my heart now, if you want it."

It was all she could do to blink back the tears. Were Nathaniel and Thomas really gone from her life? Could she believe Jon's words at last? Her resolve melted; and she could no longer remain silent.

With a trembling hand, she touched his face, something she'd only imagined doing again in her dreams. But the flesh beneath her fingers was real—warm and alive. She touched his hair then let her fingers travel around his ear, down his neck, stopping at his shoulder. With each beat of her heart, she surrendered more.

He kissed her slowly at first, gently, his hands pulling her close. Then his kiss deepened, searching and exploring, and Eliza felt as if she'd melt against him. It was as if he couldn't stop and never intended to.

When he broke away so they could breathe, Eliza clung to him and buried her face against this neck. His arms cradled her, and she felt safe for the first time in as long as she could remember. She lifted her head, and he gazed down at her, the corners of his mouth lifting and his brown eyes warm in the morning light.

"Will you marry me, Elizabeth May Robinson?" he whispered.

"Yes," she whispered back.

The galloping of two horses reached her ears; her father and the constable had arrived. Everything would be all right. Everything would be taken care of now. Helena would be put to rest, and Jon . . . she gazed into his eyes and smiled. Jon would finally be hers.

Thirty-one

*J*on's hand reached for hers, and Eliza threaded their fingers together. The only sound above her pounding heart was the crashing surf a few dozen paces from the grave marker.

Helena Talbot
1798-1819
Rest in Peace

Eliza's parents, Mr. Doughty, the constable, and several of the townspeople had left the graveside service, and now only Eliza and Jon remained. The headstone stood tall and elegant, like a buttress against the wind off the ocean and any future storm that might come.

Helena Talbot was at last buried properly. Jon had dug a small plot near the lighthouse, the place where he said his mother used to watch for his father's return. The wind was cool today, and it stirred the cloak Eliza wore over her white dress and lifted wisps of hair about her face.

Gus's body had washed out to sea, and Ruth was in jail, awaiting trial. Knowing what was in Helena's journal about Gus Senior, Eliza understood part of Ruth's motivation—she wanted to protect her brother, as wrong as it was for him to kill Helena before she could leave him. But still, Eliza didn't understand why Ruth had decided to raise Jon. The only thing she could guess at was that Ruth suffered guilt, or she didn't blame Jon for his mother's actions.

Eliza and Jon had both written and signed statements to be read in court so they wouldn't have to appear and testify. Their involvement was finally over.

He released Eliza's hand and stepped behind her, his arms coming around her waist. She leaned back against his solid chest and closed her eyes.

"Thank you for staying with me," Jon said, his mouth close to her ear.

His warm breath sent a tremor through Eliza's body, and she smiled. "I don't want to be anywhere you aren't."

His hands tightened about her waist, and his lips tickled her neck.

"Do you think she's happy now?" Eliza said.

"Yes," Jon said in a quiet voice. "Maybrook feels different. I believe it's because my mother is finally at peace."

"I believe it too. The first time she spoke to me, she told me to jump off the cliff." Eliza turned in Jon's arms to face him with a smile. She lifted her chin, meeting his gaze. Raising her hand, she smoothed the concern from his face. "Don't worry. She became more friendly once she got to know me."

Jon's expression softened, and Eliza could hardly believe this wasn't all a dream sometimes—standing here, in Jon's arms, with him looking at her like this. "If she's watching, would she be pleased about our engagement?"

One side of Jon's mouth lifted. "How could she not?" He lowered his head and brushed his lips against hers.

The touch of his mouth was divine, and Eliza wrapped her arms around his waist then laid her head against his chest. "What if she protests the wedding?"

Jon's hands moved up her back, then to her shoulders. His fingers touched her neck. "We'll find out soon enough." He started to undo the bun she'd twisted her hair into.

"Jon, what are you doing?" She drew away, until she could see him properly.

He paused, looking into her eyes; Eliza felt the heat of his gaze envelope her body. His gaze still intent on her, he finished undoing her hair. It tumbled nearly to her waist.

"I think that had my mother lived long enough to meet you," he said, "she would have fully approved of her daughter-in-law."

Jon's fingers tangled into her hair, but Eliza was having a hard time focusing on their conversation. "How can you really know?" She never wanted the nightmares to return.

"Because," he said, dipping his head toward hers, "she came to you for help. She knew she could trust you."

Eliza reached her hands up and placed them on each side of Jon's face. It was remarkable to think that during the night they'd spent in jail, she thought he hated her. But now, she understood. The darkness in his eyes had been the pain of losing both of his parents and growing up as a lonely soul.

"You look too serious," he said, brushing his lips against her neck.

Eliza let a smile escape. "I'm so glad you rescued me that night."

He lifted his head and looked at her, his brown eyes warm and intense at the same time. "You rescued me too. You are everything to me, Eliza."

She stared at him for a moment. "I love you," she whispered. Her hands moved behind his neck, and she lifted up on her toes to meet his lips.

His kiss was warm and patient. She knew he was holding back. It would not be much longer before they'd become husband and wife. Eliza released her hold on him and stepped away, then grasped his hands.

"Are you ready?" he asked.

She nodded, tears burning her eyes. She blinked them back and stooped to pick up a basket of cut flowers she'd brought with her to the grave. Jon took several flowers from it then walked to the headstone. He knelt in the newly turned earth and placed the flowers at the base of the stone. He lifted one hand and rested it on top of the stone.

Eliza joined Jon at the headstone. She spread the rest of the flowers at the base of the headstone, then knelt next to him, careful that her cloak covered the white of her dress so it wouldn't be soiled. The wind stalled, and it seemed for a moment as if nothing moved, that she and Jon were surrounded by the lightest air possible.

"Good-bye, Mother," Jon whispered. "Rest in peace." His hand reached for Eliza's, and together they bowed their heads.

A few moments later, they stood, and Jon led her away from the burial plot, away from the cliffs and the ocean, to the waiting wagon. Jon handed her up to the bench as the wind stirred again, but Eliza welcomed the salty breeze. It lifted her hair from her neck and bathed her face in coolness.

Jon climbed up beside her and flicked the reins. The wagon lurched forward then rumbled toward the road leading into town. Eliza turned for a final look at the gravesite. Three doves had landed among the flowers, settling their snow-white bodies among the petals as if grateful to have found a soft resting place.

Jon turned his head, following Eliza's gaze. Then he faced forward again, draping one arm around Eliza and pulling her close.

The ride to the Meeting House was quiet. The road seemed to be deserted—everyone must be in their fields or homes. Eliza gazed at each tree and expanse of road with fondness, a lump in her throat at all that had happened—cherished memories as well as things she wanted to forget.

When Jon reined the horse to a stop in front of the Meeting House, he helped Eliza down without a word. His eyes were moist, and Eliza knew that if she said anything, her own eyes would tear up.

Hand in hand, they walked to the open doors. Inside the Meeting House, a hush fell over the gathered assembly. It was a small group, just as Eliza and Jon had wished. Eliza's parents were there, as were Gina and her parents, Mr. Doughty, and the constable.

The magistrate stood at the head of the room, his expression as austere as his black robes.

Eliza's father rose from his seat at the front of the room and walked up the aisle. When he reached them, he shook Jon's hand, then kissed her on her cheek. She slipped her cloak off and set it on the back bench, then linked her arm through her father's.

Together they waited while Jon walked up the aisle and stood on one side of the magistrate. Then she and her father made their own journey between the pews to the magistrate. Tears burned at the back of her eyes. She heard her mother sniffle somewhere on the side of the aisle, but Eliza only watched Jon as she approached.

His smile was soft, his eyes tender as she neared him. Finally when she stood in front of the magistrate, her father released her and stepped away.

"Jonathan Porter, Jr." the magistrate said. "Doest thou take Elizabeth May Robinson to be thy wife?"

Her eyes gazed into his.

"Yes, I do," he said, his voice sure and strong.

Eliza felt the magistrate turn toward her, but she couldn't look away from Jon.

"Eliza May Robinson, doest thou accept Jonathan Porter Junior as thy husband?" the magistrate said.

She stared into Jon's eyes, seeing into his soul, knowing this was all she ever wanted and all she ever wanted to be. "Yes, I do," she whispered.

"By the law of Massachusetts, thou art now husband and wife."

Jon held his hand out to Eliza, and she placed it in his. They had married in the very building Jon's mother would have married his father in, had Mr. Porter come back for Helena. It seemed only fitting that Eliza and Jon marry in Maybrook—in the place they'd met and in the place that Helena was finally given rest.

Eliza didn't want a high-society wedding, surrounded by the eyes of New York City. Her marriage was to be a private, sacred thing, one only she and Jon, with those they loved most, witnessed.

Jon tugged Eliza toward him, ignoring the solemn gaze of the magistrate. Before anyone could give their congratulations, Jon pulled her into his arms. "I love you," he whispered into her ear, then kissed her in front of everyone.

When he drew away, her lips practically burned. The magistrate had stepped well out of the way, and Eliza was swept up in congratulations by Gina and her parents. Her mother came forward and embraced her, saying, "It's not too late to plan a reception in New York. We can keep it as small as you like."

"Mother, our steamship tickets are already purchased."

Her mother's eyes watered as she blinked rapidly, and Eliza drew her into a hug again. "We'll only be gone through the summer."

They planned to spend their honeymoon in Europe before returning to New York. They hadn't decided whether or not they'd settle in the city or purchase an estate in the country, although Jon didn't want to become too scarce, as he'd recently joined Mr. Robinson in a new business partnership.

Jon moved to her side, and his hand touched the small of her back. He leaned down. "Ready, Mrs. Porter?"

She smiled up at him. "I'm ready."

"Not before you say good-bye," her father interrupted.

Eliza laughed and turned to her father, hugging him. Tears budded in her eyes, and when her father released her, she swiped them away. She grasped Jon's hand, and they retrieved her cloak from the back of the room then walked out of the Meeting House. The clouds had darkened, and the wind had grown stronger.

In the spot where their wagon had been was a sleek black carriage equipped with two horses. A driver climbed down from the seat and opened the carriage door.

"Jon, how did you arrange this?" Eliza asked, as the first raindrops fell from the sky.

He smiled. "It's one of many surprises you'll find along the way."

Eliza wanted to kiss him right there and then, but she turned instead and waved good-bye to everyone. Large drops splashed onto the ground, and Jon ushered her into the carriage.

The ride to Boston Harbor would be long, and an open wagon would have been quite miserable, especially now that it was starting to rain. Besides a closed carriage offered more privacy. The driver shut the door. Instead of sitting on the opposite seat, Jon sat next to her.

It was their first moment alone as husband and wife. Nervousness bubbled inside her. "I can't believe we're married," she said, wondering what it would be like to be with Jon, truly with him.

Jon's brown eyes were intent on hers. "Thank you for saying yes." He grasped her hand and turned it over, then brought her palm to his lips then pressed another kiss on her wrist.

Warmth shivered through her, traveling up her arm, onto her neck and face.

"Are you blushing, Mrs. Porter?" Jon said, his tone definitely amused.

"Perhaps," Eliza said. "Close your eyes, Mr. Porter."

His lips turned up, his brown eyes steady. "Now why would I want to do that?"

"So I can do this," Eliza whispered, touching his cheek with her hand, then pressing her mouth to his. She kissed him, a feeling both familiar and new at the same time. They were now married, and that changed everything.

This time his kisses weren't patient. While the rain drummed outside of the carriage, soaking everything in sight, inside the carriage was like a blissful cocoon, and Eliza knew she would very much enjoy being Jon Porter's wife.

Dear Reader,

If you enjoyed *Heart of the Ocean*, please consider posting a review of the book on Amazon, Goodreads, or Barnes & Noble. Also, please feel free to email me—I'd love to hear from you: heather@hbmoore.com

Also, You can read Gina's story in *An Ocean Away* found in *A Timeless Romance Anthology: European Collection*

Thank you for reading!

About Heather B. Moore

Heather B. Moore is the author of a dozen historical novels, written under the pen name H.B. Moore. She's the two-time recipient of the Best in State Award for Literary Arts in Fiction, the two-time Whitney Award winner for Best Historical, and two-time Golden Quill winner for Best Novel (good things come in twos!). Heather is an author of the Newport Ladies Book Club series (2012–2014), the Aliso Creek Novella series, and writes novellas for A Timeless Romance Anthology series.

Heather owns and manages the freelance editing company Precision Editing Group. Heather lives in the shadow of Mt. Timpanogos with her husband, four children, and one pretentious cat. In her spare time, Heather sleeps.

Author website: www.hbmoore.com
Blog: http://mywriterslair.blogspot.com/
Twitter: @HeatherBMoore
Facebook: Fans of H.B. Moore

ACKNOWLEDGMENTS

I started this book several years ago, and as I took chapters to my critique group, the story unfolded with their plot and character suggestions. Often I didn't know what was about to happen next, and when a critique member asked me, I honestly couldn't say. We had fun brainstorming possibilities, and some of their ideas would show up the next week in a new chapter.

I did know one thing though: Helena Talbot was driving the story, and she wouldn't rest until the mystery of her death was revealed. It was truly her story from the beginning through the end.

With so many years having passed since the first draft, and having published a dozen other books in the meantime, I had sharpened my writing skills. So it was with a bit of humility that I dove back into this manuscript for revisions, which made me realize how patient my critique group had been with my newbie writing skills.

Many thanks to those in my critique group at the time: Lu Ann Staheli, Jeff Savage, Annette Lyon, Michele Holmes, Lynda Keith, and Stephanni Hicken Myers. Like the ghostly voice of Helena, their voices haunted me as I worked on revisions.

"Heather, where are we?"—Lu Ann

"Why is everyone smiling all the time?"—Jeff

"There needs to be more romantic tension."—Michele

"I don't buy this scene."—Stephanni

"Way too many comma splices."—Annette

"Smiley faces!"—Lynda

And of course my most favorite quote:

"What do you know about ghosts?"—Mother

As I dusted off the manuscript and plowed back through it over several stages of revisions, I possibly tortured my next round of readers. A thousand thanks goes to Lu Ann Staheli, Jillian Torassa, Mindy Holt, Julianne Clegg,

Annette Lyon, and G.G.Vandagriff, who were willing to read through the newer version and offer valuable advice and much-needed editing. Thank you!

Also, a special thank you goes out to my wonderful proofreaders: Kari Pike, Sheri Wallace, Andrea Frisby and Rachel DeVaughn, who answered the call to proof under a tight deadline.

An excerpt from

A Timeless Romance Anthology: Winter Collection

AN UNFORTUNATE EXILE

By Heather B. Moore

NEW YORK CITY, 1901

"Are you pregnant?"

Lila stared at her father, her eyes focusing on his stiff collar, stark white against his carefully shaved, red face. Her mouth opened, but nothing came out.

"By all that is holy, if you are with child. I will—" His hand came up too swift to stop and struck her across the face.

She stumbled back, knocking against her mother who sat prim-faced on the settee.

"James," her mother yelped, half-hearted as it was.

Lila scrambled away from the settee as her father turned his wild eyes on his wife. "I will not have our daughter behave like this, Annabelle! Not in my house."

Her mother's face paled even more, if that were possible, as she clenched her already clenched hands tighter. Her mouth closed into a pinch.

Making her way behind the settee, Lila spoke in a raspy voice that had already spent hours crying. "I am *not* pregnant. We did not . . . I am *not* compromised."

Mr. James Townsend looked from daughter to mother, his face darkening, disbelieving.

The knot in Lila's stomach twisted until she thought she'd be sick, right there, on her parents' talk-of-the-town Persian rug. *Now I will be the talk of New York. Either by a sudden marriage, or worse, a suspicious departure.* But how could she explain to her father that she was not defiled, that the things she and Roland had done may have been touching the fire's flames, but not *that*.

Her eyes brimmed with tears—tears she thought were already spent. They weren't from her father's slap, but because she'd sent a letter to Roland early that morning, and there was still no reply. It was now well past the ninth hour, and had been dark for three. The blizzard that had hit the upper coast the day before had just reached New York City. The snow fell swiftly outside the floor-to-ceiling windows. No one in their right mind would venture out in the face of the storm.

"Can you swear this over your sister's grave?" her father asked in a steely tone.

Her mother gasped at the mention of their younger daughter, and Lila straightened, lowering her hand from her stinging cheek. That her father had brought little Charity into this ugly argument was momentous indeed. "I swear," she whispered.

The room was quiet for a moment. It seemed as if the tick of the grandfather clock in the corner had faded with the silent falling snow. Her father turned away as if he could no longer bear to look at his only surviving daughter. He stood with his back to the women and stared out the massive windows.

Finally, his pronouncement came. "She will leave in the morning for my sister's estate. There she will stay until this whole business is completely forgotten." He scrubbed his balding head. "What will the society papers say tomorrow? There has already been enough speculation, since any woman who associates with Roland Graves is ruined, and our . . . daughter . . . has more than associated with him."

Her mother whimpered and brought a handkerchief to her mouth.

Lila's head throbbed. Her father's sister, Mrs. Eugenia T. Payne, was as austere as her name. She'd worn nothing but widow's black since her husband's passing, and her eldest daughter had converted to Catholicism and gone into the nunnery.

Who goes into the nunnery in 1901 America? That was the thing of gothic novels.

Aunt Eugenia's younger daughter, only one year older than Lila, had made a boring and dull marriage to the local parishioner. Lila had attended the wedding in Connecticut the year before, which was the first and last time Lila ever planned visiting their "estate"—which was in reality nothing more than a farm.

I can't leave the city. What if Roland comes to propose? She stared past her father into the driving snow. *Surely he wouldn't send me out in such a storm.*

Lila's father turned from the window, and she lowered her gaze. "She'll leave first thing in the morning with a letter of explanation to Eugenia. Send Fay up to pack her things. As far as society will know, our daughter is spending the holidays with her widowed aunt."

Her mother murmured assent; Lila wanted to crumple up on the floor. Instead, she turned and slowly walked out of the room then up the stairs to the second floor. Her heart hammered as she thought desperately for some sort of plan. *Should I send another letter? Could I bribe our driver to deliver it in the storm?*

Tears started immediately after shutting her bedroom door. Not tears of shame like another girl would shed at being discovered with the most notorious bachelor in the city, but tears of anger. How dare her father send her away?

She was certainly not the only woman in the world to make a mistake. Her father had made plenty of his own.

His own sister refused to come visit their home because of the corruption in the city—at least that's what she called it. *I know otherwise. Aunt Eugenia doesn't approve of my father, or his associates, or his business practices. I'll admit that I'd been pretty innocent before meeting Roland—innocent of all things. But no longer. He taught me a thing or two about the ways of men, and I'll never look at my father, or any other man, the same way again. What will my aunt think when she learns about Roland?*

Lila sat at her ivory painted dressing table and absently moved the trinkets and perfumes around. Everything in her room was ivory and gold, patterned after a distant cousin's bedroom in Paris. When Lila had visited France in the summer, she'd fallen in love with the opulent décor. Her father had ordered furniture from as far as India to achieve the right ambience, and now she'd be trading this divine room for one of splintered furniture and moldy linens.

A light knock sounded at the door. Lila didn't have the voice to answer, so she wasn't surprised when Fay opened the door anyway.

Fay shut it with a firm click before turning to Lila. The sorrow in the maid's eyes about did Lila in. Fay was her oldest friend and confidante. Only she had known about Lila's secret escapades. Fay might have been twenty years Lila's senior and would never live life beyond a personal maid, but she never judged Lila.

The tip of Fay's nose was red, and her pale blue eyes watered. "This came for you, Miss Lila, when you were in with your parents."

Lila stared at the folded envelope in Fay's hand. "Someone delivered it to the door?" She'd heard nothing. Even over her father's yelling, she would have heard if someone had arrived in the front hall.

"It was delivered to the stable boy. He brought it to me."

Lila held out her hand. She'd have to thank Tim later, since he'd done the proper thing with this sort of letter. But when she took it from Fay, her heart stuttered. It was the same envelope she'd sent Roland. Had he returned it unopened?

Lila turned it over and saw the broken seal. Her pulse thundered in her ears as she slid the letter out. She knew without opening it that it was the one she'd sent. Her throat pinched as she skimmed her note, then read his answer below.

Dearest Roland,

Do I dare believe the words you spoke to me this fortnight past? I know there have been other women for you in previous years, but I hope that I was different. My feelings are true, and I can only hope that yours are too. My father wants to send me away. Probably someplace like Africa to live among natives and to grow crops in the dry dirt.

I didn't mean for us to be discovered, and I'm sorry that it happened this way. To be forced upon you when you've lived in bachelorhood for so many years. But I hope you do not feel forced and will consider my father's request. I would be most honored to accept your offer.

Affectionately Yours,
Lillian Beth Townsend

Below her carefully constructed letter were the scrawled words:

L—.

I depart on the next steamship to England and will be gone for an undetermined time. My deepest regrets to you and your family. You knew who I was

*when you involved yourself with me, and I never
gave you any promise. Your expectations are your
own.*

    Best wishes in Africa,
    R—.

Lila read Roland's note a second time, then a third. Disbelief pulsed through her, then sorrow, anger, more disbelief. He was leaving for England. He was leaving *her.*

Her face burned, the heat spreading down her neck, to her chest. The things he had whispered to her, *promised* her, and the way he had kissed her . . .

"Fay," she croaked. "Tell Collings to have the carriage ready at midnight. I'll be paying a visit to Roland."

"Your father—"

"Shh! He'll know nothing!" Lila hissed. "I deserve a better answer than this." She held out the scribbled letter. "Roland didn't even use his own stationery."

Fay's face paled, and she peered at the letter, although she couldn't read it.

"We will pack just as father ordered," Lila said in a hurried whisper. "But my things will not be going to Connecticut to reside with my suffocating aunt. We'll be taking the same ship as Roland to England."

"There will be many expenses," Fay cut in, her eyes wide with horror.

"Roland will be sponsoring our fare." Lila's voice sounded confident, final, but inside, her heart was breaking.

"But, miss, everything I know is here."

"Then you'll stay here. I'll go alone," Lila said in a sharp voice. "I'll be a married woman soon enough, and I won't have to answer to you or anyone." She closed her eyes against Fay's stunned expression. *I hurt my only friend, but it has to be done.* She went behind her dressing screen if only to get away from Fay's gloomy face.

Once Roland saw her again, he'd remember how much he loved her. How perfect they were for each other. How she made him laugh, and how when they kissed, everything transformed into the most beautiful dream.

To read the remainder of *An Unfortunate Exile*, purchase your copy of *A Timeless Romance Anthology: Winter Collection* on Amazon or Barnes and Noble.

28083280R00177

Made in the USA
Charleston, SC
31 March 2014